# You Can Lead a Horse to Water

## (But You Can't Make It Scuba Dive)

### A Novel

ROBERT BRUCE CORMACK

YUCCA

Yucca Publishing books may be purchased in bulk at special discounts for sales promotion, corporate gifts, fund-raising, or educational purposes. Special editions can also be created to specifications. For details, contact the Special Sales Department, Yucca Publishing, 307 West 36th Street, 11th Floor, New York, NY 10018 or yucca@skyhorsepublishing.com.

Yucca Publishing® is an imprint of Skyhorse Publishing, Inc.®, a Delaware corporation.

Visit our website at www.yuccapub.com.

10 9 8 7 6 5 4 3 2 1

Library of Congress Cataloging-in-Publication Data is available on file.

Cover design by Nuala Byles for Yucca Publishing

Print ISBN: 978-1-63158-005-5
Ebook ISBN: 978-1-63158-040-6

Printed in the United States of America

For Kathryne

*"I work each day from nine to nine, turning out ads that rarely survive,*
*The deadline is four and it's already five,*
*You can lead a horse to water, but you can't make it scuba dive."*

Washroom cubicle, O'Conner Advertising, 1978

# Chapter 1

*I*'m looking out over the North Avenue Bridge, the same view I've seen for the last thirty years. The sun shines through a light gauze of clouds. I look out over the city, the river, the traffic below. In the window's reflection, I see people walking back and forth down the hall. I don't know any of them. They were brought in when Frank O'Conner—the great Frank O'Conner: businessman, entrepreneur, advertising genius—sold the agency. Most of these people are young copywriters and art directors, the new recruits. They're wondering what I'm still doing here. I'm wondering the same thing myself.

I should have been fired yesterday with Nick, Dewey, and Margot. They got their pink slips at the same time. I joined them in the bar later and we sat in a row, drinking and talking. I was the only one going back upstairs. I still had a bottle of whiskey in my desk. I wanted one more drink before I went home.

Nobody cares if I drink in my office anymore. They all know I'm going. Not even Frank O'Conner, the great man himself, can save me. That's the way the deal was structured. As soon as the ink dried, the new agency, this big multinational, would take over, put their name up outside, and all of Frank's people would get their pink slips.

What's left but to drink, put my feet up on the desk, and look at my reflection in the window? It's not much of a reflection, to tell you the truth. I'm an old man by advertising standards. I still have most of my hair but I guess that's cold comfort at this stage. I think Frank's been dyeing his. He came back from Los Angeles a few weeks ago looking all tanned, but the hair was darker, too. "That's just because of my tan, you git," he said, then went off to another meeting.

Everyone's writing about Frank O'Conner in the trades these days. They all want to know why he put everything on the table: the accounts and the building itself. He owned the works, and everything had a price. I don't know what he's getting for it all. Frank isn't saying anything yet. He can't say anything until the New York office gives the okay. He's been there all week, attending meetings and pressing the flesh. That's why he wasn't around when the others got their termination notices. Nick, Dewey, Margot—they've known Frank as long as I have. We started at the same time back in the seventies. I'm not saying he owes us anything, but he could have said thanks in person.

I never thought Frank would sell out. He always loved advertising. God knows he spent enough time at it over the years, building his little empire: his building, his image, his thoughts in every trade publication. When we started out, none of us knew anything about being an agency. I'd done a stint in radio as a copywriter. Nick and Dewey sold space for trade publications. Margot was Frank's accountant. He was in insurance back then, and before that he repossessed cars.

We were a strange lot starting an agency (well, Frank started it; it was his money). But Frank knew one thing: it paid seventeen percent commission. Seventeen percent on media and seventeen percent on production. It was easy money, and Frank saw the future. Agencies were starting up all over Chicago and he wanted a piece of the action. He went after every client back then. Some of them came and went; others stayed for years. Frank loved them all, especially the prestige accounts. He was crazy about prestige accounts. If it got his name in the paper, he'd go naked on Illinois and Michigan, and almost did in the late eighties when business dropped off. But Frank got billings back up again, and we went into the nineties with more accounts than any other time in our history.

We spent a lot of time together, more than most people in this industry. Frank looked after us, giving time off for babies, sending flowers or notes of congratulation depending on the occasion. He never stopped being generous. Nick, Dewey and Margot got three years' salary and one year medical when they left. It's not a pension, but you don't see a lot pensions in this business. They want you off the books. That's what I told my wife. I held off saying anything until yesterday when the others got their pinks slips. I knew what she'd say. "What are we going to do, Sam? How are we going to live?" I wish I knew the answer to that. I'm fifty-eight with no prospects.

Dewey and Nick will make out okay, they've got all sorts of schemes going. Margot's a different story. Money can't be a problem. Margot has investments all over the place, some you don't want to know about, others just slightly warped. Her only extravagance over the years was a Mynah named Joey, a rescue bird from a Great Lakes freighter. When he died, she bought him a lemon yellow casket with a red satin interior. Frank said it reminded him of his first Maserati.

At the funeral, Margot gave the eulogy, getting a laugh when she imitated Joey saying, "Gimme some tit action."

Joey's in the Saint Luke Cemetery out on North Pulaski.

I don't know what made me think of it. I feel sorry for Margot, but I've got my own problems. Judy, my daughter, arrives on the eighteenth with her husband, Muller. They're coming in from Seattle and Mary's been posting the latest to-do list on the refrigerator, which includes painting all the rooms on the main floor. Our house is all main floor since it's a ranch-style with a low center of gravity. I don't know how I'll get through it all, to tell you the truth. The whiskey helps.

In the office next to me is a young guy fresh out of university. We haven't talked or introduced ourselves. I hear him typing away each day, clicking those keys, missing lunches and sometimes dinner. That was my life for thirty years—thirty, long years: hammering away each day, the deadlines, the production schedules.

Over the years it consumed me, eating up my life and all the people around me. Dewey and Nick, they always had hobbies, things to keep them occupied. I wasn't interested in anything other than advertising. Fishing I can take or leave. I'll do it with Nick and Dewey; I like their company, but generally I avoid anything I find boring.

Frank's the same way. Our lives have run a parallel course over the years, but we're different. Frank's a visionary, I'm a plodder. I'm like the copywriter next door. We wait for the visionaries to tell us what to do.

I left the copywriter some whiskey earlier. I knocked on his door and put the paper cup on the rug. Then went back to my office. I ran into him later in the washroom. "Thanks for the whiskey," he said, and walked out.

He's clicking away now, music from his iPod deck tittering in the background. I sit at my desk and listen. There isn't anything else to do. They took away my accounts last week: no warning, no apology. That's the way it happens. The accounts go, then you follow. I'm sure my office is already being reassigned. They put two creatives in an office this size now. I heard a couple of art directors the other day, one of them saying, "He's got that big office all to himself," then the other one saying, "And he smokes."

I keep staring out the window, watching the North Avenue Bridge. When they replaced the old pony trusses, Frank called it "spending tax money like drunken turds." He likes the old span bridges, the way they cross the river like large straps holding the embankments in place. Chicago has a ton of them, all capable of yawning when the need arises. I've got a good view of the river and Goose Island. Some tourists got the shock of their lives when the Dave Matthews' bus emptied its septic waste onto a tour boat. The bridges are a testament to a bygone industrial age. What people throw off them is wildly rural. I still regard lift bridges as steel nightmares, like braces you put on someone's teeth, then realize they're worse than the crooked teeth themselves.

On my walls are the usual things copywriters put on their walls. There's a letter of commendation from The Boy Scouts of America above my couch. I did a campaign for them years ago when the delinquency rate was at an all-time high in Chicago. Next to it is a picture of me riding a mechanical bull at a mayoral convention. The bull proved to be more spastic than any of the mayoral candidates and I was thrown three tables over, landing on a senator's after party. Frank called it "a pisser" and got me a clavicle brace.

The Boy Scouts letter can go next to my Electrolux awards hanging up in my den. The rest I'll put down in the basement with the old appliances and folded construction paper. "Things will work out," Frank used to say. But he's a millionaire, and things work out for millionaires. His house is north of Lincoln Park, mine is a block away from an expressway. He's got six bathrooms, I've got one.

As Bukowski said, "Sometimes you have to pee in the sink."

# Chapter 2

They found our young security guard behind the building the other night. He was strapped to a broken chair with duct tape. His name is Max, and today he's back on the job, wandering the halls, tipping his hat, saying, "How's it goin'?" He comes by my office around five o'clock and we talk about life, usually his life. I can't say much about my own, other than it's not the pisser it used to be.

He takes off his hat and adjusts the newspaper he's stuck in the rim to make it smaller. It's like everything he wears, too big, bagging out in the wrong places. He sits on my couch and rotates his hat, a nervous habit I'm sure mugged people get. I tell him he should take up a safer occupation. He says he's been mugged before. From what I can gather, he's been having a run of bad luck lately.

Last fall, he brought a girl home to his parents' house. They found Otis, his father, dancing in the basement. Otis is on some kind of disability for his back. All he does is smoke dope and play old R&B albums. On this particular night, Otis was playing James Brown, and Max's girlfriend dug James Brown, so she starts dancing with Otis. Next thing Max knows, he's waking up on the rug as Ruby, his mother, is stepping over him.

"I thought she came down to do the laundry," he said. But Ruby had an armload of Otis's records. She put them in the washing machine, turned it on, and took off in Otis' pickup truck. Before she left, she told Max to feed the cat. Then she did it herself.

She's living with a guy over near Homer Park now," Max tells me. "Engineer or something. He keeps threatening to jump out the window. Ruby put up wind chimes to calm him down."

"Has it helped?" I ask, handing him a paper cup of whiskey.

"Hasn't hurt."

Every so often, Ruby still comes around Otis's house, taking food out of the refrigerator, grabbing rolls of toilet paper. Money's tight at the engineer's place. He's on disability, too. "I don't know where Ruby finds these guys," Max says, pushing his hair back behind his ears. "He's been out of work for eight years."

The other day, Max found Ruby pulling the couch out the front door. "I guess he doesn't have one of those, either," he says. He helped her put it in the pickup, then they went back inside, figuring they might as well take the matching loveseat, too.

Otis still hasn't noticed the couch and loveseat gone. Most of the time, he's down in the rec room, smoking his dope, surfing the web. He's starting his own online R&B show, a live streaming thing where he sits there, staring into his webcam, talking about old Chess and Stax artists and then playing their music. Half the time, he forgets the webcam's going. It's on all day and he's got a setup to take calls and blogs which, believe it or not, is attracting a following of sorts.

"He'll talk to anybody," Max says. "Can't trust him, though. You never know what's going to come out of his mouth."

Max says he would leave tomorrow too if it weren't for Ruby. He doesn't want to desert her. "What if she needs a dresser or something?" he says. "Who's going to help her put it on the truck?"

Ruby's had trouble with Otis before. His last fling involved a twenty-four year old mail carrier who'd joined the U.S. Postal Service straight out of ROTC. Ruby caught them in the rec room with letters all over the rug. She chased the girl out and locked Otis downstairs for a week.

"Why didn't she leave him then?" I ask Max.

"Otis plays The Stylistics. It makes her weak in the knees."

Out in the hall, people walk past. They see Max there, cup in hand, cap on his knee. They must think we're related.

"Is it okay for us to be doing this?" he says.

"They don't care what I do anymore, Max."

"So you just sit around drinking?"

"Pretty much."

"I could sure use a job like that."

"You wouldn't like it."

"It's better than being mugged."

"We all get mugged, Max. Just in different ways."

The poor guy still has glue from the duct tape stuck to his wrists.

One thing I intend to do before I leave is write Frank a note. It's official now. Just after Max left, Frank's secretary showed up with my pink slip and an envelope. "Thank God you haven't gone," she said. "This has been on my desk all day. I've been so busy with Frank's travel arrangements and stuff."

Her name's Kitty and she's been with Frank over ten years. Kitty's got that look of Masonic devotion, but she's clearly rattled with all the stuff going on around here lately. I take the envelope and put it down.

"Aren't you going to open it?" she said. "Frank asked me to give it to you personally. He's still in New York."

"Would you like a drink?"

"I wish I could. That's exactly what I need right now." She watched me take the bottle out of my drawer. "I'd better get back upstairs," she said. "I'll need your pass before you go. Just drop it on my desk on your way out. Good luck."

I look at the envelope now with the embossed coat-of-arms up in the corner, a heraldry showing two stags and a shamrock. Everything with Frank reflects a certain Irish charm. Our offices have green walls, something I'm sure will change with this new multinational. They prefer white walls and cubicles. Frank calls it "chicken breeding."

I see Max's reflection again. He's forgotten his hat. He goes quietly over to the couch where he left it.

"Want another drink?" I say. I point to one of the two paper cups. Then I look at my pink slip. "My dismissal," I shrug. "I was just fired."

He sits on my couch with his pant cuffs high above his boots.

"Give me a minute," I say, "I just have to read this." I shake open the letter and read Frank's words:

*Sam,*

*I've been detained here in New York with final details. I wish I could be there to buy you dinner. I'm off to Los Angeles tomorrow for more meetings. Tell the others I apologize for not being around. And keep your chin up. You've been through worse. Pass along my apologies to your wife. Mary has always been one of my favorite people. Best of luck.*

*Frank*

"What's it say?" Max asks.

"It says I've been through worse." I light a cigarette and take out a piece of paper. "I've got to write something here, Max."

"You want help with your stuff? I've got some boxes downstairs."

"Thanks, I'd appreciate that."

Max leaves and I pour another drink. Then I begin writing:

*Frank,*

*Apologies aren't necessary. I've had a good run. How many people can say they only worked for one agency their whole career? Quite honestly, I'm looking forward to a change. Mary's been after me to paint the house for months now. My daughter and her husband arrive from Seattle in two weeks. Anyway, I'll leave you with this memento. Have a drink on me and remember, I left here with barely a whimper. I'll pass your apologies on to the others. I'm going up north fishing with Nick and Dewey once the season starts.*

*Sam*

Frank will like the "without a whimper" part. That's him all over. "This business is a gamble," he used to say to me. "You don't pout and you don't fucking cry over spilt milk."

Frank hates anything that isn't a gamble. He thinks it makes people dull and witless. When David Ogilvy criticized clients for relying on research like "drunks hanging onto lampposts," Frank laughed his ass off. He kept telling us to read Ogilvy's book. I read it. He only wrote it to put a new roof on his chateau.

"So what?" Frank said. "Fucking roofs cost money."

I take the whiskey and letter up to Frank's office. Kitty's at her desk, separating the serious correspondence from what Frank calls "all the other crap that isn't worth a pigeon's curse."

"Did you remember your pass?" she says.

"Sorry, it slipped my mind. I'll bring it up later."

"Please don't forget. It's a legal thing."

I put the bottle and letter on Frank's desk, and then go back downstairs. Max is there with the boxes. "Why are they firing you if you won all these?" he says, taking the awards down off my wall.

"Because they can, Max."

The door opens in the next office. The copywriter comes out and leans against my doorjamb. "Sorry to see you go," he says. He's about to turn around when Max gets all excited about something. His hand goes in his shirt pocket and pulls out a joint. "You guys feel like a toke?" he says. I haven't seen a joint in years. "You're fired anyway," Max says. "Why not?"

"Sure," I say. "Why not?"

"Are you guys serious?" the copywriter says.

"Follow me," I say.

We take our drinks to the washroom and stand by the sink. Max lights the joint, inhales, passes it to me. He leans against the sink with one eye closed.

"Ruby's boyfriend tried to kill himself last night," he says. "Jumped out the bedroom window and landed on his car."

I hand the joint to the copywriter. "How's Ruby taking that?" I ask.

"Who's Ruby?" the copywriter says.

"My mother," Max says. "Otis says it serves her right."

"Who's Otis?" the copywriter asks.

"My father," Max says. "He shagged my girlfriend."

"He shagged your girlfriend?"

"Down in the rec room."

"C'mon, what did you do?"

"I was passed out on the rug. Ruby woke me up."

"Your mother woke you up? What did she do?"

Max looks at me and then we both break out laughing. "She told me to feed the cat," he says.

The copywriter looks at me slapping Max's back.

"You fed the cat?"

"My mother did."

"I thought she ran off with some guy?"

"She fed the cat first."

Max is sliding down the wall now. I try pulling him up, but we're both laughing, and I slide down next to him. The copywriter keeps looking out the door, but ol' Max is going through his pockets again, saying he's got another joint somewhere.

"If I'm going to get mugged, I might as well do it stoned."

"Good thinking, Max," I say.

"Ready for another?"

"Light it up. What the hell."

"Coming at you."

The copywriter stands there looking at us like we're crazy. Max can't even get the joint lit. The match keeps going past the end and into his scrawny beard. "Maybe we should wait a bit," he says.

We get up, dust ourselves off, and open the washroom door. Out in the hall, we get a few strange looks from the cleaners. They play Bosnian reggae on a small ghetto blaster. It's not as bad as you'd think. The copywriter disappears in his office. Max and I grab my stuff and take it to the elevator. Right next to the reception desk, there's this glass partition. It still has *O'Conner Advertising* etched in big red Helvetica letters. I figure Frank needs a parting gesture. I put down my boxes and drop my pants. "Goodbye, Frank," I say, pressing my ass against the glass.

The elevator doors open and there's Kitty. She starts pushing buttons like crazy. I'm trying to pull up my pants. "I got my pass," I say. "Wait. It's right here."

Kitty's still pushing buttons. Max is in hysterics. "Congratulations," Max laughs. "You mooned Frank's secretary."

"I did not."

"What do you call it?"

"I was facing her, Max. How's that a moon?"

"You mooned her, old man."

"I'd better find her and apologize."

Kitty isn't at her desk. She's probably off telling everybody I'm pressing hams all over the creative department. I know Frank will see this as a sad attempt at getting his goat. "Put his ass right under my name, did he?" he'll say. "Pretty juvenile, if you ask me."

I leave my pass card and go back downstairs. Max is leaning against Frank's partition like the horse in *Cat Ballou*.

"You find Frank's secretary?"

"She's not at her desk." The elevator comes and Max grabs my boxes. He wobbles a bit, losing his hat at one point, but we get everything loaded and down to the street.

A big double Winnebago is parked out in front of our building. There's a film crew shooting a commercial for some beauty product. The front entrance has been made to look like a department store complete with a doorman dressed in a uniform and white gloves. Max walks up to the Winnebago with his hat pushed back on his head. Just inside, we see a DJ sitting there at his console. "How's it going?" Max says to him. "Got any Lloyd Price?"

"Piss off," the DJ says.

One of the guards sees Max and hikes up his belt. Even in uniform, Max can't hide the fact that he's stoned. The guard tells him to move along and Max trips over a potted plant. It rolls down the red carpet and thumps against the speakers.

Max's car is parked in an alleyway somewhere just south of the office. He can't remember exactly where. We go up and down the street like idiots, finding the car about three blocks away. Max starts kicking the driver's side door, telling me it sticks sometimes. "Did you try the handle?" I ask, and he pulls the handle, falling backwards as the door opens. "You're a bit of a dumb ass," I say.

"At least I don't moon people."

"I'm not proud of that, Max."

"Where do you live, anyway?"

"Prospect. You sure you don't mind? Aren't you on duty?"

"I don't care. I'll probably just get mugged again."

"You're putting your life on the line, Max."

"I'm thinking of packing it in."

"And doing what?"

"I don't know. I'm looking at my options."

"That's good, Max. Always look at your options. Would you mind stopping at a liquor store?"

"What happened to your bottle of whiskey?"

"I gave it to Frank."

"Why would you give him a bottle of whiskey?"

"I don't know, Max. I've never been fired before."

"You don't give'em a bottle of whiskey."

"I'll remember that."

# Chapter 3

*I* wake up this morning with the sun in my eyes. Out the window, my cardboard boxes tilt precariously on the front porch. Max and I did a number of detours last night; some I remember, some I forget. We went to a bar and I guess I drank too much. I vaguely recall stopping at a liquor store after that, then Max dragging me up my steps and ringing the bell. Mary hauled me inside, giving me the skunk eye, then sent Max packing.

A radio is going in the basement now. Post-it notes are stuck to the walls. Each one is numbered according to urgency, which Mary accentuates with exclamation marks. "One to three are a *must* today," she's written. "Get started as soon as you've had breakfast."

I sit at the kitchen table, listening to Mary moving things around downstairs. My son-in-law will be sleeping down there. Muller has sleep apnea, which requires him to wear a mask that sounds like a wombat (my daughter's words). Judy can't stand the noise, so we're putting Muller next to the furnace with their two lovebirds, Meek and Beek. Judy takes them everywhere they go.

Judy calls while I'm eating my toast and starts going over diet requirements, especially birdseed. Then she says, "Did cops really bring you home last night, Daddy?"

"How did you hear about that?"

"Mom emailed me this morning."

"He's a security guard, sweetie. His name's Max."

"What were you doing with a security guard?"

"Long story. Daddy needs a coffee first."

"Did you really leave a pressed ham on the front window?"

"That could have been anyone."

"Mom says it was you or the cop."

"Security guard, sweetie. Daddy has to go now."

Hanging up, I look at the list Mary's left on the kitchen counter. We need everything at this point: paint, drop cloths, edging tape. I put my coffee cup in the sink and look out the window. The grass is growing in crazy tufts, a smattering of dandelions along the fence. The phone rings again. Max is on the other end. "What is it, Max?" I say, "I'm trying to get to the store for paint."

"Ruby's back," he says. "She left the engineer. Otis's been playing The Stylistics all morning." I could hear Max blowing smoke out his mouth. "It's awful around here, man."

"What's so awful? Don't you want Ruby back home?"

"Sure. It's the atmosphere I hate."

"It'll work out."

"Ruby says Otis crossed the line."

"The man slept with your girlfriend, Max."

"I know," he yawns. "I'm starting to hate The Stylistics."

"I thought Ruby destroyed all his albums?"

"He fished them out of the washing machine. Some are okay. He's been getting replacements. Picked up some Larry Williams yesterday."

"What's Ruby been doing since she got home?"

"She's starting a business. Not sure what it is yet."

"Tell her good luck."

"Why are you painting?"

"Because," I say, closing the cellar door, "when you come home shit-faced, you have to pay penance. I'm stuck painting. And I've only got two weeks before my daughter arrives."

"Ruby's a good painter."

"Glad to hear it, Max."

"We're both pretty good. Want us to come over and help?" I can hear a woman's voice in the background. "That's Ruby," he says. "She's up for anything that'll get her out of the house."

"You seriously want to help me paint?"

"Sure. It'll be good for Ruby. Get her mind off Otis."

"Let me see what Mary thinks."

"We're here if you need us."

"I appreciate the offer."

"We've got drop cloths, ladders and stuff."

"I'll pass it by Mary."

"Okay. Let me know."

Six rooms, a hallway, front foyer, all to do in less than two weeks. I don't know what's worse: having to paint, or waiting for my son-in-law to show up. I know Judy loves him to death, but he's a bit of a dud. Mary hates it when I call him that. "He's your son-in-law, Sam," she'll say, like I need reminding. Judy says, "Daddy, you just have to know him better," which is fine if you like guys who keep nasal flush in their pocket. I guess I'm just pissed at all this painting I have to do before they arrive. Ruby and Max could help get the job done faster. That's if Mary agrees, which is doubtful judging from the way she shooed Max off the porch last night. It's still worth asking. I go downstairs, aware that Mary is probably holding a broom.

# Chapter 4

"*H*ow do you know they can paint?" Mary is saying.

She had me filling cracks all over the house yesterday. I didn't even have a chance to pick up the paint. I point out to Mary that Max and Ruby come equipped with drop cloths.

"I'd better not find you and Max slacking off," she says. I promise her we'll be on our best behavior. "Fine," she says. "As long as this house gets done by the eighteenth. You'd better get the paint now."

At the paint store, I get everything on Mary's list, then push my cart to the cash register. Suddenly everything starts drifting in and out. I'm sweating like crazy and my heart's going boom, boom, boom.

I go outside and lean against a wall. Years ago, this art director I worked with, Don Conroy, had a stroke. He said everything went numb for a while. He was in his late fifties. He survived, but his time had come. He had to retire. Frank made a big show of it by planning an elaborate retirement party. He rented the town hall, complete with Don's favorite band, The Jazzbusters. Frank had shrimp the size of plantains. At the end of the evening, a limousine took Don up to his cottage where he planned on retiring. After a year of that, Don realized he couldn't take it anymore. He ended up back downtown, looking for work. I brought him in on a few freelance assignments. Then I couldn't even give him that. A few months later, he died in his sleep. We all went to the funeral and Frank stood there, chin out, all polished with aftershave. He said a few words at the gravesite later, calling Don a "likeable git."

Don didn't even make sixty, and here I am, two years away from that, hugging the wall, sweating like crazy. "Are you all right?" I hear someone say. I look up to see this old woman holding the door. "Why don't you come in out of the sun?"

"Thanks," I say. "I think it's just low blood sugar."

I go back inside with my heart going boom, boom, boom. Everyone's waiting in line at the cash register. I wipe my face with my sleeve. The old woman's there with her husband. I make my apologies.

As soon as I get to the car, I'm leaning against the hood, feeling like the asphalt is a trampoline. The old couple come out a few minutes later. The husband says, "Everything okay?"

"Just a little dizzy, that's all."

I'm thinking about that scene from *The Sopranos* where Tony collapses at this swank country club. He ends up in hospital, sitting on a gurney. A nurse comes along and says, "I've got good news for you, Mr. Soprano. Your heart appears to be fine."

"How the hell's that good news?" he says. "If you found something wrong, you could cut it out. You're telling me it's nothing. Why the fuck did I collapse?" Next day in his psychiatrist's office, he tells her it felt like a can of ginger ale going off in his head. "What the fuck happened?" he says, and she says, "Sounds like a panic attack."

"I can't have a panic attack," Tony says. "A guy in my position?" So he goes home and starts watching these ducks in his pool. They fly off and he starts bawling. So back he goes to the psychiatrist's office, saying, "What the fuck?" and the psychiatrist tells him it's a fear of abandonment. "But they're *ducks*," he says. Again, he goes home, the ducks are still gone; he starts bawling again.

Christ, I hope I'm not having panic attacks. I don't want to start bawling over ducks. Back at home, I put the paint in the kitchen and crawl into bed. Mary appears and says, "What's wrong?" She feels my forehead. "Is this for real or are you pulling a sicky?"

"Not quite sure," I say. "It might be the heat."

"I hope that's all it is."

She fluffs up the pillow behind my head and goes back to the basement. I start feeling better after a few minutes. The phone rings and I answer. Max again. "Sam," he says. "What did Mary have to say?"

"She's okay."

"You want us to come over now?"

"Come over in the morning." I hear music playing in the back-ground. "Isn't that The Stylistics, Max?"

"Otis keeps playing it."

"Is it working?"

"They're circling each other like cats."

"Haven't heard that song in years, Max."

"Wish I could say the same thing."

# Chapter 5

*A*nother day, birds sing, the boxes from my office tilt on the porch. Max and Ruby arrive in painter pants. "Hey, there," Ruby says, a cigarette going in the corner of her mouth. "Here we are, two painters ready to go." Her hair is done up in a bandana. "I'm Ruby, by the way. I guess that's obvious. So where do you want us to start?"

Mary takes her off to the living room, pointing out color chips. Max gets the ladder and paint trays from the truck. When he comes back inside, I pull him aside and say, "Did you put a pressed ham on my front window or was it me?"

"It was you, old man. You did one at the liquor store, too."

"The liquor store?"

"Sure. Right after you bought a case of whiskey. It's under the boxes on the porch. Don't you remember?"

"A case?"

"Go see if you don't believe me."

"I believe you."

"I put your jacket over the whiskey."

"I thought I'd left it back at the office."

"Where do you want the ladder and stuff?"

"Living room, I guess."

Mary and Ruby are still going over the color chips in the bedroom. Then Ruby comes out and holds her cigarette under the kitchen tap. "I'll start on the trim," she says to Max. "Are these all the drop cloths? I thought we had more in the garage." She lights another cigarette. "Sorry we don't have more cloths, folks. Otis probably wrapped something up in them. It could be anything from his guitar to the cat. I haven't seen the cat lately. Have you, Max?"

"Otis probably traded it for records."

"I wouldn't put it past him."

They start painting like a couple of pros. Ruby does the cutting while Max works the roller. She calls it "cutting," which is really doing the trim. They've got their own language. You'd think they'd make a mess, moving as fast as they do, but there's not a drop anywhere.

"We've done this before, Sam," Ruby says. "You should see us when we get going."

Her cigarette smoke mingles with the paint and Mary makes the occasional wave with her hand. She hates smoking. I have to smoke out on the back deck. I keep expecting Mary to say something, but she's too thrilled with Ruby's painting skills. Ruby fills her brush with paint, running a straight bead as far as she can reach. Then she's down the ladder, moving it over, and going up again. Mary retreats downstairs to put the sheets on Muller's cot.

"You're not shitting me about the liquor store, are you, Max?" I say as soon as she's gone.

"You bared your ass, old man."

"Who bared their ass?" Ruby says.

"Sam did."

"What for?"

"I'm not quite sure," I say.

"You were stoned, old man."

"I wish you'd stop calling me old man, Max."

"I didn't know you smoked grass, Sam," Ruby says.

"Blame Max for that."

"Nobody held a gun to your head, old man."

"Stop calling him that, Max."

"Sorry, Ruby."

"How long do you think all this painting will take?" I ask.

"We'll finish before your daughter arrives, Sam."

"Ruby's big on schedules," Max says.

"Very professional."

"You're just happy to be away from Otis, aren't you, Ruby?"

"Ain't that the truth."

"Had enough of The Stylistics, yet?"

"Love The Stylistics, Max. Hate the player."

"I'm hearing it in my sleep."

"So am I. That's what worries me."

"You're not going to cave, are you?"

"We'll see, Max. I've still got a pretty good hate on."

# Chapter 6

*W*ork proceeds until Ruby finds a watermark on the kitchen ceiling. "Better check your eavestroughs," she says, and Max and I spend the afternoon pulling small trees out of the gutters. By the time we come back inside, Ruby's plastered the ceiling and primed the kitchen. "Put the drop cloths in the bedrooms, Max," she says. "They'll need a coat of primer before we leave today."

Mary takes me aside. "Ruby's a miracle, Sam," she whispers and squeezes my arm.

I go and help Max put down the drop cloths. I can hear Mary talking to Ruby in the other room.

"Will we be done in time, Ruby?" she says.

"Don't you worry, honey. Max and I are in the groove."

Morning of the eighteenth, everything is done, even the closets. Around one o'clock, Muller's old Buick pulls into the driveway, oily smoke billowing up in the air. He gets out in this tie-dyed t-shirt, baggy shorts and sandals, looking like a big, sweaty Turk. Then Judy gets out, running up, going, "We're here! We're here!" She embraces everybody, including Max, while Muller starts pulling this oxygen tank out of the back seat. It's the size of a water heater. Max goes to help him and Judy comes over, all pink and glowing, giving me a sweaty kiss. "Hey, Daddy," she says.

"How was the drive?" I ask.

"Muller barfed."

Mary links arms with Judy. "Get the bags, Sam," she says. "Then we can talk."

"What's in those boxes on the porch?" Judy says.

"Your father's stuff from work." Mary says. "I told him to put everything in the garage."

Judy walks around the house, looking at the new paint and wallpaper. Everything has the freshness of a Florida beach. Max and Muller bring the oxygen tank into the front hall.

"Where should we put this?" Muller says.

"Downstairs," I say to him. "Mary's made up a bed for you by the furnace. Come on, Max, grab this end. Muller, you grab the other."

Ruby is cleaning brushes in the laundry tub. "Hey, there," she says. "You must be Muller."

Muller puts down his end of the oxygen tank and takes Ruby's cigarette from the side of the laundry tub. "Haven't had one since we left Seattle," he says.

Ruby takes out a pack from her shirt pocket. "Have a fresh one," she says. "What's with the oxygen tank?"

"I have sleep apnea. This works better than CPAP machines." He starts hooking up the mask and hose to the tank.

"Isn't that an old gas mask?" Ruby asks.

"Yeah, army surplus. I rigged it up myself."

"Aren't you the inventive one," she says. "You sure it's sleep apnea? Otis thought he had that. All he needed was a good massage."

"Who's Otis?" Muller says.

"Don't get her started on Otis," Max says.

"Grab the paint cloths, Max," she says.

"You really think a massage would work?" Muller asks.

"Course I do. Worked for Otis. Come by the house sometime. I'll have you breathing like a thoroughbred."

"That's everything, Sam," Max says.

"You did good, Max. You two should go into business."

"We are. That's what Ruby's been planning. I'm going in with her. Who's gonna mug me painting a house?"

Muller sits down on the cot. He practically sinks to the floor. "So you're saying it's just tension?" he asks Ruby.

"Sure, it's tension. I know a tense man when I see one. Get over on your stomach. I'll straighten you out right now." Muller rolls over and Ruby straddles the cot. Her fingers disappear into Muller's flab.

"You sure got strong hands, Ruby," Muller says. She digs her knuckle into his back. "God Almighty." Mary and Judy come downstairs. "Ruby's a miracle worker, Jude," he says, letting out a moan and possibly a fart. Ruby digs a knuckle in again.

"Just do this any time he's tense, honey," Ruby says to Judy. "My husband thought he had sleep apnea for years. Never needed a machine, though. Just a good solid knuckle right here." Her fist disappears into his flesh. "I'll show you how to do it, if you like."

"I'm fine, thank you," Judy says.

"Well, any time he needs it, give him a knuckle. You want help up, big fella?" she says, and he rolls over like a beached mammal.

"Get up, Muller," Judy says.

"I'm trying, Jude."

Ruby pulls him to his feet. "Well, that's it for us," she says. "Leave the brushes in fabric softener for a few hours. You got anything else needs painting, just call Max. I don't know where I'm living yet."

"You've got a home, Ruby," Max says.

"I don't trust your old man. He's a loose cannon."

"Then we'll get a place together."

"Let's talk in the truck," she says. "Say goodbye to these nice folks." She picks up some pails and a roller handle. "Watch your back there, beefcake. Losing a few pounds wouldn't hurt, either."

"I like him just the way he is," Judy says.

"Big and cuddly, huh?" Ruby laughs. "I hear you. Come on, Max, grab those pails. We'll pick up a burger on the way home."

I take out my wallet.

"Don't worry about it, Sam," Ruby says. "Max says you got fired. Darn shame at your age. You don't look none the worse for wear, though. You doin' okay? You sleeping?"

"I'm fine."

"It probably hasn't hit him yet," she says to Mary. "Everything's fine until you come home and find them shagging the postal carrier." Mary squints at Ruby. "Story for another time, honey. It's been a rough couple of years. Don't forget about the brushes. Wrap them in damp newspapers afterwards. They'll be good as new. And take care of that back, big fella. You've got a few good years left in you yet."

"Come on, Ruby," Max says.

"I'm right behind you," she says.

Muller's looking at her like she's Venus de Milo.

# Chapter 7

Saturday, going down the aisles at a Food4Less, my heart starts beating like a conga again. I push the cart to the entrance, bumping into shelves, banging into knees. Then I start to fall over and two hands grab me under my armpits. My heart flutters like a bird. Next thing I know, I'm in the parking lot with this big guy patting my back. "Just keep breathing," he says. "You'll be okay."

"Thanks," I say. "I just got a little dizzy."

"You might want to get him checked out," he says to Mary. "Just to be on the safe side." He goes back to the store.

"What happened, Sam?" Mary says.

"I got a bit dizzy, that's all."

Mary helps me into the car and goes back for the groceries. I keep seeing Don Conroy's face. When I look up again, Mary's staring at me. "I think you need to see a doctor," she says. "I'll make an appointment. Do you want to stop for a coffee or something?"

"No," I say, "let's just go home."

Muller's car is dripping oil in the driveway. "Go lie down," Mary says. "Muller will bring in the groceries."

"Okay," I say. I check the mailbox and find a letter from Frank. I use the washroom first, then read Frank's letter in the sun room.

*Sam,*
*I could be away longer than expected. They want me heading the operation here in Los Angeles until a new CEO is found. Lots of sunshine in this part of the world. You and Mary would enjoy it. Hope she took the news okay. I realized after I signed off that I*

*might have sounded glib. That wasn't my intention. Let me know if there's anything else I can do. I'll call when I get back.*

*Frank*

Strange sounds are coming from the basement. I go down and find Muller's head in the laundry sink and Judy holding a towel. "He hit it on the boiler trying to catch Beek," Judy says.

Muller's a sopping mess, hair everywhere, water streaming down his face. There's no blood, but it looks like he's going to have a lump. "What are you letting the birds loose down here for?" I ask.

"They can't spend all day sitting in a cage."

"Do you want a drink, Muller?" I say.

"Sure, Sam."

"Come upstairs and I'll make you one." We leave Judy cornering Beek behind the dryer.

Out on the porch, I reach under the boxes and find a bottle of whiskey. The brand isn't familiar. It looks Bulgarian from the script. Why would I buy Bulgarian whiskey? I take two trophy cups out of another box, pour in some whiskey, handing one to Muller. "How are things out in Seattle?" I say.

"Lousy. I got fired."

"How the hell did that happen?" He slurps like a spaniel.

"I don't know. Maybe I'm in the wrong field."

"Maybe."

"What about you?"

"What about me?"

"What are you going to do?"

"Drink this case of whiskey."

"I admire you, Sam."

"No, you don't."

"I do."

"You're full of shit." He looks hurt. "Muller, it's just a figure of speech."

"No, I'm full of shit."

"You're making me lose respect for you."

"I know."

"If Mary comes out, you're admiring these trophies, understand? You think I'm the most talented copywriter on earth."

"You are, Sam. Judy's always talking about how talented you are. We saw one of your commercials last week."

"Which one?"

"A little girl talking to her mother. Judy laughed through the whole thing. I don't remember what it was for."

"Q-tips. It's been running over a year."

"Judy thought it was very funny."

"It wasn't supposed to be."

"Q-tips, huh?"

"Q-tips."

"I wish I was like you, Sam."

"No, you don't."

"I do, really." Then he starts slurping like a spaniel again. Christ, even Bulgarian whiskey deserves to be sipped.

# Chapter 8

"Sounds like you're suffering from anxiety, Sam," Dr. Krupsky says, looking at me over the top of his glasses. A wisp of hair hangs down over his forehead. "I like the ginger ale going off in your head bit. You come up with that yourself?"

"I saw it on *The Sopranos*."

"Good show."

"So?"

"So what?"

"Why am I having panic attacks?"

"Could be anything from shock to dehydration," he says. He rubs his hands up and down his stubby legs. "We're dealing with three things here, Sam," he says, pulling on three fingers. "Serotonins, nor-epinephrines, dopamines. Don't worry about the names. Sometimes they get out of whack. We use drugs to fix the problem. It's a fiddle. See what I'm saying?"

"What sort of pills will he have to take?" Mary asks.

"He doesn't have to take any," Krupsky says. "I wouldn't. I'm just saying it's an option. What do you want to do, Sam?"

"I'd like to stop passing out."

He puts his glasses up on his forehead. "So, sit down when it happens. Take up yoga."

"What's that going to do for me?"

"Calm you down."

"And that'll cure my panic attacks?"

"Who knows?" he shrugs. "Look, we're human. You think you're the only one? People come in here complaining about panic attacks all the time. I say, 'Do meditation'. They say, 'Give me a pill.' What am I going to do? I give'm pills."

"So he either takes a pill, or lives with it?" Mary asks.

"What's so bad about yoga? Do it together. Add a little tantric sex."

"Shouldn't he stop drinking and smoking?"

"Sure he should," Krupsky says. "Take away his nail clippers while you're at it. Everything's risky. He could die planting rose bushes."

"Do you want the pills?" Mary asks me.

"I'm starting to wonder."

"Sam, look," Krupsky says. "If it bugs you so much, see a psychiatrist. Otherwise, do like the rest of us. Get lots of sleep and don't be a big shot, wear a hat." I button my shirt and Krupsky slaps me on the back. "You'll live. Get out in the sun. Good source of vitamin D."

He follows us out to the waiting room. "Any more episodes, call me. Now go forth and multiply."

"We've already multiplied," I say.

"Then I'm out of advice," Krupsky says and goes back to his examining room with another patient.

Out on the street, I light a cigarette and stare at the sky.

"Krupsky's got a point," I say.

"What point?" Mary says. "He made tons of points."

"Maybe I just have to live with it."

"I can't understand him half the time. Rose bushes?"

"He's just saying anything is possible." She takes my cigarette and throws it on the ground. "Littering," I say.

"I'll litter you in a minute."

We stop at a bookstore and check out some yoga books. Mary chooses ones with lots of pictures. Most of the positions look painful as hell. What's the point of putting your foot behind your head?

We go home and Mary shows the books to Judy. Muller's making dinner. Tomato sauce bubbles on the stove and garlic bread warms in the oven. Judy licks her thumb as she turns the pages. "We could do this, Muller," she says. "It doesn't look that hard."

Muller comes over, wiping his hands on his shirt. His stomach falls over the back of her chair. "I don't know if I'm up for that, Jude."

"Well, I want to try." She takes the book in the living room and sits on the rug. Mary changes her clothes and joins her. They find a page with warm-up stretches. Muller and I watch.

"Are you two just going to stand there?" Mary says.

Judy's trying to sit cross-legged. "Either get down here or quit staring," she says.

Muller and I go out on the porch instead. I get the bottle of whiskey and fill the trophy cups. Muller sips and sighs like a buffalo.

"I don't know what Judy wants anymore," he says.

"I thought she wanted kids?"

"I can't even get a stiffy."

"I didn't need to hear that."

"I'm just saying."

"I know what you're saying. I still didn't need to hear that."

"Sorry."

"You're talking to your father-in-law here."

"I just don't know what do, Sam. Judy finds fault with everything these days. She even pulled out all my pot plants before we left. Why would she do that?"

"Women don't want distractions. They want babies."

"But grass makes me horny."

"Cut it out, for chrissake. That's my daughter you're talking about. I don't need to know about your sex life. Especially stiffies."

"Sorry."

"And stop saying you're sorry."

Now he's got me worrying about my own stiffy.

# Chapter 9

"*C*hakras are layers of subtle bodies known as focal points of reception and transmission," I read aloud from a meditation book. We're on the living room rug, legs crossed, shoulders back. According to the book, we're supposed to embrace the fullness of our existence.

Mary and Judy are saying their mantras. Muller's lips are moving, but he's probably faking it. He makes this *hm-m-m* sound which usually turns into a burp. My foot's falling asleep.

Muller leans over and asks when Ruby is coming over again. I tell him to shut up about Ruby. She's got her own problems. Max told me yesterday she's put Otis in the basement and nailed the door closed. Otis has to come in through the side entrance. He sleeps in the bedroom off the rec room. Sometimes Ruby drops large pans on the floor just to hear him fall out of bed. He's on his computer most of the night doing his on-line R&B show. People are sending in requests. "Thirty last night," Max said. "People love the old R&B stuff. Ever hear of Lee Dorsey?"

Max still gets Otis his grass and even dropped off some joints here the other day. I keep them stashed with the whiskey on the porch. When Mary and Judy go off shopping, Muller and I smoke a joint. Then he starts moaning about Judy, especially how he wished she hadn't pulled up all his pot plants. "I used to make grass brownies," he says. "Nuts and everything. I wouldn't mind baking them again."

"You're not baking grass brownies, Muller."

"They're really good."

"Save it for when you go home. You *are* going home, right?"

"Don't you like having us here, Sam?"

"Yeah, it's a treat." I take another hit off the joint. "What's so special about grass brownies?" I ask.

"Great stone."

"Better than this?"

"One brownie can keep you going all afternoon."

"You're shitting me."

"Sure. Why don't you let me make some?"

"You're not stinking up the house with grass brownies."

"They don't smell like grass, Sam."

"What do they smell like?"

"Regular brownies. I split the tray in two, half with grass, half without. I'll leave the regular brownies out for Judy and Mary."

"You're one sneaky son-of-a-bitch."

He picks up the baggie with the joints Max rolled for me. "This should do it," he says, breaking them up then tossing the rolling papers in one of the boxes. "I'll show you how I make them, if you like. I use special ingredients."

"We're only making one batch, Muller. Understand?"

"Whatever you say."

In the kitchen, Muller starts pulling out pans and stuff. He melts unsweetened chocolate, then adds walnuts, spices, sugar and some other things. He pours the mix into two pans, sprinkling the grass into one.

"Why don't you become a chef?" I say.

"I love cooking," he says. "Judy thinks I should start a catering business. Maybe focus on pastries."

"What's wrong with that?"

A half hour later, the kitchen smells like a bakery. When the timer goes, Muller brings out the brownies. "Take one of these," he says. "I'll put the plain ones out on the table and hide the others."

The brownie burns my hand.

"Careful, Sam, they're hot."

"No kidding. Let's take them outside."

"Do you want some milk?"

"Milk?"

"They're good with milk."

"Bring milk, then."

Muller comes out with two frosty glasses of milk. He sits down and bites off the end of his brownie. "Go ahead, Sam, they're great when they're warm."

I put a piece of the brownie in my mouth, tasting a hint of cinnamon and what appears to be some kind of pepper. "You should take Judy's advice, Muller."

"About what?"

"Making pastries or something. These are great."

"I thought you'd like them."

"Seriously, you could sell these things. Forget the grass. All you need is a little marketing, some packaging, a logo design. Maybe you could call them Muller's Deep Dark Madness."

"That's good."

"You could also sell them online. Maybe do the whole thing as a cross promotion or something."

"What's that?"

"What's what?"

"What you were just saying."

"What was I saying?"

"Promotion or something."

"You sell them with messages on top. You know, company logos, that sort of stuff. Your name is on the packaging itself."

"That's clever, Sam."

"We put messages on cookies once. For one of the big bakeries."

"What were you selling?"

"What do you mean?"

"On the cookies?"

"The bakery."

"What was the message?"

"The name of the bakery."

"Why?"

"Why what?"

"Why did the bakery have the name of the bakery?"

"To promote themselves, for chrissake."

"Didn't they know they were a bakery?"

"Of course they knew they were a bakery. They wanted other people to know they were a bakery."

"Oh, right."

"You're a bit of a dumbass, Muller."

"What was it you wanted to call them again?"

"Call what?"

"My brownies."

"I don't remember."

"I think you're stoned, Sam."

"So are you." We stare across the lawn. Muller sticks his foot through the porch railing. His flip flop goes in the garden. We both look over.

"I think my foot's stuck," Muller says.

"Point your toe."

"That's as much as it points."

I start pulling at his leg. The foot's really wedged in there. Then I go down in the garden and start pushing from the other side. Muller just sits there staring at his foot.

"Pull, for chrissake, Muller. It's not going to come out by itself."

I give his foot a big shove and he goes back in his chair. His glass falls and milk flies everywhere. I come back on the porch and he's lying there with his stomach hanging out.

"You've got milk all over you," I say.

"I know."

"Here's your flip flop."

"Thanks."

"Give me your hand."

"I should probably go change."

"Bring me a cloth while you're in there."

He goes inside and disappears down the basement stairs. The milk's running under the boxes. I have to move everything and then go downstairs for a mop. Muller's putting on some socks.

"Grab that bucket," I say. "We're attracting cats."

"You have cats?"

"No, the milk, Muller. It's running under the boxes. What are you putting on socks for?"

"I don't know," he says. "I could sure use a massage. My back's killing me. Do you think Ruby would come over?"

"She's busy." He keeps sitting there. "Come on, Muller. That milk's going to stink pretty soon."

He turns on the oxygen and puts the mask over his face. He grins like a chimp. "Give me some of that," I say.

He passes it over and I take a hit. Not bad. I wish I had this when I was feeling dizzy. It straightens you right out. Muller has some sort of regulator in the mask. He tried explaining it, but the grass brownie has made me stupid. I thought he wore the mask all night, but he only has it on until he calms down, which varies depending on the weather and his job prospects. He takes another hit of oxygen, going on about its effect on the brain cells. The crazy bastard has degrees in chemistry and science and sounds like that weird scientist in the Thomas Dolby video. Supposedly, the guy was a real scientist and thought Thomas Dolby was a twerp. After ten minutes of passing the oxygen back and forth, Muller and I are two pretty relaxed characters. "What about the cats, Sam?" Muller says, and I remember the milk seeping under the boxes. I grab a mop and go upstairs, the kitchen still smelling like a bakery.

Outside, we clean around the boxes, then we're back in our chairs, feet up on the railing. Muller's eyes are starting to close. I stare at the street, seeing an old guy riding past on his bicycle. He wobbles and totters, disappearing around the corner. There's a clatter of metal and Muller opens his eyes. We get up, leaning over the railing. A few minutes later, the guy comes back, teetering and tottering, waving and taking out one of Mary's dogwoods.

# Chapter 10

*M*ary and Judy came home yesterday and found Muller and I asleep on the porch. They also found the plate of brownies, ate them all, then watched their shows in the living room. Mary scolded me later for leaving Muller out in the sun all afternoon. "You know how easily he burns," she said. "Those were delicious brownies, by the way, Muller. Judy says you might go into catering."

"He's so good," Judy said. "I love his date squares."

This morning, the phone rings. Max is on the other end. He's just come in from a painting job. Ruby's taking a shower.

"How goes it, old man?" he says. "Feel retired yet?"

"You ever try grass brownies?"

"Great stone."

"I know that, Max. Anything I should know about them? Chemical dependency, that sort of thing?"

"What's with you, old man?" Max laughs. "First, you're hanging moons. Now you're eating grass brownies? Who made them?"

"Muller. They're spectacular."

"You got any more?"

"I'll save you one."

"C'mon, Sam. How many did he make? You're giving me *one*? What about Ruby and Otis?"

"Ruby does pot?"

"She loves grass brownies. So does Otis."

"Look, Max, I don't want to make a big deal out of this. Mary watches me like a hawk. She'd kill me if she knew I was doing grass brownies. I can sneak a few over. How's that?"

"Why don't you bring Muller over here? Ruby's got an industrial oven. Then you don't have to sneak around. Come over now."

"I'll see, Max. Are you going to be there all day?"

"Sure. We're doing up mailers for the painting business. Drop over any time. Ruby's got all sorts of pans and stuff. Good ones, too."

"I'll pass that along," I say and hang up.

In the kitchen, Judy and Muller are going through cookbooks. Mary's on the computer. I pour some coffee and sit at the table. "You feel like coming with me this morning, Muller? I'm looking at lawnmowers."

"What's wrong with our lawnmower?" Mary asks.

"It's on the fritz."

"Why can't you get it fixed?"

"I think it's seen its day. You want to go with me or not, Muller? We'll only be gone a couple of hours."

"If it's okay with, Jude."

"Of course it's okay," Judy says. "You don't have to ask. Mom and I are shopping later, anyway."

Muller takes about an hour getting showered and dressed. Once we're in the car, I say, "We're going over to Otis's. I told Max you'd make some grass brownies. Big oven, double burners."

"Do you think Ruby'll give me a massage?"

"Make the brownies first."

"I don't have my special ingredients."

"How many special ingredients are we talking about?"

"Maybe I'd better go back inside and get them."

"And say what, for chrissake? We'll stop somewhere on the way."

"I need special nutmeg."

"You're not making soufflé."

"Soufflé doesn't have nutmeg."

"Look, this is simple: bake and eat. Don't overthink it."

"I could sure use a massage."

"Bake the brownies first."

Inside the J & P, Muller looks at every shelf, going through each spice like a pharmacist. Suddenly, my heart's going faster and faster. I'm all clammy. "Let's get this stuff and go," I say to Muller. We grab nutmeg, cinnamon, and a bag of walnuts. On our way out, Muller starts trying on baseball caps.

"I've got baseball caps at home," I say.

"My head's pretty big."

"Just go wait outside and I'll get this stuff rung through."

"You're really sweating, Sam. You okay?"

"I'm not great in crowded places."

"Let me run this stuff through. You get the car."

"Fine. Just hurry up."

Outside, I'm gulping air. People walk by, a few stop. When Muller comes out with the bags, I'm leaning against a wall.

"You okay?" Muller says.

"Just dandy."

We get to Otis's around twelve thirty. Max and Ruby are stripping wallpaper. Ruby's up on a ladder with a cigarette going.

"Morning," she says and looks at Muller. "Hear you're quite the baker, big fella. Max'll show you where everything is. I want to get this paper off the wall before dinner."

Music blares from the basement. "Damn it, Otis," Ruby yells. "Turn it down."

Muller makes enough brownies to feed the neighborhood. Ruby comes in the kitchen with bits of wallpaper stuck in her hair.

"You've missed your vocation," she says to Muller, running her finger along the edge of the mixing bowl. "Hm-m, no wonder you're beefy. This is sensational."

We take the brownies into the dining room with a jug of milk. Downstairs, we hear Otis moving around. Then there's knocking on the cellar door. "What's going on in my kitchen, Ruby?" he says. "Damn you, woman! All I got is Popsicles down here."

"Ignore him," Ruby says. "What spices do you use, Muller? Nutmeg. What else? I taste something I don't recognize."

"Cayenne pepper. It really brings out the flavor."

"Aren't you the mad scientist."

"I could really use a massage, Ruby."

"Sure, get down on the rug. I'll fix you up. I'm surprised you've got any tension at all with these brownies. I'm loose as a goose."

Max is already on the rug with his hands behind his head. "Shove over, Max," she says. "Muller takes up a lot of floor space. That's not a criticism, Muller. You're just big, that's all. Good to see a beefy man once in a while."

Ruby straddles Muller's back, digging her knuckles into his rolls of fat. He groans and whimpers. "You're a marvel, Ruby," he says.

"All it takes is a knuckle here and there."

Footsteps are coming up the basement stairs again. Otis tries slamming himself against the door, a yelp—"Lord Jesus!"—and he tumbles down the stairs. "Damn you, Ruby!" Seconds later, he comes crashing through the door, one eye squinting around the room. "I won't be ignored, Ruby," he yells. Suspenders hang from his waistband, his stomach bulges out. "You hear me! Dang it all, anyway. What the hell are you up to?"

Otis sniffs the air and makes for the oven. Pans clatter, the oven door slams. Max looks around the corner. "He's scarfing all the brownies, Ruby," he says.

Otis comes in the dining room with a brownie in each hand.

"Don't you look at me that way," he says to Ruby. "Driving a man crazy with fresh baking. What're you sitting on that man's back for? Who the hell is he, anyway?"

"This is Muller, Otis," Ruby says. "He's Sam's son-in-law."

"Who's Sam?" Otis says, stuffing another brownie in his mouth.

"Go easy, Otis," Max says. "Those aren't ordinary brownies."

"What are they then? Is that nutmeg?"

"A little cayenne pepper, too," Muller says.

"Not bad."

"Thank you."

"Ruby," Otis says. "You can't keep me out of my own kitchen. How am I supposed to eat? Living on Popsicles ain't no way to live."

"Your song stopped," Max says.

"Well put something on, Max. I'm trying to talk to your mother. Will you get off that guy, Ruby?"

"Oh, go back downstairs."

"I won't be ignored," Otis yells, then looks at me. "Who are you?"

"Sam."

"Who's he?"

"Muller."

"What the hell's his problem?"

"You've still got dead air, Otis," Max says.

"I'll be right back," Otis says, scarfing another brownie. "Get off that man, Ruby!"

Otis thumps downstairs, suspenders catching on the bannister, a sudden twang, a thump, and Otis tumbles down. "Hell and tarnation," he screams.

"You all right?" Max yells downstairs.

"No, I ain't all right. Where's my Jackie Ross? You seen it, Max?"

"I haven't been down there, old man."

"Folks," Otis says on his show. "You're gonna have to listen to Junior Walker and The All Stars all the way through. I got things to sort out with Ruby. Just hang tight. This here's from Junior's *Shake and Fingerpop* album, startin' with 'Shotgun'. For any of you interested, Junior's first name was Autry. Changed it when he came up from Arkansas. I'll bet"—a large belch—"'cuse me, folks, I'll bet Junior never got locked out of his own kitchen,"—another belch—"and left to fend for hisself with a few Popsicles and Puddin' Pops. I'll be back as soon as I straighten Ruby out. And, remember, folks, before you take any marital vows, get the food arrangements sorted out. Otherwise, you'll be starvin' after your first indiscretion."

The music starts and Otis comes stomping up the stairs again, eyes wide, suspenders dangling. "Dang it, Ruby, how's a man supposed to survive on Popsicles? I'm warning you, I'll kick every door down in this house if you keep—if you keep—Jesus H. Christ, what the hell's in these things?"

"They're pot brownies," Max says. "How many did you eat?"

"I don't know. Five, ten."

"Five or ten?"

"I was hungry."

"You don't look so good, Otis. You'd better sit down."

"I know how to handle a goddam pot brownie, Max. Now, Ruby"—holding out his fist—"I'm not kidding here. Are you listening to me? A man's got a right,"—belch—"as head of this household to whatever you got cookin', and that's a fact. You hear me?"

"Oh, stick it in your ear," she says. "And Max is right. You'd better sit before you fall down."

"I don't need to sit down. I know what you're doin'? You're tryin' to starve,"—belch—"starve me out of my own house. I'm warning you, Ruby . . . I'm . . . Jesus H. Christ, maybe I'd better sit down." Otis leans against the dining room table. "Lord Almighty."

"He's going over, Max," Ruby says.

"I've got him," Max says, catching Otis.

"I don't feel so good."

Otis's eyes roll back. Ruby gets off Muller and comes around the table. She slaps Otis's cheeks. "Otis? Can you hear me, honey? He really looks awful. Otis? Don't go swallowing that big tongue of yours. You'd better get the car started, Max."

"Where . . . where are you taking me?" Otis says.

"You're going to the hospital," Ruby says. "Help me get him to the car. Let's go, Otis. On your feet."

"What about my show?" Otis says. "I got a regular audience."

"You got thirty listeners," Ruby says. "They'll wait. Now get out to the car."

"Put on some Purify Brothers after Junior, Max."

"Either I'm driving you to the hospital or putting on the Purify Brothers. Which do you want? I'm not doing both."

"What the hell's in those stupid brownies?"

"Are you allergic to walnuts?" Muller says.

"No, I ain't allergic to dang walnuts."

"Might be his sugar levels."

"Are you tryin' to kill me, Ruby?"

"Nobody's trying to kill you, Otis."

"Starve me, then poison me. There's only so much a man can take, woman."

"His eyes are rolling back again."

"What the hell do you expect? That big ape poisoned me!"

"Nobody poisoned you, old man. You ate too many brownies, that's all."

"Get my gun, Max. I'm gonna shoot that big ape."

"You don't have a gun, Otis."

"I used to have a gun."

"You traded it for some Isaac Hayes."

"Dammit to hell."

We take Otis through the kitchen and out to the car. He tries to grab a brownie on the way out.

# Chapter 11

They pumped Otis's stomach last night. His sugar levels were through the roof. It's a wonder he's still alive, considering he's overweight, undernourished and, for the most part, an asshole. He got delirious at one point, talking about the injustices of the public school system, then the benefits of neutering squirrels. They gave him a sedative and he drifted off. Ruby stuck around in case he woke up and started abusing the staff. Max went back to the house to do Otis's show. Muller and I went straight to bed as soon as we got home.

This morning, Mary wakes me up, telling me it's after ten. The sun is shining, sprinklers are going, the old man falls off his bike.

"Where's Judy and Muller?" I ask her.

"In the back yard. Muller's doing jumping jacks."

Out the kitchen window, Muller's in an old track suit, hands going up and down, Judy watching from a lawn chair. Meek and Beek flap around their cage on the back porch. From the computer, I can hear Max say, "That was Sam Cooke singing 'You Send Me.' We'll be working our way to number one, so stick around. This is all music, all the time, straight from The Rec Room of Sound."

Max is working two old turntables. Behind him, there's a couch stacked with laundry.

"Muller put it on earlier," Mary says. "I like the songs."

"*The Rec Room of Sound*?"

"Max is pretty good, Sam. Ruby's around somewhere."

Max shifts around in Otis's chair. "I'm gonna leave you for a minute, folks," Max says. "Ruby's filling in while I'm gone. She's in between loads of laundry, anyway."

Ruby appears with a cigarette in the corner of her mouth. "Hi, folks," she says. "Max is getting Otis some Epsom salts. He was in the hospital last night, but he's making a speedy recovery. He'll be back with you as soon as he takes a bath. Meanwhile, I've got a few of my favorites I'd like to play. Just before I do that, if any of you need some painting done, I'm a good hand with a brush and roller. So's Max. We're trying to get our painting business going, so give us a call or e-mail us." She holds up a card with the phone number and email address. "Now I'll play you something I found in my collection upstairs. It's not R&B, but I think you'll like it just the same. You all know Bruce Springsteen from that 'Born in the USA' stuff, but Max's dad and I used to slow mo' to this one. It's called, 'Racing in the Streets,' and it's a real tear jerker."

The music starts, and Bruce is singing about his sixty-nine Chevy, a great car in its day, but it took me a long time to realize he was saying *Fuelie* heads, not furry heads. It made all those years of trying to sound like Springsteen in the shower seem ridiculous now.

"Sam," I hear Mary say. "Are you listening to me?"

"What?"

"I said, has Muller mentioned anything about having a baby?"

"Not in any detail. Why?"

"Judy's worried he's distracted."

"Maybe that's a good thing."

"How's that a good thing? Judy wants a baby, Sam."

"Muller's not exactly baby-making material."

"Why?"

"The man sleeps with an oxygen tank, Mary."

"He has sleep apnea. Besides, why would an oxygen tank interfere with having a baby?"

"I'm just saying he's a bit of a hypochondriac."

"He's down on his luck, that's all. Look at you, for God's sake. You fall down in a supermarket at the drop of a hat."

"Maybe this isn't the right time for a baby. Maybe he'll be fine once they're back to Seattle. Familiar surroundings, you know."

"Judy thinks it's more than that. I want you to talk to him."

"I've tried talking to him. He keeps telling me about his stiffy."

"So?"

"I don't want to hear about his stiffy."

"Did he say anything else?"

"He mentioned something about Judy being critical."

"Did you ever think he might be opening up to you?"

"I don't need to hear about his stiffies. He'll be discussing positions next. I'm just trying to be a good father here, Mary."

"So what do you suggest?"

"Maybe he should talk to Krupsky."

"Krupsky? I don't understand him half the time."

"What do you want me to do?"

"I want you to have a frank discussion with him, Sam. He respects you. Give him some pointers. Tell him how we had Judy."

"I don't remember how we had Judy. Besides, if he can't get a stiffy, what's the point?"

"That's a terrible thing to say."

"Just an observation."

"Look, Sam, Judy wants to get pregnant, preferably before they leave."

"She's got a schedule now? No wonder he can't get it up. Why don't *you* talk to him? You're his mother-in-law. Don't sons listen to their mothers more than their fathers?"

"You're evading, Sam."

"So I'm evading. Let nature take its course. If he gets it up, he gets it up. I can't do anything about it."

"I think those panic attacks have diminished your compassion."

"I've got plenty of compassion."

Mary takes the laptop into the sunroom and turns up the volume.

"That was 'Racing in the Streets', folks," Ruby is saying. "Hope you didn't mind me straying from Otis's format. That song just turns me to jelly. Thanks, Bruce. You paint a good picture."

Fast cars and a girl waiting on the porch. I'll bet Bruce never had a problem with stiffies.

# Chapter 12

*M*uller's cutting the grass while Judy meditates in the sunroom. I'm sitting at the computer watching Max and Ruby guide Otis into frame. He's wearing suspenders over a tank top. Pieces of toilet paper hang from his ear. At least his eyes aren't rolling around anymore.

"I'd like to send this one out to all the girls—" Otis starts off and a hand smacks him across the head. "Ouch! Okay, *women* out there who have known some level of sadness in their lives. This is from the early days of Stax Records. It's by Isaac Hayes and David Porter called, 'When Something is Wrong with My Baby.'" The needle makes a popping noise. "I remember Sam and Dave singing this at the Lyceum," he says. "Imagine those boys in their prime. They sure knew how to build up a sweat." He sits back, closing his eyes.

Ruby goes to the laundry room and turns on the washing machine. "Ruby, cut it out!" Otis yells. "I got laundry to do, Otis," Ruby yells back. "Tell your listeners this is a working household. We got chores like everybody else."

She comes out and pulls a shirt over his head. The record pops and hisses to the end, then Otis goes straight into Little Milton's, "Baby I Love You." Ruby's folding towels in the background. When the song ends, Otis cues up another. "Here's one for Ruby," he says, grabbing her by the hand. It's The Stylistics and Ruby is noticeably touched but still tries squirming away.

"Cut it out, Otis," she says. "I'm try to fold here. Lay off."

"You're my everything, Ruby," he says.

"Damn you, Otis."

They disappear out of frame, making enough racket to bring Max downstairs. "For crying out loud," he says, as Ruby squeals and Otis bangs his head. Max steps over them and sits in Otis's chair.

"Pardon my folks," Max says. "They've had some setbacks these past few months. I guess they're ready to kiss and make up. I just wish they wouldn't do it here."

Ruby lets out another squeal. Max quickly tilts the computer screen up showing the acoustical ceiling with watermarks.

"I'm leaving if you're going to do that," Max says to them. "Seriously. I mean it, you guys. Knock it off."

"I want to make a request," Otis calls out.

"Make it a short one," Ruby says. "I got a cake in the oven."

A shirt is flung through the air. "I just ironed that, Otis," Ruby says. "That's why I took it off."

"I'm out of here," Max says.

"Put Wee Willie Walker on the other turntable, Max."

"Put it on yourself, old man."

"I'm busy here."

Max goes back, finds Wee Willie Walker, and cues it up.

# Chapter 13

*I*'m back at the agency, walking down the hall past Nick's office. Dewey's in there, talking away. Margot's further down the corridor at the Xerox machine. I hear Frank on the phone in the distance telling some client to fuck off. Margot appears in my office with a photo of Joey, her Mynah bird. He's in his yellow coffin, claws crossed. "He was the best friend I ever had, Sam," she says and starts to cry.

I wake up feeling terrible. I must have groaned because Mary tells me to go back to sleep. I close my eyes, but I keep thinking about Margot. The last time we were together, she said, "All I want to do now is Sudoku puzzles." It's her one true addiction. "Outside of my poor Joey," she said. "Bless his little heart."

When I wake up again, it's morning, and I hear Muller in the bathtub. Judy is in the sunroom with the paper on her lap. Meek and Beek jump around nibbling at each other. Mary must be downstairs trying to straighten the frame on Muller's cot. As I walk by the computer, I see Max filling in for Otis again. ". . . and that was Little Johnnie Taylor with 'Honey Lou' . . ."

"Hey, sweetie," I say to Judy, kissing her on the forehead. "Do you know anything about Mynah birds?"

"Why Mynah birds?"

"Friend of mine lost hers a few years ago. We worked together for a long time. She was here at one of our Christmas parties. Do you remember Margot?"

"Aunt Margot?"

"That's right, you used to call her Auntie Margot."

"You *told* me to call her Auntie Margot."

"I probably did."

"She brought me a book of puzzles. She still alive?"

"We think so, sweetie. Hard to say. Thing is, Margot had her Mynah quite a few years—"

"She never shut up about it."

"That's true. People get like that sometimes. One day your mom and I will be eating through straws. Anyway, Auntie Margot is all alone now. I thought I'd buy her another Mynah."

"That's sweet, Daddy. Love birds are nicer, though."

"I think Margot's got a thing for Mynahs."

"Okay. Do you want me to go with you to the pet store?"

"I'd like that. Where's your mother?"

"Downstairs changing Muller's sheets."

"Why don't you and I go to the store now? Give Mary and Muller a chance to bond."

"That would be great, Daddy."

"Could you get your love muffin out of the tub? Daddy wants to shave and brush his teeth."

"Sure."

She goes down the hall, knocking on the bathroom door. Muller comes out. "Washroom's free, Daddy," she calls out. Muller's wet footprints are everywhere. I shave, brush my teeth, and step around Muller's puddles. When I come out again, I find Mary in the kitchen. "I'm taking Judy to look for a Mynah bird," I say.

"Why does she need a Mynah bird?"

"It's not for her. I'm getting one for Margot. I had a dream about her last night. She lost Joey a few years ago."

"That's a sweet gesture, Sam."

"You don't mind me taking Judy, do you?"

"Of course not. She's your daughter, for God's sake."

I hear Max on The Rec Room of Sound. He's saying Otis is still in bed. ". . . I'll be with you until he gets up. Here's Percy Sledge's 'When a Man Loves a Woman,' going out to my parents who kept me up half the night with their frickin' noise. Thanks for that, folks."

Judy is giggling in the bedroom.

"We won't be long," I say to Mary. "You'll be okay here alone with the love muffin?" Mary swats me with a dishtowel. "Anything you need at the store?" I say.

"Oh, walnuts. Muller says he's going to reveal the special ingredients of those brownies of his. What's wrong? You went all pale there for a second. You're not having another panic attack, are you?"

"No, no, I'm fine. You enjoy your day with Muller. Judy and I will get your walnuts."

Judy comes out with her arm around Muller's waist. His hair is plastered across his forehead. "Ready, Daddy," she says. "Muller and Mom are making soufflé."

"That's nice, honey. Let's go."

She gives Muller a big sloppy kiss. "Bye, Big Bear," she says to him.

"Off we go," I say, pushing Judy out the door. "And, Muller," I say. "Let's not give away too many of your culinary secrets."

"What's that supposed to mean?" Mary says.

"Just saying he shouldn't give everything away. Every chef needs to leave a bit to the imagination."

"Do you know what he's talking about?" Mary asks Muller.

Muller just stands there like a dummy.

"Honestly, Sam," Mary says. "Go find your Mynah."

There's still a milk stain around Muller's crotch. You'd think Judy would notice these things. Maybe that's what love's all about, ignoring the obvious, tolerating the stupid. We're blinded, we accept, we find lip-smacking and jaw-grinding cute and endearing.

We're all pretty sick when you think about it.

# Chapter 14

"They're highly imitative birds," the pet store guy is saying. We're in the back where parakeets carry on like a church social. An orange-billed black Mynah sits in a large cage. It walks back and forth, making a strange squawking sound. Then it rises up on it haunches and bobs. "Mynahs have very strong feet," the guy says. They look like something you'd find on a trapeze artist.

"What's his name?" Judy asks.

"Bisquick," the guy says. "No idea why. He's clever as hell, though. Ask him if he wants a sauna."

Judy goes close to the cage. "Do you want a sauna, Bisquick?" she asks. Bisquick squawks.

"He can imitate sixteen consonants and four vowels," the guy says.

"Is that good?" I ask.

"Better than some pet owners." He opens the cage and Bisquick hops out on his arm. "They're common as anything in Malaysia and India," he says. "Not like the Bali Mynah. This is a Hill Mynah." He strokes the bird's chest. "Tell them you want a sauna," he says.

"Mango," Bisquick replies.

"You want a sauna first. Sau-u-una. Sauna."

"Sauna," Bisquick says.

Judy laughs and Bisquick jumps over on her shoulder. "You might want to be careful," the guy says.

"Why?" Judy says.

"He's got a bad habit. That's why I'm not charging a lot. These birds can run up to twelve thousand dollars."

"What are you charging?" I ask.

"One thousand."

"Why the discount?"

Bisquick plunges his head down and goes for Judy's right breast. "Nipple grabber," the guys says.

"Ouch," Judy says.

"Can't get him to stop."

"Auntie Margot isn't going to like that."

"I might come down to eight hundred," the guy says.

"Fuck, suck, fuck," Bisquick says.

"Five hundred's the best I can do."

"Are you sure Margot wants a Mynah that swears, Daddy?"

"She'll be fine, sweetie."

Margot swears worse than that on a good day, anyway.

# Chapter 15

*M*argot lives in one of the older high-rises just off North Kingsbury. It was an exclusive area once, but now there's a feeling of a bygone era. Coming off the elevator, I put Bisquick's cage behind my back. Judy knocks on Margot's door. There's shuffling around inside, then Margot answers with her bifocals down her nose. Bisquick lets out a squawk.

"What have you got there?" Margot says.

"Ta da," I say, pulling the cover off Bisquick's cage.

"Tatas, tits," Bisquick squawks.

Margot pushes up her bifocals and examines Bisquick. "That's a mighty fine bird."

"Ask him if he wants a sauna," I say.

"Get in here before the neighbors start looking out their peepholes," Margot says to us. "What's the bird's name?"

"Bisquick," Judy says.

"This is my daughter, Margot. You remember Judy."

"Of course I remember Judy. I'm not senile. How are ya, Judy? You've grown up to be a fine looking young woman."

"I'm in my thirties."

"I'm in my sixties. Take the compliment."

Margot clears a space for the cage on the dining table. Every square inch is covered with newspapers and Sudoku puzzles. Out on the balcony, Margot has three plastic owls wired to the railing. She opens the cage door and Bisquick hops out. The place is adequate in his opinion. He gives the owls and pigeons equal consideration. "Sit down," Margot says to us. "You want coffee or anything?"

"We're fine," I say. "We just came over to surprise you."

"What made you think I wanted a bird?"

"Daddy saw you in a dream."

"A dream?"

"I dreamt of the office last night," I say. "You were showing me a picture of Joey. I thought you might be missing him."

"Poor, Joey. Bless his heart. Keeled over one day like a downed Spitfire. Wish I had more pictures of him. So you figured I needed company, did you? That's very thoughtful." Bisquick jumps over on her shoulder. "A bird's a big responsibility, Sam. Especially at my age."

"You're not old."

Bisquick pecks at her breast. "Lord love him," Margot laughs. "Just like Joey." Bisquick takes another peck at her breast. "Persistent little rascal," Margot says.

"He did that to me in the store," Judy says.

"Just like my Joey." She pets Bisquick's head and smiles. "Okay, Sam," she says. "You done good." Bisquick bobs his head up and down.

"He does grow on you, doesn't he?" Judy says.

"That's a Mynah for you," Margot says. "Hell of a nipple grabber, though. Guess I'll have to get used to it. How are you doin', Sam?"

"Not bad. Judy and her husband are here for their holidays. Maybe we can get you over for dinner."

"That's a great idea, Daddy. You'll come over, won't you Auntie Margot?"

"I'm not loaded with invitations. What's your hubby's name?"

"Muller," Judy says. "We're trying to have a baby."

"Well, honey, it's not rocket science. When you say 'trying', that mean someone's not pulling his weight?"

"Muller's a little down lately."

"Men are all the same. They're only really good during Lent and halftimes. Got yourself some cute girlie stuff?"

"I've tried the stockings, the garters—"

"Let's leave it at that, shall we?" I say. "I'm sure Auntie Margot can figure out the rest."

"What's the bug up your ass?" Margot says.

"Asshole," Bisquick lets out.

"I'm just saying we get the picture."

"Look, Judy, you know the drill. Get both parties hot and bothered and let nature do the rest."

"Asshole," Bisquick says.

"They'll figure it out, Margot."

"Good thing it wasn't you telling Judy about the birds and the bees. She'd be working in an aviary right now."

"Daddy never told me about the birds and the bees."

"You're a slacker, Sam."

"She's in her thirties, for chrissake."

"It might have helped, Daddy."

"I'll give you one piece of advice, Judy," Margot says. "Don't leave it to science. Men operate on blood flow only. Right, Sam?"

"Okay, enough."

"Just trying to help."

"We should get going. Glad you like Bisquick."

"Like I said, you done good."

"Good luck with him, Auntie Margot. Hope you come for dinner."

"I'll be there with bells on, kiddo. Good luck with the baby making. Just grab Muller by the ears, Judy. Works every time."

"Bye, Margot," I say. "Enjoy the bird." Bisquick makes another play for Margot's nipple. He never gives up.

# Chapter 16

The grocery store is full of kids banging their toys against canned goods and end-of-aisle displays. We get the walnuts and go next door to the liquor store. "It should be French if we're having soufflé," Judy is saying. I look around nervously, wondering if this is the place where I pressed my ass against the window. I honestly don't remember. We go to the French section and get a wine neither of us can pronounce. It's good having a little time with Judy. She freaks me out a bit, a grown woman calling me "Daddy" all the time, but Judy's always been like that. She has names for everybody. Mary was the same when she was younger. She used to call me "The Bean" because I was so skinny. My weight's stayed pretty much the same over the years, probably because of ruffage. These days, Mary occasionally calls me "Cranky Face" because of my sunken cheeks. "How are you and Muller doing?" I ask Judy. "Any problems?"

"Like what? Why are you looking so nervous?"

"Nothing, sweetie. So everything's fine?"

"I think so. Why, did Muller say something to you?"

"About what?"

"He seems distant these days. It's not like him."

"Maybe he's not used to sleeping in the basement."

"He says I'm putting too much pressure on him. Like the other night. I wanted to try something—"

"Keep the graphic stuff to yourself, sweetie. I'm trying to be a parent here. Let's talk about something else."

"How are you and Mom getting along?"

"I think she wants me to be a greeter at Lowe's."

"I wish Muller would find something."

"How about a chef's course?"

"He has a chef's degree. Muller's got lots of degrees. He just has to apply himself. He's really a great cook."

"I know he is, honey." I keep seeing Otis's eyes rolling back in his head.

"Will you talk to Muller, Daddy?"

"And say what?"

"He listens to you."

"We'd better get going. Your mother needs the walnuts."

Out by the car, I see the old couple from the paint store. The woman recognizes me. She nudges her husband. "Hello there," she calls out. "How are you feeling?"

I push Judy towards our car like we're in a hurry. "Just fine," I call back.

"Who are they?" Judy says.

"I think I met them in a waiting room."

"Are you sure you're okay? You seem jumpy."

"Let's get in the car." The old couple watch us drive way.

Turning off Canfield later, Judy says to me, "Muller should cook. He's happy when he cooks. He's very creative."

"Seattle must have a lot of restaurants."

"Stop trying to get rid of us, Daddy."

"Sorry. I think Muller will make a great chef."

"I liked what you did for Auntie Margot, by the way."

I keep seeing Bisquick pecking at Margot's boobs. "Determined little bugger, isn't he?"

Margot kept saying. And priced accordingly.

# Chapter 17

The Rec Room of Sound plays, the soufflé rises, and Otis stares out at us from his computer. "Here's Percy Sledge doing another Dan Penn, Spooner Oldham composition called, 'It Tears Me Up,'" he says, "which I intend to do myself, shortly, thanks to our friend, Muller. We're on our way to 'I Want to Be Free,' by Joe Tex. Here's a little known fact. James Brown stole Joe's dance moves, especially dropping to his knees and the cape. Stay tuned. I'll be back after I eat my wacky brownie."

I jump up and head for the door.

"Sam—" Mary says.

"I left my wallet at the liquor store." I run out, jump in my car, and drive like crazy over to Otis's house. Max and Ruby are out front trimming roses. I run past them up the front steps. "Crisis," I yell, and they follow.

"What's up?" Max says.

"Your father's naming names," I say.

We find Otis downstairs, licking his fingers. "I'm gonna take a short siesta on the couch, folks," he says. "I'll just let Albert King play through. In the meantime, look around your houses and see if you need any painting done. My wife's affordable and thorough. Don't believe that crap about College Painters. They're all immigrants getting ripped off left and right."

I drag Otis out of frame and upstairs. "You said Muller's name *on air*, you dumb bastard," I say. "My daughter can hear that."

Otis's eyes remind me of a bass. "Freedom of speech is guaranteed under the First Amendment"—he hiccups and slaps his chest—"of our beloved Constitution."

"Fuck the Constitution," I say. "Quit saying Muller's name on air. Quit saying it *period*. If my wife finds out we're making grass brownies, there won't be any more. Understand?"

"Duly noted," he says.

"Sorry, Sam," Max says. "On that same subject, though. Any chance of Muller making another batch? Otis cleaned us out."

"Not according to him," I say.

"Have you been hiding brownies, old man?" Max says, grabbing Otis. "Is this my shirt? Stop wearing my clothes."

"I put clean shirts in your drawer yesterday, Otis," Ruby says.

"I have to go," I say. "Muller's making soufflé."

"God, I'm starving, Ruby," Otis says. "Make a soufflé, will you?"

"I don't know how to make a soufflé."

"Make your own soufflé, old man," Max says. "Hoarding our brownies. You're lucky we don't lock you downstairs again."

"One little soufflé!"

"Forget it, Otis, we got gardening to do."

# Chapter 18

The soufflé turns out light as cotton candy, and like cotton candy, you wonder if you ate anything at all. You remember opening your mouth, chewing, rolling it around, but then you're wondering if it's a hoax. You don't feel like you've eaten, even if there are a few walnuts and turnip French fries left on the plate. "I've gotta hand it to you," I say to Muller as we're clearing the table, "you've got talent. I might need a snack in an hour, but the food was delicious."

"What's delicious, Daddy?" Judy says from the living room. She's going through the channels on the remote. Half the time, she runs right past the show she wants to watch. "Mom, it's on," she says, and Mary comes out of the washroom. It's American Idol night. Muller and I do the dishes and then slip outside behind the garage.

"We'd better lay off the grass brownies for a while," I say. "Otis can't keep his mouth shut on air."

"He says there's a market for grass brownies, Sam."

"Don't listen to Otis, for chrissake. The man's a walking identity crisis. Do you want to end up like him?"

"I would if I had Ruby."

"If you—what?"

"If I had Ruby."

"What the hell are you talking about?"

"I really like Ruby, Sam."

"Come again?"

"She makes me feel good about myself."

"So she makes you feel good, so what?"

"I think I'm falling for her, Sam."

"You—you're telling me you've got the hots for Ruby? Are you out of your fucking mind?

"I'm just telling you how I feel."

"I don't give a rat's ass how you feel. Christ, you're one fucked up prick. That's my daughter in there. Your *wife*, for chrissake. Doesn't that mean anything to you?"

The back window opens. May calls out. "Sam? Are out there? Is Muller with you?"

I push Muller into the garage. "Get in the car," I say. "I'll tell the girls we're taking a drive." I go inside and grab my keys off the kitchen counter.

"Where are you going now?" Mary says.

"I'm taking Muller out for a drive by the lake. Won't be long."

"Pick up some ice cream, Daddy," Judy says.

"Okay, sweetheart."

My heart's going zip-a-dee-doo-dah and my tongue is at the back of my throat. You hear about domestic violence and wonder what pushes people over the edge. All the neighbors say, "Nice couple, quiet," but that's a front, a ruse. Next thing you know, there's tape across the front door. Read the papers. I've been a calm man up to now, loving husband, doting father. All that could go in a heartbeat with Muller around. I'm gripping the steering wheel so hard, my knuckles look like ping pong balls.

# Chapter 19

All the way to Montrose Beach, Muller sits there, smoking these bent cigarettes he keeps in his back pocket. They're shaped like his ass. I park, turn out my headlights, then light my own cigarette. I puff, seeing ghostly eyes in my rearview mirror. "Boy, I'd like to knock your teeth in right now," I say.

"Sorry, Sam."

"You're a grown man. You're married. You have responsibilities."

"I can't help how I feel."

"For chrissake, Muller. You can't go around getting stiffies every time someone sticks a knuckle in your back."

"I know that."

"Give me one good reason why I shouldn't go tell Judy."

"I wouldn't blame you."

"You want to end your marriage, is that it?"

"I love Judy, Sam."

"Then what? What is it?"

"I just feel good around Ruby."

"Don't give me that crap."

"I've never felt like this before."

"You're one sick dickhead, you know that? Do you know what this would do to Judy if she found out? Do you, you fat fuck?"

Muller lets out a short sob. "I'd kill myself before I hurt Judy."

"Yeah, well do it then. Go kill yourself. There's the lake. I'll say you tried to help a terrier in distress. There's probably one out there somewhere." Muller opens the car door and climbs out. "Get back in the car, Muller."

He shakes his head and walks off down the beach. At the water's edge, he kicks off his sandals, goes in the water up to his waist, and then disappears below the surface.

I wait a minute. Then two minutes. The stupid bastard's not coming up. I toss my cigarette and jump out of the car. I run down the beach and make a shallow dive. Water goes up my nose. I come to the surface, then dive down again. Under the murky water, I see Muller's face, cheeks puffed out, hair rising. I pull him up coughing and belching. "What the fuck are you playing at?" I yell.

We stumble up on the sand and collapse. I can hardly breathe. The asshole rolls on his stomach, his pants stuck up his butt crack. I pull him to his feet and push him towards the car. We're covered in sand and smell terrible. I get in, slam the car in reverse, and drive out along Lakeshore to Foster. I can't even look at him I'm so mad. "Why would you do that?" I say.

"I don't know."

"You could have drowned us both."

"I'm confused."

"You're a moron."

"You should have left me."

"And tell my daughter what? Sorry honey, Muller isn't coming home. He wasn't as good a swimmer as he thought he was."

"I'm an excellent swimmer, Sam."

"Shut up, Muller."

"I'm just saying I'm certified."

"And I'm telling you I don't give a shit."

"Just saying—"

I grab my hat off the floor and start smacking him. His big arms come up covering his head. "I don't care, you hear me?" I yell. "I don't care! I don't give a rat's ass if you can swim!" I'm breathing hard, my eyes getting more ghostly in the rearview mirror. Muller takes out his cigarettes. They're soaking wet. He still tries to get one going. "Give me that," I say, throwing it out the window.

I pull into a parking lot next to a variety store. I get out, slam the door, kick the trim. Then I go in, grab Judy's ice cream, and ask for a carton of cigarettes. "What happened to you?' the guy at the counter asks.

"Just bag the stuff." I take everything out to the car. Muller's throwing up out the window. I go back in the store and buy paper towels.

Coming outside again, I toss everything through his window. "Here," I say, "I got paper towels and cigarettes." Muller sits there with the stuff on his lap. "Give me a cigarette," I say.

He fumbles around, tearing things, the ice cream container falling on the car floor. He finally gets the carton open and hands me a cigarette. He doesn't take one for himself. "Do you want a cigarette?" I say.

"I don't smoke that kind." He takes out his wet cigarettes again. I grab the pack and throw it out the window. We drive home without talking.

As we pull in the driveway, I say to him, "Let me do the talking, okay? Just shut up. Don't say a fucking word." He belches up a bit of Lake Michigan. "You slipped on some rocks."

"Okay."

"I tried to grab you and fell in, too."

"Okay. . . . thanks, Sam."

"For what?"

"I don't know." He starts sobbing again.

# Chapter 20

*M*uller's in bed with an ear infection. Judy brings him warm tea while Mary watches me over the newspaper. She's been eyeing me all morning. There's sand in the carpet and a few spots on the kitchen floor where we dribbled water last night. I told her we went out on some rocks and Muller slipped. I went after him. It sounded believable, but you never know with Mary. She likes to ruminate. It's the ruminating that kills you in the end. "Sam," Mary says.

The phone rings. "Hold that thought," I say. I grab the receiver. It's Margot.

"Sam?" she says.

"Hey, Margot. How're you liking your bird?"

"Over the moon, Sam. Over the moon. Bisquick's a natural performer. I bought a video camera. He's up on YouTube right now. I've got eight hundred views already. Check him out. He's adorable. Smart as a whip, too."

The doorbell rings. I hand Mary the phone and answer the door. There's Max standing on the porch, looking at the boxes.

"Hey, Sam," he says. "Just thought I'd drop by, see how you're doing." He looks past me. "Muller here?" He keeps making facial gestures. Mary looks around the corner. "Hi, Mrs. Bennett," he says. "Hope I'm not disturbing you."

"For heaven's sake, Sam," Mary says. "Don't leave him standing there. Come in, Max. We're watching Bisquick on YouTube."

Mary and Judy are at the computer. He's sitting on Margot's shoulder, talking away. I'm more impressed with Margot figuring out how to operate a video camera.

"Is she a ventriloquist?" Max says.

"It's a Mynah," I say. "I gave it to her last week."

"How does she get him to swear like that?"

"That's what Mynahs do, apparently."

"Tell the folks what you've been doing today, Bisquick," Margot's saying and Bisquick bobs up and down. "Did you take a sauna?"

"Sauna," he squawks.

"Bless your little heart."

"Gimme some tit action."

"Bisquick."

Christ, she's teaching him Joey's eulogy.

"That's pretty cool," Max says. "Otis has to see this." He calls the house. Ruby must have picked up the phone. "Hey, Ruby," Max says. "Tell Otis to get on YouTube. There's this bird I want him to see. Go to Bisquick, The Talking Myna. I'll hold."

Muller comes in the kitchen with a piece of cotton baton in one ear. Max switches from YouTube to The Rec Room of Sound. Otis is checking the video out on his other computer. He still hasn't shaved. The phone is tucked between his shoulder and his ear. "Excuse me, folks," Otis is saying. "Max wants me to look at this video on YouTube. Got a talking birdie or something here." Ruby's looking over his shoulder. "Is that old girl a ventriloquist?" he says to Max on the phone.

"No, it's the bird, Otis," Max says. "Mynah's can talk."

"If you call that talking. Foul-mouthed little bugger, isn't he?"

"Listen, Otis. Sam knows the woman. He gave her the bird. What do you think about interviewing Bisquick on your show?"

"You want me to interview a bird?"

"Why not? Bisquick's a natural."

"I think he's adorable," Ruby says.

"See?" Max says. "Ruby thinks it's a good idea. What have you got to lose? All you do is sit there tapping pencils."

"Okay, Max," Otis says. "Hear that, folks? I'm gonna interview a talking birdie. Set it up, Max. Until then, let's hear the Box Tops' singing 'The Letter.' Coming at you from The Rec Room of Sound."

We call Margot and she's over the moon. "Any wardrobe requirements?" she says, and I tell her The Rec Room of Sound is pretty casual. "When are we doing this? Bisquick's ready to go."

"When do you want her to do the show, Max?"

"Why not now?"

"We'll pick you up in about fifteen minutes, Margot," I say.

"Fine with me. Just let me clean Bisquick's cage."

"Isn't this great?" Judy says. "Margot's going to be on TV."

"It's a web show, sweetie. Don't get your hopes up too high."

"Why are you being so skeptical?" Mary says.

"Otis has the attention span of a fruit bat, for one thing."

"C'mon, Sam," Max says. "It'll be fine."

"Let's go get Margot then."

"Take, Muller, Daddy," Judy says. "We'll watch from here."

"If you're sure you don't mind, Jude," Muller says.

"Of course I don't mind. You and Daddy go bond."

"Just stay out of the lake, Sam," Mary says.

Out by the car, Max starts in again about the brownies, telling Muller he might as well bake a batch while he's over there.

"Maybe we should lay off the brownies for a while," I say.

"What for?"

"Otis can't keep his mouth shut, for one thing. Seriously, Max. Mary and Judy watch his show. They're watching it right now."

"We already talked to him. He won't do that again."

"He's a nutcase, Max."

"Ruby says he won't get any sex if he opens his mouth."

"He'll just go find a mail carrier or a meter maid."

"I promise, Sam. Not a word out of Otis."

"I could make a small tray," Muller mumbles.

"Fine," I say. "One small tray, and that's it."

# Chapter 21

---

"*L*et me just finish up my segment, folks, and we'll get started," Otis is saying while Bisquick jumps from Margot's shoulder to the turntable. Otis is already onto his next program; something called *Otis Cries for You*. It's a concept that only Otis could invent, meaning it's the dumbest thing I've ever heard. He invites people to send in their saddest blogs and he commiserates by crying. The blogs and emails have been coming in all morning.

"This one's a corker," he says. "A woman in Rocksmith just lost her dog. Came face to face with a cement truck. You know who wins in circumstances like that, ma'am. I feel your hurt. You keep your chin up. Chester's in a better place." Otis chokes back a sob, and then wipes his eyes. "I hope you folks will continue to share your sad tales," he says. "We'll get back to them at two o'clock. Meanwhile, let's bring a little smiley face to your day with Bisquick, the talking Mynah birdie."

Otis pulls a chair over for Margot. "So, Margot," he says. "You've only had Bisquick a few days, I hear. First impressions?"

"He's a wonderful bird," she says. "His language isn't the greatest, but that's the fault of his former owner."

Bisquick jumps over onto Otis's big stomach. He bobs up and down.

"Friendly thing," Otis says.

"He's going for your nipple."

"Why would he go for my—ouch! Ouch!"

"Don't jerk around. He thinks you've got a berry."

"A berry? Ouch!"

"Bisquick, bad bird."

"Son of a bitch—ouch!"

Margot tries pulling Bisquick away. He keeps hanging on to Otis's nipple and flapping his wings. Ruby comes out of the laundry room with folded shirts. "What are you doing to that bird, Otis?" she says.

"I'm not doing anything! He's got my nipple!"

"Bisquick thinks he's got a berry under his shirt," Margot says.

"Want me to get him some blueberries?"

"Do something!" Otis yells. He falls off his chair, bringing Bisquick down with him. Wings flap, Ruby laughs, and Max has to take the controls.

"We'll be back with more Bisquick in a minute, folks," Max says. "Meanwhile, send in your saddest stories. We'll read 'em right here at two o'clock, four o'clock and six o'clock on The Rec Room of Sound."

Ruby comes back downstairs with some blueberries. Bisquick jumps right in the bowl. "All he wants is a berry," Ruby says.

"Like hell," Otis says below the turntables. His head appears, hair disheveled. He gets back in his chair and moves his lips around trying to get his dentures back in place. "Okay," Otis sighs, rubbing his nipple. "Is that bird gonna talk or just grab my thingies?"

"Tell Otis what I taught you, Bisquick," Margot says. "Come on. What did Joey always say? Joey says? Joey says?"

"Get—get that thing away from me," Otis says, swatting Bisquick. "Bird's got a one track mind. Go peck someone else's nipple."

"He really likes yours," Margot says.

"So did Max when he was a baby," Ruby laughs

"You didn't have to say that on air," Max says.

"Don't scratch my records, you stupid bird," Otis says. "Can't you cage this thing, Margot?" Margot opens the cage door but Bisquick isn't interested. "Come on, Bisquick," she says.

"Do like your mama tells you," Otis says.

"He's wants more berries."

"Ruby, go get him some berries."

"I've got laundry to do, Otis." Margot starts helping Ruby fold sheets.

Otis cues up a record. "Here's a favorite of mine called 'Hungry for Your Love' by Joe Perkins," he says. "Listen away while I find this dang bird something besides my gibblies. More Bisquick coming your way at the top of the hour, so stick around."

Muller and I are upstairs watching on Ruby's computer. The latest batch of brownies has just come out of the oven. Downstairs, Bisquick says "cocksucker" every time Joe Perkins hits a high note. Otis comes into the kitchen rubbing his right nipple. "Bird's wearing out its welcome," he says, grabbing a brownie.

Ruby and Margot bring up the laundry. Max follows with Bisquick on his shoulder, bobbing up and down. He jumps on the counter and goes after the brownie crumbs. "You're gonna have one sick bird in a minute," Otis says.

"Why?" Margot says.

"Them brownies aren't to be trifled with."

"What's he on about?" Margot asks Ruby.

"They're grass brownies," Ruby says. "Have one."

"Don't mind if I do."

"Margot," I say.

"Oh, go fly a kite, Sam."

"Dang bird's going after my nipple again," Otis says. "What's his problem? You train him to do that?"

"Not me," Margot says.

"Get away from my brownie, damn you," Otis swats at Bisquick. "Go lie down or something."

"Bird's don't lie down," Margot says.

"He chewed off a corner of my brownie."

"They don't chew, either."

"Look at that little bastard."

"He sure loves brownies," Max says.

"I don't know about putting a stoned bird on air," Otis says, popping the last of the brownie in his mouth. "Probably get us both arrested. Fuck it. Come on, bird. Try to keep your language civil."

As soon as Otis sits down, Bisquick jumps over to the screen, pecking at his own image. "Go on now," Otis says to him. "You're not on yet." He swats at Bisquick pecking at the stylus again. "Before I put this bird back on, I got a few emails that need immediate attention. I read a message earlier from Emma out in Peoria. Her husband left her a few weeks ago—"

"Asshole," Bisquick says.

"I just want to say, we're pulling for you, Emma"—fist to the mouth—"just like we're pulling for all of you—"

"Sauna," Bisquick says.

"Button it."

"Gimme some tit action."

"For those of you just joining us," Otis says, "I've been interviewing Bisquick. He's a Mynah bird. I'll try interviewing him again after a musical interlude. This one goes out to all you folks living with a broken heart called, 'I Never Loved a Man as Much as I Love You.' If anyone has any pearls of wisdom for Emma, just blog here. I'll read them out later." Bisquick and Otis are both staring at the screen.

"Ain't that sweet," Margot laughs, picking crumbs off her shirt. "Bless his little heart. He sure loves performing, doesn't he, Sam?"

"He certainly does."

Margot finishes her brownie and licks her fingers. "He's almost as smart as Joey," she says. "I want to thank you for all this, Sam. I'm having fun."

"I'm glad, Margot."

"How much did Bisquick cost, if you don't mind me asking?"

"Not as much as you'd think."

"Well, it was a wonderful gesture, Sam."

We look at Otis and Bisquick staring at us on Ruby's computer. Bisquick jumps over on the stylus as the song ends.

"And to think all that personality comes out of a brain the size of a pea," Margot says.

"Otis or Bisquick?"

"Probably both."

The record jumps. Bisquick is pecking the stylus. "Get off there," Otis says. Bisquick drops down on the record and rotates.

# Chapter 22

*Otis Cries for You* is dedicating an hour to deceased pets, or what Otis refers to as their "unintended departures." A long list of tragedies are showing up with photos posted via Instagram. Otis reads them on air while Bisquick pecks at his bald spot. "Christ! Ouch!" Otis says at one point. "Do the goddamn show yourself, stupid bird."

Otis comes upstairs rubbing his head.

"You've got dead air, Otis." Max says.

"Go tell them I'll be back. I need an aspirin or something."

Max goes down and puts on a record. "Here's a funky tune by Albert King called 'Hey Pretty Woman,'" he says. "Otis will be right back with more sad stories. Just sit tight." Bisquick jumps on Max's shoulder.

They come upstairs as we're cleaning the brownie pans. Max talked Muller into making another batch of brownies. Margot looks ready for a nap. Her eyelids droop like old curtains. "Go use the bedroom downstairs," Ruby tells her. "It's made up."

"And take that goddamn bird with you," Otis says. Otis gets some milk out of the fridge. "Max," he says, "you'd better take over for a while. Play some more Albert King or Spencer Wiggins." He lies down on the dining room rug. His eyes close. Bisquick jumps on his stomach. "Give it a rest, Bisquick," Otis mumbles.

Max starts with some O. V. Wright, a tune called "Don't Let My Baby Ride", and we listen while Otis snores in rhythm. Muller helps Ruby clean up the last of the plates. He keeps giving her looks until

I finally take him by the arm. "Come on," I say. "The girls are waiting."

He hands Ruby his dishcloth. "Thanks, big fella," she says. "You're a good man to have around."

"Any time, Ruby."

Ruby gets her cigarettes off the window ledge. "Don't tempt me," she says patting her stomach. "You're one helluva cook, Muller. But I have to watch my waistline."

Margot's head hits the kitchen table. "Help me get her downstairs," Ruby says. We take Margot to the bedroom and head off.

All the way home, Muller just sits there. The man's on a different playing field, somewhere between Star Trek and The Flintstones. "Stop looking so miserable," I say when we pull in the driveway. "Mary already suspects something."

"I like Mary."

"Yeah, well, another stunt like the other night and she'll be a distant memory. You'll be locked up somewhere."

"I'm not crazy, Sam."

"Difference of opinion."

He takes out a cigarette and puts it in his mouth. He lights it, draws in some smoke, and then exhales. "I would have come up," he says.

"You might have told me that before I swallowed half the lake." He blows out some more smoke and wipes his eyes. "Here," I say, handing him my handkerchief. "Come on, wipe your face. And blow your nose."

When we come in the house, Judy jumps up and gives Muller a big hug. "What's the matter, Muller?" she asks. "You look miserable. Have you been mean to him, Daddy?"

"I haven't done anything."

"Is your ear still bothering you, sweetie?"

"I'm just tired, Jude," Muller says. "I'm going downstairs."

"Do you want me to make you some soup?"

"I just need to lie down for a bit." He goes downstairs, closing the cellar door behind him.

"What am I going to do with him, Mom?" Judy says.

Mary gives me a look. "Is there something you're not telling us, Sam?"

"Nope."

"Are you sure?"

"Absolutely."

The Rec Room of Sound is on the computer. Otis is sitting there wiping tears from his face. The man's decrepit. Mary keeps looking at me until I finally say I'm going for a bath.

One of these days, I need to get the washroom renovated. The tub's barely big enough to hold me. I don't know how Muller does it. He sloshes around like Flipper. Half the water is on the floor when he gets out and he leaves wet towels everywhere.

I slip down in the water. I'm practically submerged, breathing out my nose, watching the water ripple. Out in the kitchen, I can hear Wilson Pickett singing, "Land of a Thousand Dances."

There's a clatter of pans in the kitchen, a spoon falling on the linoleum. I finally get up and towel myself off. Then I go in the bedroom and put on a clean shirt and pants.

When I come out again. Mary and Judy are cooking away, The Rec Room of Sound is playing, and Meek and Beek are chewing their bars. I get a beer and watch Judy peeling potatoes. "You smell good, Daddy," she says.

"Thanks, sweetie."

On the computer screen, Bisquick's bobbing up and down, Max is working the turntables, and Ruby and Margot are doing the camel walk. Margot's bifocals are hanging from one ear. Max tells everyone Otis is on his way. "He's grabbing a shower," he says.

I go downstairs and find Muller hooked up to his oxygen machine. He's breathing like Darth Vader. I kick him in the leg. "Take off the mask, Muller. Sit up, for chrissake." Muller props himself on his elbow. "Look," I say. "Judy's not stupid. She knows something's wrong. Every time you come down here, I'm covering for you."

"You don't have to lie for me, Sam."

"I've already lied for you. I'm sick of lying."

"I should talk to Judy."

"And say what?"

"Tell her how I feel."

"You bring up Ruby and you're dead meat."

"Maybe I should talk to Ruby."

"Shut up about Ruby, for chrissake. What's the matter with you?"

"I just feel affection for her somehow, Sam."

"I should have left you in the lake. You're a fucked up asshole."

"I'm sorry."

"And stop saying you're sorry." I sit down on the edge of the cot and take a hit of the oxygen. Then I hear Mary calling us to dinner. "We'd better go up," I say.

"Sam, thanks for worrying about me."

"I'm worried about Judy. You I could kick to the curb."

# Chapter 23

*W*e live in an established neighborhood: old homes, nice lawns. Back in the seventies, everyone planted shrubs and hedges. Nobody gave much thought to care and maintenance. You stuck the shrub in the ground and hoped for the best. Now it turns out some shrubs don't get along with other shrubs. Some hog all the nutrients and the others just sit there feeling sorry for themselves. That's what this article's telling me while I sit in Krupsky's waiting room.

He comes out and waves me into his office. "Anything new, Sam?" he says, and I tell him my shrubs may be at war. He undoes my shirt and thumps my chest. "Your lungs sound like a popcorn factory," he says. "You still smoking?"

"I'm stopping."

"When?"

"As soon as my son-in-law hits the road back to Seattle."

"Not getting along?"

"He's got the hots for my friend's mother."

"She attractive?"

"You're not funny, Krupsky."

"I'm not trying to be funny. Your heart's going like a conga. This son-in-law—"

"—Muller."

"Has he made advances?"

"No, he just gives her goo-goo eyes."

"So he makes goo-goo eyes," Krupsky shrugs, looking like Edward G. Robinson. "It's not the end of the world. Why get so upset?"

"He's married to my daughter, for chrissake. She wants a baby."

"Isn't that for them to work out, Sam? Your son-in-law—Muller—is probably having anxieties of his own. Babies are a big step. Maybe Ruby is a way of avoiding the issue."

"So what should I do?"

"Let him goo-goo eye the woman. He'll get it out of his system. Stop thinking you have to solve everything, Sam. It's not healthy. Why do you think you have panic attacks? What are you doing for exercise?"

"I pull people out of Lake Michigan."

"On a regular basis?"

"Just the one time."

"Well, Sam, I don't see anything wrong with you other than those panic attacks. You try the yoga?"

"My legs fell asleep."

"Are you getting out, other than on the lake?"

"Daily."

"So it's just Muller you're worried about? What does your daughter think of his infatuation?"

"She doesn't know, for chrissake."

"It's not a criminal act, Sam. It's a crush."

"How many daughters do you have, Krupsky?"

"None. You're saying I can't offer advice?"

"Are we done?

"I am if you are."

"I'm leaving."

"Go with God then."

I don't know what it is about Krupsky. Every time I see him, I leave there either more upset or more confused. Getting in my car, I look up and see him standing there at his window. It's one of those full-length jobs. He waves and I feel like giving him the finger. The man irritates the hell out of me. All this 'live and let live' 'try a little yoga' and 'go with God'. Believe me, if there was a God, he would have cleaned up Lake Michigan years ago.

I drive home and check the mailbox. There's a letter from Frank. I take it inside, smelling something on the stove. Muller and Judy are out back lying on a towel. Judy makes swirls in Muller's chest hair with sun tan lotion while Meek and Beek doze in the shade. Mary's in the sunroom. I sit across from her and open Frank's letter.

"Sam," she says, "Put that down a minute. I want to know again what happened the other night."

"When we fell in the lake?" I say. "Muller slipped and I went down with him."

"Muller told Judy you pulled him to shore."

"The place isn't exactly teeming with life guards."

"Well, he's very grateful. What did Krupsky say, by the way?"

"I'm fine physically."

"Did you tell him you've had more panic attacks?"

"I didn't want another lecture on tantric sex."

"Why would he do that?"

"I don't know. He gets on a roll."

"Who's the letter from?"

"Frank."

"I still think there's something fishy going on, Sam. Are you listening to me?"

"There's nothing fishy except Lake Michigan."

"Sam?"

"Let me read Frank's letter." I put on my glasses.

*Sam,*

*I'm back here on some unrelated matter. Kitty showed me what you did to the partition. Nice touch. I also hear a security guard's gone missing. Listen, Sam, Iris brought this up, so don't blame me. She thinks you might need some counseling. If you want a shrink, she has a good one. Call the house. She'd love to hear from you. Thanks for the whiskey, by the way.*

*Frank*

*P.S. Kitty hopes you get better. I asked her what she thought of your ass. Can't get a straight answer out of her. Next time, move your shirttail out of the way.*

I fold the letter and rub my eyes. So now everyone wants me to see a psychiatrist. Mary's still giving me the skunk eye. "What?" I say, and she asks what Frank has to say. "He's back in town on some 'unrelated matter.' No idea what that means." I keep thinking about

Frank telling Iris about me and his partition. I've always liked Iris. Funny and sarcastic. Now she's wondering if I'm a headcase. I don't know whether to feel offended or mildly grateful. Knowing Iris, she probably laughed her ass off. *Put a pressed ham on your partition, Frankie. That's a hoot.* It wasn't much of a mark, to be honest. As Frank would say, "I'm surprised his skinny ass made any mark." In Frank's world, you either make a splash or you keep your pants up.

Mary keeps staring at me. I wonder how we'll make out, two empty-nesters, getting under each other's feet. We've never spent a lot of time together. Work kept me at arm's length. We'd meet over coffee and mortgage payments. I know we're on the same page now, imagining life in the sunroom, daily comments on obituary notices and new sugar substitutes. Having Muller and Judy here is a bit of respite. We're distracted and therefore civil. Once they're back in Seattle, given time, one of us will probably go for the carving knife.

"I don't know what you're saying to Muller, Sam," she says. "He looks worse every time you take him somewhere. What exactly are you doing over at Ruby's house?"

"Technically it's Otis's. Max pointed that out."

"You're being evasive." I fold Frank's letter and put it in my pocket. "What else did Frank have to say?" Mary asks.

"Iris thinks I should see her psychiatrist."

"Why does she think that? I mean, you probably do, but what makes her think so?"

"There were a few complaints at the office."

"What sort of complaints?"

"I may have acted out near the end. Frank likes to be informed of anything untoward."

"How exactly did you out?"

"My pants fell down as I was leaving. I was carrying two big boxes. I might have rubbed up again Frank's partition."

"You dropped your pants?"

"Accidently."

"Just like you did with our front window?"

"Very likely."

"You said you weren't sure before."

"Max confirmed it. Anyway, Frank told Iris about the partition business and now she thinks I need counseling."

"Maybe you do. You've been acting immature lately."

"I'm doing my best given the circumstances."

"I have no idea what that means."

"According to Krupsky, I overreact."

"Well, that's very possible, Sam. Muller isn't getting any better. Maybe he should see Iris's psychiatrist, too."

"I'll ask about a family discount."

"I'm being serious, Sam. You make a quip about everything. That's what I mean by being immature. I hope you're not regressing."

"Krupsky hasn't mentioned it."

"Seriously, Sam."

"I'll talk to Iris's psychiatrist. What more do you want?"

"Ask if he can see you and Muller together."

"I don't want to see a psychiatrist with Muller. The man's got problems up the ying yang. He'll take hours."

"More quips."

"So I quip. Krupsky says I overreact, you say I quip. I don't know if I'm coming or going with you two."

"Stop feeling sorry for yourself."

"I'm not feeling sorry for myself," I say, going to the kitchen window with a little pouty look on my face. Judy's massaging Muller's back. I'm sure he's telling her to give him a knuckle. "How does he do it?" I say. "Everyone wants to rub his back."

"Judy says he's big and cuddly."

"He's also frying like an onion."

# Chapter 24

*I*'ve been taking naps lately, usually in the early afternoon when Mary and Judy go out for something. Maybe my body's adjusting to being unemployed, or I'm just trying to get away from Muller. He takes naps, too. He's downstairs now, hooked up to that oxygen tank. Judy's always saying, "I don't know how they do it, Mom. Can you sleep in the afternoon? I can't." They came home about ten minutes ago with bags rustling. Judy barely packed anything for this trip. Every day, Mary tells her, "That looks pretty worn out, Judy. Let's go over to Target and get you a new one." Personally, I think it's all planned. Judy and Muller are on a shoestring budget. This is a chance to spruce up the wardrobe. Judy is always coming back with a new t-shirt for Muller, or some socks. "Mom's treat," she'll say.

I get up and find Judy in the sunroom, the computer on her lap.

"Daddy, Bisquick's on TV again," Judy says.

"So, birdie," I hear Otis say. "Got any plans for the holidays?" Margot is standing behind him with her arms crossed. "Why isn't he answering?" Otis says.

"What do you want, a travelogue?"

"That was Bisquick, folks," Otis says, "the talking Mynah birdie. If you're tuning in for first time, Bisquick will be back periodically with his own brand of birdie wisdom. We're coming up to the top of the hour with a special edition of *Otis Cries for You*."

Margot looks over his shoulder. "Why's it special?" she says, putting on her bifocals. "All you're doing is reading a bunch of sob stories."

"This is Margot, folks, Bisquick's owner. Somehow I've inherited the two of them. They'll be around, so stay tuned."

"I'm helping Ruby with the laundry, then I'm going."

"I need that bird, Margot. He's a prop. Go upstairs and have a ham sandwich or something. Or maybe we could take a minute—interview like—and talk about your living arrangements with Bisquick."

"It's a bird, Otis. He's got a cage. You've seen the cage."

"Are there times when you and Bisquick cadoodle? Hop around the room like The *Jungle Book*? Maybe sing a song?"

"You're an idiot, you know that?"

"Who's an idiot?" Ruby says on the stairs. "Otis? What else is new?"

"Hear that, folks?" Otis says. "My own wife's turned against me. You're supposed to defend your man, Ruby—which, I might add"—winking at Margot—"happens to be the subject of *Otis Cries for You* today. Abandoned love, folks: who's turned against you, let you down or said you had a small willie. Send in your stories, at this address"—holds up a card—"and we'll get to them right after I grab a sandwich. Here's Otis Redding, *Live in Paris*, with 'Can't Turn You Loose' and whatever follows. Enjoy."

He shoos Bisquick off the turntable. Bisquick flies back and forth, throwing out the occasional invective, landing on his head again.

"Craphound," Bisquick says.

"Get off me," Otis says. "Bird's giving me a mountain of a headache." He disappears from frame with Bisquick following. Ruby brings a load of laundry to the couch and Margot and her start folding, swaying away to the music. As the song ends, Ruby goes in the back bedroom and comes out with a record. She puts it on the other turntable. "Here's a slight format change, folks," she says. "Something by Lesley Gore called 'Maybe I Know.'"

The song starts with Lesley complaining about her boyfriend, saying she's pretty sure he's cheating—well, she says, *maybe*, but she sounds pretty sure—and that opens up a can of worms, because all her friends are *really* sure, and that's really got her back up.

There's a thump on the stairs and Otis comes tumbling down. "Dammit, Ruby," he says. "I won't having you sullying my show with Lesley Gore." Ruby and Margot grab his loose suspenders. "Let go. Let go of me, dammit!"

It's pretty funny watching Margot and Rub swing Otis around, his big gut hanging out. Judy's all giggles. Muller comes upstairs covered in red patches where Judy missed with the sun tan lotion. "Ruby and Auntie Margot are dancing," she says, and Muller looks at the screen. He smells like a big coconut. "Why doesn't Otis like Ruby's music?" Judy says. "It's a good song."

"He doesn't like format changes, sweetie," I say. "Tends to drive away the purists. All thirty-two of them."

"He's got over two thousand views, Sam," Muller says.

"What? Where?"

"Says at the bottom there. Two thousand and twelve, actually."

"Son of a bitch," I say. "People really watch that asshole?"

"*We're* watching," Muller says.

"I know we are. I didn't think anyone else was."

"Two thousand and fifteen."

"Good Lord."

"It's pretty funny, Daddy."

"It's two women swinging a fat slob around."

"Two thousand and twenty, Sam."

I push the computer away. "Listen, you two—where's your mother?"

"She went to the store."

"Okay, look, we're a little worried about you two. Mary's talking to you, Judy. I'm talking to Muller. Thing is, are you really communicating with each other?"

"We talk all the time," Judy says.

"Do you ask each other what you want?"

She tilts her head like a cocker spaniel. "What do you mean, Daddy?"

"Okay, I guess what I'm saying here—and please don't take this the wrong way—you have to get past the lovey dovey stuff and ask hard questions. Do you know what each of you wants? Are you even sure you're right for each other?"

"Daddy!"

"I'm not saying you're not, sweetheart. I'm just saying, it's good to ask the question. Even your mother and I have doubts . . ."

"Are you and Mom getting a divorce?"

"Of course not. I'm just saying—"

"O, my God," Judy wails. "Does Mom know?"

"We're not getting a divorce—"

"You just said you're having doubts."

"I just mean—"

Judy goes running off down the hall. Muller just stands there like a big dummy. "Don't be afraid to weigh in here," I say to him, just as Mary comes through the door with the groceries.

She hears Judy crying. "Sam, what's wrong with Judy?" She goes down to Judy's room, then she's back giving me the skunk eye. "So you want a divorce, do you, Sam?"

"No, I don't want a divorce," I say. "I was just trying to get Muller and Judy on the same page."

"Your daughter's crying. How's that on the same page? Go talk to her before she jumps out the window."

The house is a ranch style, but there's no point telling Mary that. She's pissed and when she's pissed, you don't bring up the fact that Judy's window is only five feet off the ground.

I go and tell Judy that everything's okay.

"Then why did you say it?" she says.

"I was trying to make a point."

"I don't understand."

"Let's talk in the kitchen." I take Judy out and sit her at the table. "First of all," I say, "I don't want a divorce, okay? I was just saying you have to ask hard questions. Right, Mary?"

"Keep going. I'm still thinking of braining you."

"For instance, are you giving each other what you need?"

"I think we are," Judy says. "Aren't we, Muller?"

"I just want to make you happy, Jude."

"I know you do. I want to make you happy, too." They lock lips like they're sharing a carrot. "Let's go snuggle," Judy says. She takes Muller by the hand and they go off to the bedroom.

Mary's giving me the skunk eye again. "What exactly was that all about?" she says.

"I have no idea. They confuse the hell out of me."

Behind us, Otis lets out a loud wail on *Otis Cries for You*. "I feel your pain, ma'am," he's saying. "Maybe your cat got in a tussle with a big dog. You know who wins in those situations. Might be time to hit the pound and get a faster cat. Anyway, here's another big cry from ol' Otis"—he takes out a handkerchief and dabs his eye—"We're pulling for you. Just like we're pulling for all you cat owners out there. Watch your cats, folks. The slow ones particularly."

I look at the bottom of the screen. Two thousand fifty views.

# Chapter 25

*I* go to McDonald's and get served by a man in his sixties. We look at each other like this is a bad joke. "Four Big Mac's," I say and he says, "Will that be for here or to go?" He's looking at Muller's big gut.

"To go," I say, and then the ginger ale can goes off in my head. I tell Muller I have to go outside, making for the door, tripping over strollers. Muller comes out with our burgers and stands next to me by the car. I'm smoking a cigarette with shaking fingers.

Muller suffered panic attacks a few years ago. I remember Mary telling me about it after our last visit to Krupsky's office. Judy took Muller to specialists. They told him it was stress. His video department was made redundant, and since most video departments were redundant, Muller joined the unemployed. The attacks kept coming. Then he collapsed in a mall. An ambulance brought him to emergency, tests were done, and no major arterial plaque was found. Muller's heart, as one doctor described it, "beat like a tribal drum." A week later, he dropped like a stone in a Taco Bell.

He got over it somehow, and I guess I have to do the same. I still can't understand what sent me over the edge. Getting fired, sure, but I knew it was coming. Why weren't Nick, Dewey, or Margot having panic attacks? Then I thought of Iris. Why would she need a psychiatrist? She's the sanest individual I've ever known. She and Frank grew up dirt poor in Belfast. The thing about Iris, rich as she is, she still listens with the ear of a local barkeep. If she's seeing a psychiatrist, it's probably doing him more good than her.

After dinner, I give Iris a call. We haven't talked in a couple of years. I take the phone out on the back deck, stepping on a bottle of Muller's sun tan lotion. Iris answers on the third ring. "You poor man," she says with her cooing Irish accent. "All those years of loyalty. Do you want me to sock Frankie for you?"

"That okay, Iris."

"Well, let me know if you do. Your Mary must be beside herself. Tell her to call me if she wants to talk." She gives me the name of her psychiatrist and some advice about trimming hydrangeas. She thinks we have hydrangeas. "Good luck, Sam," she says and hangs up.

I sit there in the dark, listening to The Rec Room of Sound through the window. Otis is throwing out a song to some woman who just got back from having a nose job. "Here's The Dramatics singing, 'What You See is What You Get', and let's hope that schnoz of yours turns out to be a good one, Whitney."

Three thousand twenty views. I guess moral turpitude sells, but you'd think at least one person would shoot him in the ass. I go back inside as Otis announces he needs another pee break. He leaves us with Rufus Thomas singing "Walking the Dog."

I'm wondering about this psychiatrist business. The whole thing is a bit of a doddle as far as I'm concerned. Where does talking get the average person? Nothing really changes. At least Krupsky admits it's a crapshoot. And it's probably true that psychiatrists take more pills than their patients. People go to psychiatrists because nobody else will listen to them. They've worn out everybody else's eardrums.

I'm also thinking about this fishing trip coming up with Nick and Dewey. Judy and Muller should be back in Seattle by then. I asked Judy the other day when they're leaving. "Why are you trying to get rid of us?" she said. I told her about the fishing trip in August. "Can't you take Muller with you?" she said. Muller came up the basement stairs holding his oxygen mask. The strap was broken. He was looking for scotch tape or a stapler.

I tried calling Nick this morning and got his answering machine. Dewey said he's probably down in Florida, deep sea fishing or buying local artifacts for his craft shows. Dewey's been filling in at his brother's picture framing shop. "I'm waiting for a lull," he told me on the phone. "The place is crazy right now, Sam. All you do is take orders and send the pictures to a framing factory. Everyone uses the same company. Nobody undercuts anybody." He wants to check out the towns up north, maybe corner the market in Wausau. "Come in with me," he said. "We'll be the framing kings."

I told him I'd think about it. Now I'm sitting in the kitchen, watching The Rec Room of Sound. Bisquick is hopping about, pecking at the computer screen. I think of my family and friends, the strange scenario playing out all around me. Everyone is moving on, getting things done. Look at the obstacles they've overcome. Nick, Dewey and Margot lost their jobs just like me. They've picked themselves up. Christ, Otis has over three thousand viewers now. Sponsorship is in the wind. Ruby and Max have their own painting company. All I'm doing, as far as I can see, is babysitting my daughter's husband, and attempting the occasional water rescue.

The next morning, I'm sitting around the sunroom. There's dead air over at Otis's place. Half the time he just lets records play through, catching catnaps in his chair. I watch him suddenly jump up, push Bisquick off his turntable, and cue up another song.

"We're back"—he coughs—"This one goes back to when Ruby was still in short dresses."

Ruby is carrying paint cans from the laundry room. "What song are you talking about?"

"I'm getting to it, Ruby."

"All I heard was me in short dresses."

"Like I was saying, folks," he said. "Here's a song done by Linda Lyndell called 'What a Man' recorded around 1968."

"Damn right I was in short dresses." She goes upstairs.

"Any of you wondering what Ruby's doing with all the paint," Otis says, "she and Max have a bunch of new contracts. According to our business manager—" he turns the computer to show Margot sitting at a desk in the corner—"Ruby and Max are booked all summer. Right, Margot? It's really hopping, huh?"

Margot looks over her bifocals. "Nothing's hopping til the money's on my desk."

Max comes downstairs in painter pants and a red bandana. He and Ruby obviously have a uniform worked out.

"How's it going, Max?" Otis says.

"I'm working my ass off, old man. Try it some time."

"There you go, folks," Otis says. "Capitalism in motion."

I watch the computer screen with everyone rushing about. Things are really moving over there. It gives me an idea. I go downstairs and pull the oxygen mask off Muller. His eyes pop open. "Get dressed," I say. "We're going to work."

"Where?"

"Painting with Max and Ruby. The sun will do us good." He practically flies off his cot.

"I don't know how good a painter I am," he says.

"Just get your socks on." I go start the car and sit there smiling. What better way to get Ruby out of Muller's system? The man moves at the speed of a possum. How long before Ruby kicks him in the pants?

Muller comes out wearing one of his tie-dyed shirts. I thought those things went out in the sixties. He takes a bent cigarette out of his back pocket and lights it. "What do you think Ruby'll have us doing?" he asks, and I tell him I don't know. Probably scraping eavestroughs. "I'm not great with heights, Sam," he says. "I get dizzy."

Driving across Division to Clybourn, Muller fiddles with his hair, patting down wandering curls. I'm surprised he hasn't licked his hand and tried to tack them down. "This isn't a church social," I say to him.

"I could have used a shower, Sam." He keeps looking at himself in side mirror.

We arrive just as Max and Ruby are getting the last of their stuff out of the basement. Otis is reading the paper with Margot's bifocals.

"You've got yourself two painters," I tell Ruby.

"Painters?" Otis says. "We need Muller up in the kitchen."

"Not today, Otis," I say. "What about it, Ruby?"

Ruby looks Muller up and down. "Have you ever worked with a brush, Muller?" Ruby says.

"A few rooms around our house."

"I guess you'll get the hang of it. You're not going to fall off the ladder, are you? You look at bit tipsy."

"I just woke up," he says. "Sam dragged me out of bed."

"He'll be okay," I say.

"He'd better be okay," Margot says. "We don't have medical." We all look over at Otis's computer screen.

"Do you think anyone heard that?" Max says.

"Like a church testimonial," Otis replies.

"Boogaloo," Bisquick squawks.

"Let's get moving," Ruby says. She starts taking a bunch of rollers upstairs while Max grabs some paint sheets. "Muller, you go with Sam."

"Can't I ride with you, Ruby?"

"There's no room in the truck." She brings out two bandanas. "Here's your headgear," she says us. "Buy yourself some painter pants on the way home. We have a strict dress code."

We get in our respective vehicles and drive off. *"Can't I ride with you, Ruby?"* I imitate Muller. "You're embarrassing yourself, you know that?"

"I just like being with her, Sam."

"You're not going to be with her. You're going to be up a ladder." Muller starts fiddling with his hair again. "Here," I say, grabbing his bandana out of his pocket. "Tie this on your head. You'll be getting a lot of sun."

"I wish I brought my baseball cap."

"You can wear your baseball cap tomorrow. Today you're going to work your ass off. Eight hours of scraping and you won't give a shit about Ruby. You won't give a shit about anything."

"If you say so, Sam."

"Ever see painters when they finish for the day? They look like crap. You're going to look like crap, too. So's Ruby."

"I can't imagine that, Sam."

"Imagine it, Muller."

He ties on the handkerchief with the flap down over his face.

# Chapter 26

Ruby put some zinc oxide on Muller's nose earlier. He kept giving her those stupid goo-goo eyes most of the afternoon. I kicked him going out to the car later and he went "*Urumph.*" His eyes go a dull brown, a sickening color brought on by ardor and, no doubt, a certain element of guilt that I place there whenever the opportunity arises. "You're beating a dead horse," I said to him.

Now we're sitting around Otis's kitchen, eating brownies. Bisquick is a crumb hound. He flies from one plate to another, snatching up crumbs faster than you can blink.

*Otis Cries for You* is building a steady audience. Tears flow, the burden of grief is lifted, and Otis takes all the credit. He's out to lunch and seriously bordering on a class action lawsuit from seriously offended individuals. He tells one woman her daughter is simply expressing herself by taking on four guys in a Grand Caravan. Margot finally pushes him out of his seat. "Scratch that last comment," she says. "Listen, Mavis, your daughter's a messed up little boob. She obviously lacks self-esteem." Margot leans into the computer, squinting. "And you, Estelle, you're giving your mother the heebie-jeebies. Men want smart girls. They don't want floozies who can hook their toes on door handles."

Otis comes up off the floor. Margot pushes him over again. "Look, Estelle," Margot continues. "You can't spend your life taking on the whole Little League and expect sympathy. Get off your keister and make something of yourself. It wouldn't hurt you to do the same, Mavis. Both of you need to wise up."

Ruby comes downstairs and starts folding laundry. "Look at Ruby," Margot says. "Otis cheated on her. She caught them in bed right here in this very house. What did she do? She picked herself up, dusted herself off. Now she's got a good painting business. She didn't get it feeling sorry for herself. She got it using good old-fashioned initiative. Here's the deal, Estelle, and you too, Mavis, stop relying on men. They're just mainframes for dicks."

"Steady on, Margot," Otis says.

Ruby laughs. "Did you tell them it was Max's girlfriend?" she says.

"For Christ's sake," Otis says.

"I didn't know that," Margot says.

"I think it's time for a song," Otis says. "Here's The Purify Brothers, doing, 'I'm Your Puppet'."

The blogs and phone calls fly in after that. Everyone's crazy about Margot. They want her to do her own show. "Bullshit baffles brains," she says, but they keep asking for her advice, and wouldn't you know, the next thing we hear, Margot's starting her own internet show called *Reality Check*. It's positioned right after *Otis Cries for You*. The highlight is Margot pushing Otis out of his chair which, surprisingly, never gets old. Comments come in from as far south as Oklahoma. The audience hates Otis and loves Margot, creating a perfect counterpoint. The format never changes. Otis can say what he wants, telling people to protest or fall out of trees. Then Margot gets on, calls everyone "bubbleheads," and tells them they'll never get anywhere following the advice of a craphound like Otis. Believe it or not, they've got the demographic in their pockets.

People call in, happy to hear Otis rant away about the lack of moral fabric in society today, and happier still when Margot tells him he's a Fruit Loop. Just the other day, Otis informed a woman she was being too chummy with her dog. Margot sent him flying. "You should be horsewhipped, Otis," she told him. "Don't you worry, Mary Beth. His mind is a sewer. Loving a pet is a wonderful thing, and it takes a sick individual like Otis to turn it into something sordid. Which is like men in general, I might add. They're all dickswingers."

That just sends the feminist groups into hysterics. "You are a shining light in a maelstrom of chauvinism," one feminist wrote, to which Otis dropped his pants, Margot shoved him over again, and Bisquick went for his balls. The screams brought more comments from women, some claiming Otis led their daughters astray. "Well, if your daughter's are dumb enough to listen to him," Margot says, "they deserve what they get." Sometimes a guy will offer up some defense, like, "Girls dress like whores," but Margot tells him if every girl wearing a short skirt wanted to be raped, we wouldn't get any work done. "Try taking the mirrors off your shoes," she said to him.

Feminists keep sending her buttons, saying "No means no," which Margot claims is about the stupidest thing she's ever heard. "You wouldn't have to say no if you tried having an intelligent conversation. Half the time, these guys stick their hands up your blouse just to break the monotony." Even Otis nods to that. Then Bisquick starts nipping at his nuts, he's holding his privates in one hand, and swatting Bisquick with the other. The feminists think that's a hoot.

# Chapter 27

*M*uller spends most of the drive home taking paint chips out of his hair, leaving them everywhere. It's hard to know what he's thinking. On the one hand, he isn't argumentative, on the other, you're never sure if he's even listening. Most of the time, he just sits there, or stands there, making the odd complaint about his vertigo or his back or the way the sun shines in his eyes. In his slow, inoffensive way, he takes life as it comes; part survivor, part complainer, carrying on despite all the troubles that seem to pop and grind in his head.

When we get home, Mary and Judy are on the yoga mats while Meek and Beek clean their beaks on the cage bars. A recording of waves plays on the stereo. Incense smoke rises from a cockleshell. "That's some burn, Muller," Judy says. "What's on your nose?"

"Ruby gave me some zinc oxide."

"We're working for Ruby's Painting," I say to Mary.

"What's Ruby got you doing?"

"Scraping paint, mostly."

"We saw Margot on air earlier. I didn't know she had it in her."

"She's a pistol," I say.

"How did Otis end up sleeping with Max's girlfriend?" Judy asks.

"Long story."

"He shouldn't treat Ruby that way," Muller says, taking off his bandana. There's a tan line across the middle of his forehead.

"Muller, look at you," Judy says, rubbing his forehead like she can blend the red and the white together. "Who shouldn't treat Ruby that way?" she says.

"Otis," he says. "Ruby could do better."

I give Muller a warning glance. "What's for dinner?" I ask.

"Pot roast," Mary says. "It'll be ready in about twenty minutes. So, Margot's got her own show, huh? I've never heard her talk so much. It's quite funny, actually."

"She's getting tons of feedback."

"Just for telling mothers to suck it up?"

"They like the message."

Judy takes Muller's arm. "Come on, Muller," she says. "Let's get you in the shower and I'll scrub your back. Where did you guys get those painter pants?"

"We bought them on the way home," he says. "Ruby says we have to wear them. I'm feeling a bit funny, Judy."

"What kind of funny?"

"I think I need to lie down."

"Can I get you anything?"

"Just give me fifteen minutes or so." He starts downstairs and I follow him. "What the hell's wrong now?" I say.

His eyes suddenly go a little wonky. "I don't know, Sam. I feel funny."

"What kind of funny?" I help him down on his cot. "Do you want the oxygen?"

"Maybe a little."

I put the mask over his face and turn on the juice. Muller starts to relax. He's breathing like Darth Vader again. I leave the mask on him and go upstairs. Mary and Judy are putting dinner out while Meek and Beek chirp, or whatever it is lovebirds do. "I think he's got a touch of sunstroke," I say to them.

"I've never seen his face so red," Mary says.

"Me either," Judy says. "I'd better see how he's doing."

She starts down the basement stairs, but Muller is already on his way up. "Feeling better?" she says to him, and he looks at her like a tranquilized dog. "Come up here and have something to eat," Judy says. "Maybe you're hypoglycemic. Did you eat lunch today? Muller's a bit diabetic," she tells us. "He gets tired easily, don't you Big Bear? You'll be okay once you eat something."

She sits him down and stuffs a napkin in the neck of his t-shirt. Then she spoons out mashed potatoes and green beans. He just sits there, looking all dopey. It was hot as hell on the ladders today. Muller doesn't mind first floor work around the windows. It's anything over ten feet that gives him vertigo. He'll stop halfway, saying maybe he needs to use the washroom. "Ruby's going to think you're a slacker," I told him at one point, and he went up the rungs like a trapeze artist. It's like dealing with Pavlov's dog.

# Chapter 28

*W*hat did John Lennon say? Success happens to you while you're busy doing something else? Somewhere along the way, I guess I was doing something else and this happened. I haven't felt dizzy since I started working outside. The agoraphobia still kicks in occasionally, but other than that, I'm doing okay. I feel pretty good, to tell you the truth.

The psychiatrist called yesterday, saying Iris talked to him. "You still getting panic attacks, Sam?" he asked. I told him I was better. "Better in what way?" I told him I was walking, talking, taking out the garbage. We agreed it might be better to wait. I wasn't having any attacks lately, although he warned it might be temporary. "Some people only have a few attacks and it's over. Others go on for years. Call me if they come back with any regularity. We'll go from there."

I got off the phone feeling partly relieved, partly offended. These psychiatrists only seem to want the meatier cases. Give them a straightforward occasional panic attack and they practically yawn on the phone. He made me curious about one thing, though. I'd like to know why some people only get a few attacks while others have them all the time. After supper, I do a little research on the Internet. Most information sites are sponsored by the drug companies. They obviously want to get you hooked on their latest product. None of them tell you to pick up a paintbrush. It's all about endorphins, and you're seriously fucked if you don't take their medication. To use Bisquick's words, they're all *cocksuckers*. I checked The Rec Room of Sound. Otis was passed out with his face on the keyboard. A record was skipping—*funky chicken, funky chicken*. Bisquick was asleep on Otis's head. Every so often, Otis swatted at him like a fly.

We came home tonight, fighting the usual traffic on Lincoln. I was taking back streets for a while, cutting along Burling. Everyone's trying to get home. Pulling up at one stoplight, I saw this old couple. The woman could barely see over the steering wheel. The light changed, but the car didn't move. Horns honked, the car jolted forward, then it stopped in the intersection. The light turned yellow and she backed up.

"God damn old people," I said, realizing the irony. One of these days, Mary and I will be driving around like this. Mary's reasonably tall, so seeing over the dashboard won't be a problem. But I can imagine her hesitating. Whenever we're driving now, and I start harping on about old people on the roads, she'll look at me and say, "They've got as much right to be here as you do, Sam."

Muller sits there with one of his bent cigarettes. He still keeps them in his back pocket. By the end of the day, they're a twisted mess. He smokes and looks out the window. I think he was in better spirits today, probably because Ruby told him he had a cute jiggle on the ladder. He started attacking the blistering paint, sending the chips down on my face below. "Take it easy, Muller," I said.

We both ended up with paint chips all over us. Muller never shakes himself before getting in the car. The floor mats are covered in the stuff. Pulling in the driveway, I say to Muller, "Shake yourself before you go inside," and he gets out of the car doing what looks like a hula dance. "Why can't you shake like normal people?" I said to him. Now there's paint chips mingling with oil, running down my driveway to the culvert. Muller doesn't even notice. Sometimes I think his eyes only see as far as a cookbook or Ruby's bandana.

Lasagna is waiting when we come through the door. We shower, eat, and then watch a movie. Mary found this place where you get ten movies a week for a set price. Her taste runs to sad tales, people wailing as the boat leaves, kids holding their dogs before the father grabs his shotgun. Muller blubbers through them all, grabbing tissues, while Judy hugs his face. "He'll get another dog, Muller," she'll say, taking him off to bed. Mary and I stay up to watch the news, then we turn in as well. "How was Muller today?" Mary asks.

"He's coming along." Most of the time, he makes a hell of a mess, tripping over cans, tracking paint into people's houses. Ruby's more patient than most, but you see her give the occasional sigh. I think he's only tolerated because he's a loveable lug with an innocuous disposition. At the end of the day, he'll make his brownies and all offences will be forgiven.

Kept within reason, his brownies calm me down. Go beyond one or two and it's lights out. Otis gobbles them up like potato chips, and then starts telling people the dumbest things. One woman called to say she's putting her father in a home. Otis started sobbing away until she explained she'd won a lottery and was buying him a split-level up near Seward Park. "Oh," he said, and then Margot pushed him out of the way.

"What part of *Otis Cries for You* don't you get?" Margot said. The woman said she just wanted to talk about it. "You're barking up the wrong tree here, sister." she says. "Otis doesn't know good deeds from bad ones. How old's your father?" The woman said he was eighty-four. "In a split-level, for God's sake? They've got beautiful retirement homes all over the place. Friendly staff, physicians, psychiatrists, the works. Didn't you think of that? What happens when he takes a header down the stairs?"

The woman started crying. Margot pulled Otis back in his chair. "She's all yours." Otis let out a few sobs and the woman thanked him.

I drift off thinking of Margot the way she used to be, sitting in her office, bifocals low on her nose. I see Frank, standing at her door, saying, "We need to charge these bastards more," and Margot saying, "You're a vulture, Frank."

That always sent Frank over the edge. He'd rant away about capitalism and free markets. She'd finally push him out of her office, and Frank would storm down the hall saying, "I should put that woman in a facility." I wake up laughing and get an elbow from Mary. I try to get back to sleep again, and when I do, I dream of the time Frank pulled us all in on a new pitch, a sports equipment manufacturer out in West Town. We worked for two weeks, taking stuff into Frank's office each morning. Nothing got him excited. "Bollocks," he said, getting up and going to the window. Down below, these two guys were walking along carrying two cases of beer. It was a hot afternoon. They put the cases down, took out a beer, and sat down, using the cases for seats.

"There's ingenuity," he said. "Take your bar with you." Frank went back to his office. Ten minutes later, he was shouting down the hall, "Get in here, all of you!"

We came in his office and he was standing there at the window, pointing down at the two guys. "See those bastards there?" he said. "Fucking geniuses." Then he started laying out this campaign, telling us his idea for hockey equipment. "They're selling everything separately," he said. "Skates, gloves, upper body protectors. We gotta start bagging all this shit together. The bag's the thing. Every kid wants a hockey bag. Why sell all this shit separately? Start selling the whole getup. Make your money on the package."

Was that how people bought hockey equipment? We didn't know, but Frank made the bag concept work. One commercial had this kid coming home, seeing his father on the front porch. The father takes him inside. There's this full hockey bag in the hall. The kid's over the moon, the mother's wiping away tears. It was a hell of an emotional spot and parents ate it up. Frank had those bags everywhere: commercials, end-of-aisle displays, contests to win a bag of hockey equipment. The slogan became an instant catchphrase in the industry: "Now, play!"

That fall, the client sold more sports equipment than he could manufacture. Frank was a hero, a legend, and O'Conner Advertising took home awards, big awards; gold, silver, bronze awards. The trades called him a genius, another Leo Burnett. "They're comparing me to Burnett?" he laughed. "I never put a homo in green tights on a can of peas. A right pansy."

"I'm starting to worry about you, Sam," I hear Mary say. I open my eyes. She's up on her elbow, staring down at me. "What's so funny?"

"Frank," I say. "He was calling Leo Burnett a pansy."

# Chapter 29

*J*udy's singing to the song, "Dedicated to the One I Love." It's a nice piece, a little sappy. Otis did this whole stupid opening about how it goes back way before The Mamas and the Papas. John Phillips adapted it, and Otis wanted everyone to hear the original version by The "5" Royales. "This was recorded by King Records back in the fifties," he says. "John Phillips was still doing his wacky doodle folk stuff. Listen to this version, folks. I ain't got nothin' against The Mamas and the Papas. I had a good little cry when Mammy Cass choked on that chicken sandwich."

Judy laughed and then sang along. She loves to sing. She just can't carry a tune. As much as I love Judy, I'd like to put her out in the garage when she sings. She's making Meek and Beek all flappy, probably figuring she sounds like a hawk, one of their sworn enemies. At least The Rec Room of Sound is expanding her repertoire. When she first arrived, she kept singing that if you want it, you need to put a ring on it or something. I asked Muller what that meant, but he's as clueless about modern music as me. He also tends to morph songs together when he sings, which bugs the crap out of Otis. "You ain't got a dang full song in that head of yours, do you?" Otis told him the other day. Muller was bringing the brownies out of the oven. Otis gets all dreamy-eyed when the oven door opens, smacking his lips. "At least you can bake," Otis said. "You sure can't sing worth a shit."

We're finishing this place on Carlyle, so this morning I tell Muller we'd better get going early. Then Judy says, "Can I help you paint?" and Muller gets all fidgety.

"You have to wear painter's pants," he tells her, acting like there's no way around Ruby's rules.

"It's Ruby, for God's sake," Judy says. "What's she going to do?"

"I don't like to buck authority."

Mary wants to pick up the new barbecue today, so Judy goes with her. They walk out the door singing about love making a woman. It seems pretty obvious from a breeding perspective, but somebody puts it out on a record and suddenly it's an inspired thought.

On the drive to work, I tell Muller he's a sneaky shit. "I know what you did back there," I say.

"I can't help it, Sam."

"Yes you can, you dumb bastard. Krupsky says this is just a crush. Well it's getting old. I'm sick of this cow-eyed crap."

"I've tried to stop. I feel awful."

"What was all that shit the other night? *I just want to make you happy, Judy.* You're so full it, Muller."

"I do want to make Judy happy."

"By thinking about Ruby? You really are one fucked up asshole. Maybe you should go back to Seattle."

"Judy doesn't want to."

"I mean you. Leave Judy here. You don't deserve her." He looks out the window. "I'm serious, Muller. You don't deserve Judy."

"I'm sorry, Sam."

"Cut out that sorry shit."

"I can't help how I feel."

"Ever since you showed up here, you've been telling me how you feel. Forget how you feel. Nobody cares. Try *not* feeling for a change. Try not even thinking."

It works for most men in America.

# Chapter 30

"What's wrong with Muller?" Ruby asks. "He barely said a word when I zinced his nose. Is he okay?" I tell her he was like that when he woke up.

He's been up on the ladder all morning, doing the soffits. His fear of heights doesn't seem to be bothering him today. He looks like a primate, toes hanging out over his sandals. It reminds me of the joke where a man finds a gorilla on the roof of his house. He calls the zoo and tells them to send somebody over. Two men arrive, one carrying a net, the other a shotgun and a bulldog on a leash. "Here's how it works," the one guy tells the homeowner. "I go on the roof, push the gorilla off, and my assistant releases the bulldog. It goes straight for the gorilla's nuts. The gorilla's distracted, my assistant nets the bastard, and we're out of here." He then hands the homeowner his shot gun. "What's this for?" the homeowner says. The zoo man replies, "If I get pushed off, shoot the bulldog."

As I'm thinking about that, Muller's shadow passes overhead. He hits the ground with a dull thud. Max and Ruby come running outside all in a panic. Ruby kneels beside Muller, listening to his heart. Max calls an ambulance on his cell. We end up racing to the hospital behind the ambulance, following a gurney down the hall. Muller opens his eyes and takes Ruby's hand. "Ruby, I—I—" Two orderlies wheel him into an examining area. "The poor man," Ruby says. "I thought he looked kind of tipsy this morning. We shouldn't have put him up on the ladder if he's got sunstroke."

I get Judy and Mary on the phone. They rush right over. Then Margot shows up, taking me aside. "The man's a liability, Sam," and I tell her he probably did it on purpose. "Why, for God's sake?" she says. Then I tell her about Muller's crush on Ruby.

"Ruby?" she laughs, looking around for a coffee machine. "Let's go down to the cafeteria." We take the stairs and Margot decides she needs something to eat. She orders a full breakfast, putting on her bifocals to look at the menu overhead. "Is that the biggest breakfast you got?" she asks the girl at the cash. The girl tells her it's the *only* breakfast they have. "Gimme an extra order of toast then," Margot says. "You want anything besides coffee, Sam?"

"No, I'm fine."

The food comes and Margot takes her tray over to the far corner. She starts slathering her toast with jam. "So Muller's got the hots for Ruby, huh? Has he made any advances yet?"

"Thankfully, no."

"Ruby's not bad looking for her age," she says with her mouth full. She takes a gulp of coffee, washes it down, and then gets a sausage on her fork like a mallet. "It's probably just a passing fancy. Judy know anything?"

"No, and she's not going to know anything," I say. "I told Muller I'd throw him in Lake Michigan before I let him hurt her."

"Spoken like a true father, Sam," she says. "Maybe you should talk to Ruby. Tell her the big guy's got a bad case of puppy love." She takes another gulp of coffee. "At least get it out in the open. Saves having him jumping off roofs." I tell her that's not a bad idea. "Glad I could help," Margot smiles. "Strictly speaking, my real concern is the liability issue. Muller's a sweet guy, but we ain't got the money for his high jinks. Sure you don't want anything to eat? Have some toast. My eyes are always bigger than my stomach."

I take a piece of toast and watch Margot shoveling the rest of the eggs away. She probably doesn't weigh more than a hundred and five pounds, but she's got the appetite of an entire fire hall. "Ruby," she laughs, shaking her head. "That's a hoot."

"Why's that a hoot?"

"I got a better ass than she does. I do butt squeezes at my desk. Two hundred a day. They really work, Sam," she says and gets up. "Feel my ass. Go on, grab a handful."

Not even if you did three hundred butt squeezes a day, Margot.

# Chapter 31

*M*uller's back is sprained, but that's about it. The official story is he slipped and fell. Judy reads him *The Road Less Traveled*, which I'm sure goes right over his head. I had trouble with it myself, especially the bit about holes. Supposedly, we all have these emotional holes. Relationships are based on how well we fill the other person's hole. Muller must have one the size of a tanker truck. How Judy even makes a dent in it is a mystery to me. I wish she didn't love him so much. One of these days, Muller's going to do something really stupid (not that he hasn't already), and Judy's going to fall apart. I know how easily that can happen. I don't want her ending up like those people writing into *Otis Cries for You*. I can see Margot pushing Otis out of his chair and saying, "Move on, Judy. He couldn't even give you a kid. What was he waiting for? A coronation?"

To be honest, I don't know where Margot gets her advice. She's never been married, never had kids. In all the time I've known her, the closest she came to a meaningful relationship was with Joey. Maybe that's what makes the Internet an equal opportunity medium. Anyone can sit there weeping like a baby, or dispensing tough love.

If the Internet brings the masses together, it also lets anyone with a computer be a quack. Look at Otis. He's not even wearing pants half the time. How can anyone take advice from him? The man's a moron, but he's already up over four thousand viewers an hour. The other day, he told a woman she could get rid of crow's feet by watching horror movies. Fourteen people blogged saying it really worked. Margot had to get on and tell them they're all ninnies.

Feminist groups send Margot messages every day, inviting her to conferences and rallies. The other week, she told Ruby she's thinking of attending one on the fifteenth. "I'll go with you," Ruby said. "We'll get the fur flying," which is just the sort of thing Margot should avoid. She's never been able to keep her opinions to herself, and I doubt they're flattering to feminists. She hates them as much as Frank does. You still don't fuck with those women. I read about a feminist in Evanston who had a man in court, claiming he was using his telescope to watch her undress. The guy was a noted astronomer and taught at the university. Even after giving his credentials to the judge, the woman still complained that she was being observed. If not by him, at least by someone in the galaxy. The judge found the astronomer in contempt when he casually said, "I think alien life forms are more selective than that."

The astronomer was ordered to move the telescope nearer the university and do community service. The woman got a lot of press, appearing on talk shows, getting feminists all worked up. The university didn't need the hassle. They took away the astronomer's tenure and now he's gazing at stars in the Nevada desert somewhere.

If Margot and Ruby start something with the feminists, I hope I'm up on a ladder, scrapping paint, and not anywhere near Otis's place. Imagine him telling a bunch of angry women to go hook their toes on door handles. We'll have every feminist in the country out there looking like hyenas. Some of them are more bug-eyed than Otis.

# Chapter 32

*B*rownies are baking again. Otis eats them straight out of the oven, tossing them back and forth in his hands as he goes back downstairs. He's really getting on his high horse these days, going on about abortion, speed limits, and the right to assembly. Margot thinks he's getting too evangelical. When he crosses the line, she sticks a cattle caller in his ear. His dentures flew out the other day. "Stop being such a sanctimonious shit," she said, and went back to her invoicing. The cattle caller sits right next to her. She uses it on delinquent clients. "Send me a check tomorrow or you'll get worse than this," she says, blasting the cattle caller into the receiver. As of today, we only have one outstanding payment.

Bisquick takes it all in stride, cleaning up Otis's crumbs, going for his nipple now and then. Otis tapes them down when the air conditioning's running. He swats Bisquick away, and Bisquick flies over to Margot's desk. She's got him saying, "Pay, or else." Some clients think it's cute, others see it as a form of extortion.

We've started a new house over on Webster Avenue. Ruby has Muller painting the basement floor. I'm outside on the ladder, getting all the sun I need. After work, we wash up, have brownies, then drive home for dinner. We eat like there's no tomorrow. Judy figures it's because we're outside all day. Mary's suspicious. She gets me in the sunroom later and says, "I know something's going on. It better not be why Muller jumped off the roof." I tell her I don't know what she's talking about. She flashes me a look, then she's back on the baby business. "You'd better do something with Muller," she says. "How are they going to have a family if he's jumping off roofs?"

I take Muller aside later and tell him we can't come home stoned anymore. "Mary suspects something," I say. He gives me his typical *woe-is-me* expression. He looks forward to getting stoned with Ruby and Max. He doesn't say anything. I think that high wire act off the roof did something to his head. He takes naps on the basement floor. Ruby's being sympathetic, but not the way he'd hoped. She pets him like a dog. "I wish she'd give me a back massage," he says, driving home. "My back hurts more now than it ever did."

"Shut up about your back, Muller. Mary's on my case about this baby business. Have you talked to Judy?"

"I'm not sure I can, Sam."

"You took a header off a roof. What's the worst she can do to you?"

"I can't think straight these days."

"You know what Krupsky says? He says this crush on Ruby is avoidance. You're scared of having a baby so you fall for someone else."

"You talked to him about Ruby?"

"I'm looking for logical reasons not to kill you."

"I wish I could talk to Ruby."

"Forget Ruby."

"Maybe I should write her a letter."

"I'm telling you she's not interested."

"You missed the turn off."

Mary and Judy are waiting on the front porch when we get home. Everything is out of the boxes, the trophies, the awards, the bottles of whiskey. They're lined up on the railing like a shooting gallery. Mary has her arms crossed as we come up the steps. "So," she says, "look what we found cleaning up. Have you been drinking the whole time?" She gives me a long cold, stare. Most women tend to soften with age. It wouldn't hurt her to sag a bit. "I'm waiting, Sam."

Judy takes Muller inside but Mary blocks my way. "Another thing," she says, pulling something out of her apron pocket. "I found this in your shirt this morning. Honestly, at your age I thought you'd know better." It was one of the grass brownies. "What am I going to do with you?" she says. "You're drinking on the sly, eating brownies between meals. Is there anything else you're not telling me?"

"That's about it."

"Are you sure?"

Well, Margot asked me to grab her ass.

# Chapter 33

Two in the morning, I'm wide awake. Muller's crush on Ruby is driving me crazy. Margot's probably right, I should talk to Ruby. I roll over and get a poke in the ribs from Mary. "Go to sleep," she says. I drop off and have another weird dream. I'm back in that coffin again. Frank comes up and says, "Not a bad job. A little too much blush." Then Iris is standing there going, "Do you want me to sock Frankie?"

Ruby's bringing paint cans out to the truck when we arrive this morning. We get everything loaded, then drive over to Webster. Ruby and Max work inside, Muller's down in the basement, I'm finishing the soffits. Ruby comes out for a cigarette, but I'm way up in the far corner. Then Max comes out and goes off behind the garage. I decide to fill him in on Muller's crush. "Muller has the hots for Ruby?" he says. "He does kinda get weird around her. What's the problem?"

"You don't see a problem?"

"Does Ruby know about this?"

"No, Max. That's why I'm talking to you. I don't know what to say to her. She's your mother. How would you approach it?"

"Just talk to her," Max shrugs. "Ruby's cool. I wouldn't let Otis know. He's got a jealous streak."

"He slept with your girlfriend, for chrissake."

"What can I say? He's Otis."

Ruby comes outside, shaking her bandana over the railing. She sees us talking and comes over. "I hit a cobweb the size of a circus tent in there," she says. "What're you two talking about?"

"Muller wants your body, Ruby," Max laughs.

"That's not what I said, Max," I say. "I thought you were going to let me handle this."

"Tell me something I didn't know," Ruby says.

"You know?" I say.

"Have you seen him after a massage, Sam? He's got a package the size of a corn dog." Max doubles over on the grass. "You want me to talk to him?" she says.

"I'd appreciate it. He says he can't help himself." Max and Ruby are both laughing now. "It's not funny," I say. "I dragged him out of the lake last week."

"The big lug," she says. "I'll see what I can do."

"By the way," I say. "I've gotta watch the brownies. Mary found one in my shirt pocket yesterday."

"What did she say?"

"I shouldn't eat between meals."

"Okay, Sam, I'll check your pockets before you go home and I'll talk to Muller. How are things out here? Can you have the windows done today? The family's home Friday."

"They should be ready."

"Max, get the other ladder from the truck and start the bedrooms. I'll see how Muller's making out in the basement." Ruby goes inside and Max gets the ladder.

Muller comes out while I'm back behind the garage. "Did you finish the basement?" I ask him.

"I'm waiting for the second coat to dry."

"Can you help me out here?"

"Ruby says she can't give me massages anymore."

"I know, Muller. I asked her to talk to you."

"She says I should get Judy to massage me."

"That's exactly what you should do."

"I need to talk to Ruby again."

"Why?"

"I need to tell her how I really feel."

"She knows how you really feel. She's telling you to bugger off."

"I need to explain."

"You're on the wrong expressway."

He goes back inside and I climb up the ladder. Next thing I know, Ruby's pulling Muller out on the porch. She's got two fingers down his throat. "I turned my back and he started chugging," she says.

"Chugging what?" I say.

"Paint."

I get the garden hose and stick it in his mouth. He laps at it like a dog. Then he coughs and sputters out green paint. "Stick your finger down his throat again," I say, and turn the hose nozzle to a hard spray. I let him have it in the face and Muller starts spewing green all over the porch. "How much did he drink?" I say, and Ruby takes off her bandana. "I don't know," she says. "He's got an appetite."

I shove the garden hose right in his mouth. He gags and heaves, drooling strands of green saliva. "I think that's it," Ruby says.

"What do we do with him?" Max says.

"Leave him in the sun," I say.

"Don't be hard on him, Sam," Ruby says. "Come on, big fella. Let's get you inside. Max, fetch that loaf of bread out of the truck. Maybe we can sop up his insides with it."

I push Muller through the sliding doors. "Sit down, Muller," I say, pulling out one of the kitchen chairs. He coughs and drools more green paint. At the sink, Ruby soaks a dishcloth and brings it over, pressing it against his forehead. The zinc oxide is running down his face. Max appears with the loaf of bread. Ruby starts shoving slices in Muller's mouth.

"Just keep eating, honey," She says. "You don't want that paint hardening. Chew, chew, chew." She works his jaw up and down. "That's a good boy."

"Is the bread helping at all?" Ruby asks, "Do you want warm tea? I've got some in my thermos." Muller shakes his head and Ruby keeps dabbing his forehead. "Maybe we should take him to Emergency."

"I'm sorry, Ruby."

"Enough of that."

"I just wanted you to know how I feel."

She sits down and takes his hands. "Look, Muller, I know how you feel. I'm flattered, really. But I'm married to Otis. One goofball is all I can handle."

"I didn't mean any harm. I just feel good around you, that's all."

"I feel good around you, too, big fella. Why the paint, though?"

"Dunno."

"Drinking paint ain't doing it for me."

"Drinking paint's pretty desperate, you gotta admit," Max says.

"I'm not feeling so good," Muller says. He goes to the sink and all the bread comes out green.

"Give me the phone," I say.

"Why don't we just take him over to the hospital?" Max says.

"I've had enough of Emergency rooms." I call Krupsky and give him a short version of events.

"How much paint did he drink?" Krupsky asks

"It's hard to say. We got most of it out, I think."

"He's conscious?"

"Yes."

"That's a good sign."

"He's not going to start having seizures, is he?"

"I treat symptoms, Sam; I don't predict them. Bring him over now and I'll have a look. How far away are you?"

"About ten minutes."

"I'll be here. I'm having a sandwich."

"His name's Muller, by the way."

"I know. You told me."

"I wasn't sure I had."

"So bring him over. Let me eat my sandwich. And stop worrying so much, Sam. You'll give yourself a coronary."

"The man's horking green, Krupsky."

"At least he's horking."

"That's a good thing?"

"I'll know better when I see him, Sam."

"We'll be right over."

"I'll be waiting with baited breath."

"What's he saying, Sam?" Ruby asks.

"He's waiting with baited breath."

Man, he's a sarcastic prick.

# Chapter 34

*M*uller sits on the examining table with his shirt open. Flecks of green paint dapple his chest hair. Krupsky listens to his heart, taps his back, and then sticks a penlight in his ear. "How are you feeling these days, Sam?" he says. "Meditation helping?"

"I'm okay," I say. "How's he look?"

"Not bad. Can't say the same for you. Ever think about taking a vacation? Argentina is nice this time of year. Great beaches. You and Mary should try it. Might be just the thing."

"I'm fine, Krupsky. I'll handle stress my own way, thank you."

"You need to relax, Sam," Muller says. "Stress kills."

"Where would I get stress from? You just drank paint, for chrissake. That give you any clues?"

"Muller's right," Krupsky says. "You need to relax. Take up dancing. It works wonders."

"Stick to Muller, will you?"

"He seems okay," Krupsky says. He taps Muller's back. "Some old bruising down here. Any falls lately, Muller?"

"He dove off a roof," I say.

"How high?"

"Two-storey."

"That's quite a drop."

"Not enough of one, obviously."

"No internal injuries?"

"Nothing. His heart beats like a tribal drum."

Krupsky takes his glasses off. "I'm going to say three things to you, Muller"—holding three fingers—"Drinking paint is dumb. Diving off two-storey buildings is dumb. Going out in the sun without a hat is dumb. Find yourself a vocation that doesn't involve those three. You'll thank me on your sixty-fifth birthday."

"That's it?" I ask.

"What do you want me to say?"

"You could tell him he's crazy."

"You a psychiatrist?"

"No."

"Neither am I. That's why I didn't touch it."

Down in the parking lot, I kick Muller in the pants. "You're giving me advice? Who the hell drinks paint?" I push him around to the passenger door. "Get in, for chrissake."

"Can we stop somewhere for food, Sam?"

"We'll take burgers back for Max and Ruby."

Muller stares down at the ground. "I forgot about her for a minute."

"Forget about her completely, Muller."

"You think we should go back to Seattle?"

"I want *you* to go back. Leave my daughter here."

"That would break Judy's heart."

"What do you think you're doing now?"

"I'm just trying to be honest."

"Honest?"—I start hitting him with my ball cap— "I'll give you honest, you dumb bastard!" The ginger ale can goes off in my head and I sink to the pavement. Muller kneels next to me. He takes a folded paper bag from his back pocket, shakes it out, and puts it over my mouth. "Just breathe, Sam," he says. I try pushing it away, but Muller keeps putting it back over my mouth. As I breathe in and out, Krupsky appears in the window above. He's munching away on his sandwich. Then he points at me and starts doing the twist.

# Chapter 35

Krupsky should be reported to the American Medical Associa-
tion. The man's a fucking menace. He didn't even ask Muller
why he drank paint. He was more interested in *my* stress levels. Of
course I'm stressed. Who wouldn't be stressed? Muller's suicidal,
Judy's oblivious, and Mary thinks I'm an alcoholic. I admit, Bulgarian
whiskey does have a hint of desperation to it. I'm getting stress from
all sides, Muller all day, Mary all evening. Between the two of them—
and Krupsky—it's a wonder I haven't had more attacks. "You're a
piece of work," I say to Muller on the way home. We pick up corn and
steaks at the supermarket. The new barbecue was delivered this morning. When we get to the house, Mary and Judy have nuts and bolts
everywhere. Muller starts reading the instructions, lining all the pieces
up according to a diagram. The girls husk the corn while I stand there
feeling dizzy. "I'll go get charcoal," I say. Mary tells me it's propane.
"Then I'll get propane," I say.

I jump in the car and drive around, going down by the lakeshore,
watching the beach where Muller tried to drown himself. I smoke a
cigarette. The wind blows ashes back on my lap. I start thinking back
to this incident years ago when we were doing a presentation to Jack
Baines, the worst client in the industry. Jack was a former World War
II fighter pilot. He lost a leg during training exercises. Every time he
came into meetings, he'd throw his artificial leg out in front of him.
Jack liked to rattle people, and this particular time, just the way he
was sitting, you knew he was up to something. Don Conroy and I were
starting to present when Jack suddenly said, "Any of you remember a
copywriter named George Burton? Worked in our business years ago."

None of us could recall the name. "Maybe he was at Young and Rubican," he says. "Anyway, he killed himself the other night. Did it in a hotel room with his belt. Left a wife and two kids."

I didn't sleep for a week after that. Don was the same way. The only person it didn't affect was Frank. I remember him coming by my office one day saying, "Who the fuck's George Burton? Did I fire him?" I told him the guy never worked for us. "Didn't think so," he said. "Frigging hotel room," he said, shaking his head. "That's one way of doing it, I guess. At least you've got a mini bar close by." He went off down the hall, whistling away, making some joke to Margot. She had to get up and push him out the door.

I finish my cigarette, pick up some propane at Walgreens, and drive home. Everything's ready to go when I get back: steaks, corn on the cob, a big tossed salad. Mary and Judy are sitting at the picnic table, going through books on children's nurseries. I hook up the propane tank and everything starts okay. I leave Muller to the cooking and go inside, taking some gin out of the liquor cabinet. Judy comes in and stares at me. "Are you okay, Daddy?" she says. "You're starting to worry us. Mom thinks it's a sugar spike from Muller's brownies."

She puts her arm around my waist. Judy's a sweet girl. It makes me want to brain Muller even more. "*Are* you okay?" Judy asks. "Muller says you had another attack. What did Dr. Krupsky say?"

"He thinks I should take up dancing."

"What's wrong with that? Muller loves to dance."

"Good for him."

"We used to dance together all the time. Muller's a terrific dancer. We went three times a week at one point."

"Where did you and Muller dance?"

"At a dance studio."

I swirl the ice around in my glass, imagining Muller doing a fox trot. "Do you have to be any good?" I ask. "What if you're terrible?"

"Everyone's terrible starting out, Daddy. I couldn't even do a simple waltz. You pick it up pretty quick."

"Do they grade you and stuff?"

"They have different levels. You move up from beginner to intermediate to senior."

"What if you really suck?"

"Everyone's real supportive, Daddy. You should try it."

"Maybe I should."

"I can find a dance studio near here," she says. She's already at the computer on the kitchen counter. "There's probably one close by. They're all over the place."

"Okay, sweetheart. If you find something, book us all in there. I think it's a foursome kind of thing, don't you?"

"We'd love to," Judy says. "I know Muller would."

I pour another drink and take it outside. "We're taking dance lessons," I say to Mary and Muller. "The four of us. It'll be a good family exercise." Mary looks at me over her glasses.

"I didn't know you liked to dance, Sam," Muller says.

"You seriously want to dance?" Mary says.

"Sure, why not?"

"You've never danced in your life."

"So I'll start now."

Muller turns the steaks and licks his fingers. "I love to dance," he says. "Judy and I are pretty good."

"Keep that under your hat," I say to him. "We need you in the beginner classes with us. Moral support, and all."

"No problem," Muller says.

Mary gets up and comes over to me. She puts her arms around my neck. "Nice one, Sam," she says. "You're quite something, you know that? I'm proud of you. What made you think of it?"

"Krupsky," I say.

"Krupsky?"

"I saw him twist."

# Chapter 36

The dance studio is a low-slung affair tucked between a child's shop and a Jiffy Lube. Posters sit on easels announcing dance contests and Salsa Nights. Rows of plastic palms separate the lobby from the main dance area. A man with silver hair and a silk shirt takes us through. Other couples are waiting. Everyone's nervous, the women tossing the bottoms of their dresses.

Muller has on this old blazer Mary found at a rummage sale. She thought would fit me, but I was practically swimming in the thing. On Muller, it stretches at the seams, riding up his back. Mary and Judy both wear culottes and high heels. They look like a couple of gaucho twins ready to start a hat dance.

As soon as everyone arrives, the silver-haired man introduces himself as Silvio and, as he explains it, pressing his palms together, we're going to be learning basic steps common to most Latin dances. "Stand in a line facing me, please," he says. "I will show you each step. Place your feet like this to start. Your right foot now goes back here, the left here."

He does it a few times. "Now you try," he says and walks back and forth, watching each of us. "Very good," he says. "Now, if you take these steps like this,"—moving his feet back and forth—"and put it together with this"—sliding one foot back from the other—"you have a Latin dance step."

"Now," he says, "I will play some music. You'll see that you can dance many dances with these simple steps." He presses a button on this big ghetto blaster and Latin strains fill the room.

"Now then," Silvio says, standing in front of us with his hands clasped. "The emphasis here is on the first beat. DA,da,da,DA,da,da."

He takes a step forward with his left foot, then rocks back with his right. "Follow me, please. Step into the beat like this. You do not count the beat. You *feel* it. DA, da, da, DA, da, da."

We're all pretty stiff off the top, except Muller, who despite my warnings, can't help showing off in front of everybody. He attracts Silvio's attention right away. "Good, my friend, Very nice rhythm. I think you've done this before. That's all right. You'll be an inspiration to the rest. You look Cuban. Are you Cuban?"

"Seattleite," Muller replies.

Silvio cocks his head like he doesn't understand. "Very nice, anyway," he says, and moves on down the line, hands clasped, looking now at Mary and me. "DA-A-A, da, da," he says to me. "Watch me, please," taking Mary by the hand. He leads her out on the floor. "One hand here,"—holding one hand on her hip—"and one hand on her wrist. This is how you guide her." He steps in and out between her feet. "You see?" he says to me. "Your wife follows very well. Now you come here." He puts one of my hands on his hip and dances with me. "DA, da, da, DA, da, da," he says. His hair smells kind of floral. "Okay," he says, leading me back to Mary, "take your partners."

"You two make a lovely couple," Mary says to me.

"I think he tucks."

We dance away, Silvio watching, straightening someone's arm, moving a hand down another's hip. Muller and Judy are dancing away, her eyes all glistening like a Sandra Dee movie.

Judy loves the dope and you can tell he loves her, too. I told Ruby yesterday, this crush business is giving me chest pains. "He's already jumped off a roof and drank paint, Sam," she said. "What else is he going to do?" I told her I feel I've let my daughter down. "You haven't let anybody down," she said. "The big lug will get over it. Let it be, Sam, or you'll have heartache coming out the wazoo."

Silvio comes over and takes Mary by the hand. "You guide her this way, Sam," he says to me, moving Mary's hips back and forth. "Let her know who's boss. You must show her authority. Always *guide*. That is the secret." He turns her left and right. "You try now," he says. "Take her hand." He gives Mary back to me.

"God, he's good," Mary says.

Silvio moves over beside Muller and Judy. His arms are crossed. He extends his first finger to his lips and nods. "Excellent," he says, clapping his hands. "Everyone," he says. "Watch him, please."

Muller and Judy dance while Silvio smiles. They make the rest of us look like hillbillies.

"You're very good, my friend," Silvio tells Muller. "I like how you dance. All of you must learn to dance like him. Remember, always listen to the beat. It is not hard if you listen."

We dance to three or four more songs, each of us forced out into the middle at some point. Silvio has an eye for detail. He catches every little thing, pulling a hand up higher, pushing a knee back.

An hour later, he slaps his hands together. "That is enough for one night," he says. "Now go home and practice. I want you all to dance like this couple here," pointing at Muller and Judy.

There's coffee and biscuits in the corner. Muller goes over with some other people. Judy stands with us. "I'm so proud of Muller," she says to us. "Wasn't he fantastic?"

"He was swell, honey," I say. "Let's drink our coffee and go."

"What's the rush, Daddy," Judy says. "We should mingle. It's good to get to know people. You'll have to dance with them at some point."

"Why?"

"Because, Daddy, you have to be able to dance with different partners."

I look around the room. There's nobody I want to dance with. That's why I never learned to dance in the first place. Sock hops scared the crap out of me. "We'll mingle another time, sweetheart," I say, seeing Muller talking to a couple. He's a suave son-of-a-bitch when he wants to be. Judy goes over and joins him. Everyone's singing Muller's praises. They wouldn't be if they saw him a few days ago, making green puddles.

Muller and Judy finally come back and we leave the studio. Out in the car, I can feel Muller right behind me, like a damp sheepdog breathing down my neck.

I try to adjust the seat to give him more room, but the seat ends up sliding back instead. His knees are digging into my back. I try again only making it worse. "Sorry," I say. "Want me to get out and pull the seat forward?"

"It's okay, Sam."

"Wasn't Muller amazing tonight?" Judy says. "He's so *mucho machismo*. I'll bet he could teach. That's what you should do, Muller."

We stop off for something to eat and Judy keeps going on about Muller's dancing, calling him her Latin Stud Muffin. Back at the house, Judy goes straight to the computer, downloading Latin songs to her iPod. I get myself a drink and go outside. Standing in the dark, I hear familiar strains, the same beat. Mary and Judy are dancing away in the living room. Muller joins them. I feel a headache starting just behind my eyes as my head pounds to batucada rhythms and bongos.

"Sam," Mary calls to me. "Join us. Muller knows how to salsa."

"I'm fine," I say.

"Don't be a spoilsport, Daddy," Judy says.

For all his faults, Muller does cut an impressive figure. I watch them dancing away and then slink off to the bedroom with *The Road Less Traveled*. I flip through the pages, reading about holes again. Muller's a poster boy for this stuff. He's all circles and holes. I know he's not a bad person, but I can't understand how he's attached to an oxygen tank one minute, yet still manages cazas and flambés.

Mary's all hands when she comes in the bedroom later.

"What the hell's gotten into you?" I say, and the next thing I know, my pajama top is unbuttoned. "I'm reading here," I say, but she's pulling down the sheet.

I know this sort of thing happens in Latin countries all the time, with a population to prove it, but I'm not in a Latin country, and I'm too tired for even a half-hearted olé.

"I'm horny, Sam."

"It's the endorphins."

"The what?"

"Endorphins. I read about them online. All that dancing is increasing your production of endorphins."

"I don't care what I'm producing, I'm horny."

"Is this going to happen every time we go dancing?"

"You tell me. You're the endorphin expert."

"You could channel it into a hobby."

"Put the book down, Sam."

"I'm learning about holes."

"You've been on that chapter for a week."

She pulls the drawstring on my pajamas. "Lift up."

"I'm lifting."

"Higher, Sam, I want them off."

"When did you start caring if they're off?"

"Stop being difficult."

"Okay, they're off."

# Chapter 37

*M*ary lets me sleep while she helps Muller with breakfast. I hear skillets banging and Mary humming. The phone rings, I pick up, but Mary's already on the extension. Otis is telling her he misses Muller's baking. "We'd appreciate his attendance in our kitchen," he says. The crazy fucker is too spaced out to care. All Mary can say is, "What? Who is this?" I tell her it's Max clowning around and once she's off the line, I explain to Otis that he needs to fuck off. "That's a fine howdy-do," he says and hangs up.

Out in the sunroom, I hear Otis back on the air: "That's 'It's All Over Now', by The Valentinos. You probably remember The Rolling Stones' version. They were nothing special 'til Bobby Womack pulled their nuts out of the wringer."

The Rec Room of Sound is going constantly in this house, even when Otis is just sitting there, slack-jawed, sleeping through another album. Sometimes Margot just slides his chair back, does her show, then slides him in front of the screen again. Amazingly, the numbers are growing, especially for *Otis Cries for You*. The crazy bastard can cry on a dime and still be an insensitive asshole. Fortunately, Margot anticipates these critical moments, pushing Otis out of his chair before he gets into real trouble. As I make my breakfast now, I hear Otis, talking to some girl on line. Then I hear something crash, and Margot saying, "Listen, Susie, Otis is feeding you a line of bull. Contraception *is* your responsibility. Just because your boyfriend's all thumbs doesn't mean you stop protection. Practice makes perfect. Try putting it on a banana . . ."

I take my cereal over to the computer, watching Margot slipping a condom over a banana. "That's my breakfast," Otis is saying. Margot ignores him and keeps talking. "Practice your technique, Susie," she says. "Craig isn't going to lose his stiffy if you're fast. I can't believe I just said stiffy."

"I can't believe it, either," Max says.

Ruby laughs in the background. Margot tosses Otis the banana. "Take your stupid banana, Otis."

"I don't want it now."

"I'll take it," Max says.

"Get your own banana, Max."

"Stop being a baby, old man. Look, you've got blogs."

"Get out of my chair, Margot," Otis says, pushing her aside. "Okay, here we go. A woman in Rockford just lost her son in a kayaking accident. That's a tragic loss, ma'am. Hope he's not your only kiddie—" Margot leans in to read the screen. "He's not dead, you idiot," she says. "He just hasn't called."

"Correction," Otis says. "We don't know if the kid's alive or under a deadhead somewhere. Either way,"—fist to his mouth—"Otis is feeling your pain and your loss—"

"Read the next message, for God's sake, Otis," Margot says. Bisquick jumps on Otis's head. Otis swats him away. Max is standing behind them, eating the banana.

"Okay, her kid just walked through the door," Otis says. "Hallelujah for that. I'm happy for you, ma'am. Little Johnny came marching home, eh? Here's a cry for the happy reunion of mother and son. You hold him in your arms. Hold him good and tight, 'cause one day, things won't be so rosy."

"Just cry and shut your yap," Margot says.

Bisquick pulls at a hair on Otis' arm. "Ouch! Fuck off, Bisquick!"

"Shove over," Margot says, pushing Otis out of the way. "Just a little perspective on that last story. Mrs. Klein, if your kid's doing water sports, make sure he's wearing a good life jacket. Better than sinking like a stone, honey."

Ruby comes out of the laundry room, holding a monkey wrench. "Something's clogging up the drain, Max," she says. "You got any whites, Margot?" Margot disappears into the bedroom next to the laundry room. I guess she's been crashing there since Ruby let Otis move back upstairs. "Otis, give me your shirt," Ruby says.

"Why?"

"It's filthy," Ruby says, pulling the shirt over his head. "Anything else you want washed? Speak now or forever hold your peace."

"I'm half-naked here, Ruby."

"Nobody cares if you're half-naked."

Mrs. Klein is laughing her head off.

# Chapter 38

The kitchen smells of peppers and Gorgonzola cheese. I come in and find Mary and Judy licking tabasco sauce off their fingers. The plates show the last remains of Muller's cooking. "You want a tamale?" Muller asks me. He's holding the pan like a tambourine.

"Just coffee for now, thanks," I say.

"We're getting proper dance outfits today," Mary says.

"What's wrong with what you wore last night?"

"We need Latin clothes, Sam. Get in the game."

"What game?"

"I can get you something, too. Maybe a silk shirt like Silvio's."

"I don't do silk."

"Come on, Daddy," Judy says. "Muller's getting one."

"If Muller jumped off a roof, would you expect me to follow him?"

"That's not funny, Dad."

"I'm making a point."

"Why does it have to be at Muller's expense? And he didn't jump off the roof. He fainted." I'd like to tell her his arms were spread like a dove. Judy gets behind Muller and gives him a hug. "My big bear," she says.

"Your big bear put a dent in someone's lawn," I say.

"Sam," Mary says, "Muller's made us all a wonderful breakfast. Can't you be nice and show some appreciation?"

"I appreciate the effort, Muller. Now let's read the news and see how the world is doing. Any favorites? Simple assaults? Purse snatchings? Renegade Islamists?"

"You're not funny," Mary says. She puts her coffee mug in the sink.

"I'll do the dishes," Muller says.

"You've done enough," she says. "Sam can take care of the dishes. Can't you, Sam? Are you staying here or coming with us?"

"Staying here. I might take a dip in the pool next door."

"You realize the Andersons don't live there anymore?"

"Since when?"

"Since March."

"We have new neighbors?"

"What do you think?"

"Have we introduced ourselves?"

"No, we haven't," Mary says. "And, just in case you decide to say hello, they're nudists. At least I think they're nudists. They like to swim naked, in any event."

"How did you find that out?"

"I looked through that hole in the fence."

"That's illegal, Mary."

"So's flapping your package out in the open."

I shake the newspaper. She takes it out of my hands. "Make yourself useful."

"I really don't mind doing the dishes," Muller says.

"Go with them," I say. "I'll clean up."

"Let's go, babykins," Judy says. "We're buying you a silk shirt."

"With patches under the armpits," I say.

"Ignore him," Mary says. "He thinks he's being funny."

Judy and Muller go down the hall to the washroom. The giggling starts as soon as the door's closed.

"Sam," Mary says, snapping her fingers in my face. "Listen, I've put up with the drinking, the panic attacks, and the snide remarks. It's time to stop feeling sorry for yourself. Everyone else is making the best of things. Look at Margot. She's having the time of her life."

"She just put a condom on a banana."

"She's helping people," she says. "Which is more than I can say for you. Stop making fun of Muller. He has feelings, you know. Will everything be cleaned up when we get back?"

"Yes, it will."

She goes out to start the car.

The toilet flushes. "Bye, Daddy," Judy calls out.

"Bye, honey," I say

"Bye, Sam."

"Bye, Big Bear."

I put my coffee cup in the sink and look out the window. A pool skimmer is going back and forth. I step out on the porch, then walk across the lawn. Looking through Mary's spy hole, I see a whole family sitting there, wrapped in towels. I step back and call out, "Hello."

A man's head appears wearing a fishing hat. "Hello to you, too," he says.

His face is bright red. I wonder if his wife is standing below him, making a stirrup with her hands. "Sam Bennett," I say, extending my hand up.

"Riley," he says. "You wanna come over for a swim?"

"I heard you're nudists."

"We'll put something on if it makes you feel any better."

"Can I bring you some whiskey?"

"At this hour?"

"Sorry, I keep thinking you're the Andersons."

I go in the house and put on my bathing suit. On my way out, I wake up the computer. Margot's telling a woman she shouldn't smoke in bed. Behind her, Max is sleeping on the couch. Otis is trying to get Bisquick to say, "Howdy doody."

". . . smoking in bed is about the dumbest thing I've ever heard of," Margot is saying. "You people need your heads examined. Put on some music, Otis. I've got a headache the size of an amusement park. Max, you're wrinkling my shirts there."

When I get over to Riley's, everyone's wearing t-shirts. There's lemonade in tall glasses, a blue and white umbrella, a cabana with a matching bar. The filter bubbles away. The skimmer drips. Riley's wife walks around the perimeter, an attractive, leggy, mother of three. Her t-shirt features a pornographic Disney character. As soon as I'm through the gate, she hands me a glass of lemonade. Her nail polish is the color of tangerine. "I'm Pam," she says. "These are the kids, Cassidy, my eldest, Shawn, Lisa. Say hello, kids." The two girls and a boy wave. "I was just about to jump in the pool," she says, then dives in the deep end. When she comes up, she swims on her back, showing two dark circles under her t-shirt. "Get in, Sam," she says. "The water's beautiful."

I take off my shirt and make a shallow dive. Pam's now sitting in the shallow end. "We should have come and introduced ourselves earlier," she says when I surface. "Riley's a big fence talker. I saw your wife and daughter yesterday. I said to Riley, 'Let's ask them over,' but they were talking."

"My daughter wants to start a family."

"Our Cassidy just turned nineteen. I guess it's only a matter of time. How old's your daughter?"

"Judy turns thirty-four next month."

"Time does fly by."

"Like an albatross," I say.

She swishes the water around with her toe. Cassidy stands up and dives in the deep end. Her tanned body ripples beneath the surface. She goes from one end to the other without coming up for air. When she finally surfaces, she pushes back her hair and hangs onto the diving board. "What's your wife's name, Sam?" Pam asks.

"Mary."

"Tell her we'd love to have you all over some time."

"We're learning Latin dancing."

"How exciting."

"My son-in-law knows how to salsa."

"I love to dance. What's your son-in-law's name?"

"Muller."

"Do you think he'd teach us to salsa?"

"He's pretty busy right now."

Cassidy eases herself out of the water, shaking her hair. The others are playing a board game. Cassidy picks up a comb and runs it through her hair, tilting her head back and forth. Lisa goes to Shawn, "That's not a word. You're making it up."

"Challenge me then, idiot."

"Be nice," Riley warns from his chair in the shade.

"There's no such word as *burate*."

"Challenge me."

"Up yours."

Riley gets up and runs the skimmer down the pool. He raises his arms, exposing his package. Mary's right, it shouldn't be flapping around. "You're welcome to stay for lunch, Sam," Riley says.

"Yes, stay for lunch," Pam says. "I'm making tomato sandwiches."

"I should get going. The lovebirds are calling me."

"Say hello to Judy and Muller."

"No, they have real love birds. Meek and Beek."

"How sweet."

"Not really."

I climb out of the pool and get my towel. Cassidy is lying on a lounge chair, one hand above her head, tanned legs shining in the sun. Her toenails are pink. Lisa gets up and dives in the deep end. She comes up on her back with small areolas showing through her top. She glides across the pool. I walk around to the gate, waving as I go.

"Tell Muller we'd love to learn to dance," Pam says.

I walk away with three words in my head.

Nudists shouldn't dance.

# Chapter 39

*M*argot's changed. I don't know what's changed, exactly. She's still the cranky, sullen woman I've known for years, but now she wears blue contacts. They're a light blue, almost grey, and I detect flecks in the retina. Sitting there at the computer screen, she's a pistol, a blue-eyed terror, exploding myths and goofy lifestyles. Last night, some girl asked if it was okay to blow someone as a favor. "A favor?" Margot said. "Young lady, do you know what a favor is? It's doing a kindness. Blowing every Tom, Dick and Harry ain't a kindness. It's using your mouth like a big box outlet." Another girl sent a video clip showing her technique. "What's the matter with you?" Margot says. "It's not only offensive, it's tacky. Have you got no sense of pride?" Margot chastises, but it doesn't make any difference. They like freaking her out. Our generation was taught to think before you speak. These kids act on reflex. One girl sent in a blog, saying, "My farts smell these days," then followed up by saying, "I like giving myself Dutch ovens." Margot lambasted her, pointing out that it wasn't very dignified. Then the girl asked if you could catch anything from sharing a milkshake straw. "Oh, shut up," Margot said. Then she started giving some livestock farmer in Mattoon shit for going on about his cows. "A cow's a cow, for God's sake," she said. "It's just going to end up on someone's plate." He wrote back, saying she wouldn't know a Guernsey from a Black Angus. "If it sizzles, Gomer," she said, "I don't care if it used to wear a saddle." Blogs, texts, emails—they keep coming like a tide of dead fish. Otis and Margot practically live on air. They take breaks now and then, running off for washroom breaks, eating, then someone blogs or texts and they drop what they're doing.

Someone's even posted a video on YouTube of Margot dumping Otis out of his chair, running it back and forth in slow motion. "That's so funny," Judy says, eating toast, getting crumbs everywhere. Otis bounces up and drops like a stone, and Judy giggles like a million other viewers.

I still don't understand how YouTube makes money. People watch, they post messages—that's all they do. What's in it for YouTube? I know they have advertisers, but nobody cares about the ads. Not when you can see someone like Otis make a fool of himself. Margot says it's all about sponsoring. Otis and Margot have already being approached. They could make a lot of money, but it's a crowded marketplace. Nobody sticks around long enough to be loyal, and you can only attract so many new viewers. Even when people are watching Otis fall out of his chair, they're doing other things. It's hard to keep anyone's attention. And it seems they're taking as many videos as they're looking at these days. Those end up on YouTube as well. How do you make money when you've got as many providers as consumers? Maybe I'm too old to figure it out. How Margot makes sense of it, I'll never know. I guess, in the end, it's no different than traditional advertising, but, like I said, I still don't see how it can keep going. One day, someone's going to realize the craziness, and they'll go back to The Daily Show, where at least you know who's running the country. Until then, I guess it's Dutch ovens.

# Chapter 40

*M*ost days, we do our work, pack up, then go back to Otis's house for brownies. Max found a new supplier with a grow-op in his basement. The stuff turned everyone into wacked out fools. Margot ate her brownie down at the computer, taking over Otis's time slot. He was too blitzed to move. Margot wasn't much better. She started out telling one blogger she didn't do crying. "That's Otis," Margot said. "What's your problem, anyway?"

The woman had a failed boob job. Her tits looked like squashed marshmallows. Nobody wanted her squashed marshmallows. "There's more to life than your tits, Lola," Margot told her. Another message followed: "But I'm an exotic dancer."

"Well," Margot said. "Maybe it's God telling you to get off the pole. Did you ever think of that? Surely, a well-spoken girl like you has other options. What about telephone sales?" Another message: "I do telephone sales—check my prices."

"That's not what I meant, Lola, and you know it."

Meanwhile, Ruby's learning to tango in the living room. She and Muller practice a few cazas under the critical eye of Otis. He sits off in the corner with Bisquick on his head, grunting like a warthog. Bisquick loves Latin music. He bobs up and down, getting all fluffed up. "Tango," he says. "Tango." I finally have to drag Muller away, telling him he's got two women waiting to dance at home. We leave Otis swatting at Bisquick, and Ruby trying a few moves on her own. Max is passed out on the couch.

As we leave, Otis is saying, "That's the devil's music, Ruby." She tells him to go fly a kite. "I'm tangoing whether you like it or not, Otis," she tells him.

"I won't have my house turned into a dago hall."

"Shut your piehole."

"I'm warning you, Ruby."

"Dammit, old man," Max says. "You woke me up."

"Your mother's dancing the devil's music."

"You still woke me up."

"Stop doin' that dago shit, Ruby."

Margot's cattle caller go off downstairs, probably making Lola's marshmallow tits shake like crazy.

# Chapter 41

The mail comes with another letter from Frank. He's still down in the Los Angeles office, filling in until they find a new CEO. He says it could take another month at least. After that, Iris wants him to slow down, take things easy for a change. I can tell by his writing that it scares the hell out of him. He'll still have to spend six months in the Chicago office after Los Angeles. It's a standard arrangement to prevent existing clients from bolting. All he has to do is attend a few meetings. "Just your usual wank," he says. Then he throws something in at the end that really has me worried.

> *Once things settle down, we'll grab a drink and a steak dinner. Iris has me booked up the first month I'm back. After that, my time is my own (she won't want me under her heels). Hope Mary is holding up okay. Iris would love to hear from her. We'll get together after Iris's treatments. I'm sure the doctors make it sound worse than it is. I'll keep you posted.*
>
> *Frank*

I get Iris on the phone. She sounds the same as always. I tell her about Frank's letter and find out she has a form of lymphoma. "They caught it early," she says. "They expect I'll be completely cured. Fingers crossed. How are you doing? Still dizzy?"

"I'm making out. I think Mary wants to talk to you."

"Lovely. Put her on."

Mary gets on the phone, they talk away, then make plans for lunch. Judy wants to go with them. She still calls Iris, Aunt Iris, because Iris gave her a doll one Christmas. It was thirty years ago, but Judy has a long memory where dolls are concerned, and she's all hopped up about seeing Iris again. "We're going to a fancy restaurant," she says. "Uncle Frankie is paying for it."

"When did you start calling him Uncle Frankie?"

"Iris calls him Frankie."

"If Iris jumped off a roof, would you do it?"

"What's wrong with calling him Uncle Frankie?"

"Nothing, sweetie. He's been called worse."

Mary comes out of the bedroom in a new dress. "Whoa!" Judy says. "You look gorgeous, Mom! I didn't pack anything really good. Do you have a dress I can wear?"

Off they go down the hall again, closet doors banging, hangers scrapping together. They come out looking like sisters. Judy's really matured these last few years. You don't notice it when she's in shorts and a tank top, but now she looks great. I've never seen Judy in heels. Her wedding was a bit of a hippy affair, everyone with garlands in their hair and bare feet. This is a completely different Judy. She's actually got nice legs. "What do you think?" she asks, and then takes a last look in the hall mirror. "We'd better get going, Mom," she says. "Bye, Big Bear." She gives him a hug. It doesn't look like he wants to let her go. "Don't get me wrinkled," she says. "What are you doing today?" Muller shrugs and looks like he wants to go with them. "We won't be too long," she says, giving him a, sloppy kiss.

Muller waves from the living room window as they leave.

"Get dressed," I say to him. "We're going to work." He just stands there. "What's wrong now?" I say to him.

"Nothing, Sam."

"Are you coming or not?"

"I was thinking of making étouffée for dinner."

This is second time in a week he's begged off work. It nearly caused a riot over at Otis's place. Without their brownies, everyone wandered around like derelicts, getting all fidgety. "The man's got no consideration," Otis kept saying. "No consideration at all. What are we supposed to do now? Ruby, make some brownies."

140

"*You* make them. I'm trying to get this stain out of your shirt."

To be honest, we need a few days off those brownies. Everyone's putting on weight. Even the switch to skim milk hasn't helped. "This is worse than yogurt," Otis kept saying. I don't know what's going on with Muller. Normally he jumps at the chance to see Ruby. Now he stands there, saying he wants to make étouffée. "What's gotten into you, Muller?" I say. He shrugs, gives the stove a longing look, then goes and gets changed. On the way over to Otis's, he tunes in a Latin station. The announcer is talking in Spanish and Muller nods. "You speak Spanish?" I ask.

"Not really," he says.

"Then why are you nodding?"

"I like the sound of his voice."

"So he could be speaking Farsi."

"I guess."

A bent cigarette goes in his mouth and he pats his pants, looking for his lighter. "You could ask for a light," I say to him, but he shrugs, telling me he's changed his mind. He turns up the music. When I look over, his eyes are closed. "You sure you're all right?" I say, and he opens his eyes. He stares at the car stereo. He doesn't say anything.

Over at Otis's, Muller makes up the brownies, then we drive to a house up on Cedar Avenue. All the outside needs to be scraped and sanded and then painted. We get out the heat guns, scrapers and paint stripper. It's hot work up on ladders. By noon, Muller's covered in paint chips. Both his hands are burnt from the heat gun.

Ruby finally takes pity on all of us and calls it a day. We go back to the house and have brownies and milk. Margot is giving someone shit downstairs. We watch her on Ruby's computer, munching away on a brownie while she talks. "I'll tell you why you can't share your antibiotics, young lady," Margot is saying. "You're the one with gonorrhea, not your girlfriend. What do you mean she's got gonorrhea, too? How do you know that? Who's she been with? Who's Brain? Your boyfriend's name is *Brain*? What was she doing—oh, God, never mind."

She comes upstairs. "Honestly," she says. "Is the whole world into three ways? Why in God's name would you share your boyfriend with your best friend?"

"I did in college," Ruby says.

"When did you go to college?" Max says.

"I went to barber college."

"I didn't know that. Why did you give it up?"

She jerks a thumb at Otis. "Lamebrain there didn't think it was ladylike."

"You were too familiar with the customers, Ruby," Otis says. He goes to the fridge for more milk. Bisquick jumps on his head, Otis swats at him and milk spills on the floor.

"I could sure use a haircut, Ruby," Muller says.

"I'm pretty rusty."

"Goddamn it, Muller," Otis says. "I sure appreciate your brownies, but, boy, you're getting my hackles up."

"Ignore him," Ruby says.

"Get your own wife to cut your stupid hair."

"You're just jealous," Ruby says. "And who are you to talk?"

"I paid for my indiscretions, Ruby. I don't have a decent Otis Redding in my collection because of you."

"If Muller wants a haircut, that's the least I can do. Look at all the brownies he's made. Go sit on a stool in the kitchen, honey," she pats Muller on the back. "I'll get my good scissors." She finds her scissors and a comb in a drawer, then wraps an old sheet around Muller's neck. Otis circles behind. "Stop hovering, Otis."

"I'm watching."

"You're making me nervous."

"Why're his eyes rolling back?"

"How the hell would I know?"

"Stop massaging his head."

"It's good for the follicles."

"Quit rolling your eyes back, Muller." Max is wheezing he's laughing so hard. "It's not funny," Otis says.

"Yes it is," Max says.

"Go put on some music."

"*You* go put on some music, old man."

"Everyone's a friggin' anarchist around here," Otis mumbles, going downstairs with Bisquick following. "Stop sneakin' up on me, you damn bird."

"Sauna," Bisquick says.

"What the hell are you doing, Otis?" Margot yells.

"He wants a sauna."

"You better not be putting him in the toilet."

# Chapter 42

*M*y dreams come in Technicolor these days, like those old Alfred Hitchcock movies: everything bright, crisp and clean. Ever noticed how good they all look, even when birds are pecking the hell out of them. The guy that really drives me crazy is Cary Grant. Look at him in *North by Northwest*. Two days without a bath, crop dust all over his clothes, and he's still fresh as a corsage.

I spent most of the night tossing and turning, getting an elbow from Mary. I don't dream until the sun starts coming up, and then it consists of flashbacks, usually going back to my agency days. I guess it stands to reason. I spent more time there than anywhere else. This morning, I remembered an incident back in the seventies. We're sitting in Frank's office, working on the new campaign. The client is a local department store, one of those old five and dime chains. They've been replaced by the dollar stores today, but it's basically the same concept. We'd been working on this campaign for weeks but Frank wasn't happy. So this account guy comes up with *We make people happy*. "What do you think, Frank?" the account guy says. Frank looks around the room at the rest of us. "What do the rest of you think?" he asks. "Is it campaign or not?"

"It's interesting, Frank," Reynolds, the creative director, says. "Do you want us to do something up?"

"I want to know what you fuckers think," Frank says. "What about you, Sam? You're the copywriter."

"Honestly, I don't know if we make people happy," I say.

"Why not?"

"The stuff's cheap."

"Watch your mouth. That's our client."

"All I'm saying is, people go there *because* it's cheap. They get a bunch of stuff without spending a lot of money."

There was this song on the radio that morning, a stupid disco hit where the singer kept going, *"More, more, more."* I couldn't get it out of my head. So I say to Frank, "What if we used a song. Something that's out there now. I heard one this morning that just keeps going, 'More, more, more.'" Frank sits up and twists the cap off his tortoiseshell pen. "Yeah, so what's the angle?"

"Low prices mean you can have more. That's what the store's all about, isn't it? You want more, we've got more."

"Not bad," Frank says. "What do the rest of you think?"

"Everyone could dance around the store," Reynolds says. "Maybe bring in one of those disco balls."

"We're not selling disco balls, for fuck's sake," Frank says.

"What if we had contests?" I say.

"What kind of contests?"

"The kind they used to run at the supermarkets. They gave you five minutes to fill your grocery cart. Whoever filled their cart up first won the groceries. What if we bring that back?"

"Where does the song come in?"

"It's playing the whole time."

"While the people jump around like monkeys," he says, "which we turn into commercials. What would something like that cost?"

"Dirt cheap."

Frank looks around at the other people, then the account guy. "See why he's creative and you're not?" he says. "We need the rights to that song. Any of you know what it's called?" Everyone's looking at their shoes, straightening their bra straps. "Well, get production working on the rights. Sam, put some scripts together. Just the general idea. The client's in on Friday."

Friday comes along and we bring all the storyboards into the conference room. Frank's telling the client a joke. "So the guy says to the priest . . . Wait, here's the creative. Arthur, this is Sam. Sam, this is Arthur. Set up the boards, Sam. I'll give Arthur a brief introduction. Arthur, we got a song here we want you to hear. Sam, play the song first, then we'll go through the concepts." I play the song and Arthur nods his head. "Catchy tune," he says.

"Damn right it's catchy," Frank says. "Take a look at the storyboards. Remember those supermarket contests? First one to fill their cart wins the groceries? We do the same thing, only we turn them into commercials. Dirt cheap, Arthur. Not actors, no talent fees. Someone falls on their ass, leave it. Someone does a header into a display, leave it. Everyone's having a great time. It's a fucking party."

"What if someone falls and gets hurt?"

"Ever seen your place on Boxing Day, Arthur?"

"That's true."

"Fucking right, it's true. You ready to sign off, or what?"

"I'm thinking, Frank."

"What's to think about? Money goes in your coffers. End of story. What more do you want?"

"You trying to hard sell me, Frank?"

"Sam, take off. Arthur and I want to talk."

Frank comes out later with everything signed. The campaign goes out, people love it, the media budget doubles. "You did good, Sam," he says. "Now let's go find that fat fuck Reynolds. Cocksucker thinks he can coast. You want his office? You wanna be creative director?" He's already standing at Reynolds' door. "Has anyone seen Reynolds? The little prick's probably gone to lunch."

"Where are you going to put him?"

"I'm not gonna put him anywhere. I should have kicked his ass to the curb years ago. Do you want his office or not?"

"Do I get more money?"

"You think I'm soft?"

"I could use a raise. I'm getting married."

"Good for you. I like married people. You starting a family?"

"We want to settle in first. What about the raise?"

"Fucking hell. You're worse than Reynolds. Okay, you get your raise. Find Reynolds for me. He's around somewhere."

"What do you want me to tell him?"

"I don't care what you tell him. Tell him he's fired. You're the creative director. Use some initiative."

# Chapter 43

"*W*hy's your hair lopsided?" Judy asks Muller this morning. She's running her fingers through his hair while he cooks. Mary's out in the sunroom watching Margot's show. How people can talk about their problems at this hour is beyond me. I take my coffee out there and sit across from Mary. Meek and Beek are going at each other. The cage rattles, feathers fly, birdseed falls on the rug. Mary takes off her glasses and stares at me. "What's with Muller's haircut?" Mary asks.

"Ruby tried to clean him up a bit," I say, flipping the paper open. "She had to stop halfway through. Otis got jealous." I pretend I'm reading.

"I thought he slept with Max's girlfriend?"

"He did."

"And he's jealous of Ruby cutting Muller's hair?"

"Otis is Otis."

"How can Margot live with these people?"

"Beats me. They gave her the downstairs bedroom. It's better than commuting and Margot doesn't like buses." I flip through the paper, hearing Margot doing her show. "Anything good this morning?"

"A woman thinks her husband loves the dog more than her."

"What did Margot say?"

"If the dog's not wearing women's panties, it's okay."

"Sounds like Margot. I'd better get to work." I grab some fruit out of the fridge. "Get your clothes on, Muller," I say. "Let's go."

"Can he have the day off, Daddy?" Judy asks. "He's got sun stroke."

"I'm okay, Jude," he says. "Sam needs me." He puts on his martyr's face.

"Give me a hug before you go," she says. They start necking. It's so damn sloppy.

"Don't be late tonight, Sam," Mary calls from the sunroom. "We've got our dance lessons tonight."

"What if I fall off the ladder?" I grab some scissors from the washroom on the way out.

"Don't you dare."

"Bye, Jude," Muller says.

"Bye, Big Bear." They start necking again.

We finally get in the car and I try to even out Muller's hair. He looks in the mirror on his side. "Hold your head still," I say to him.

"You're not much of a barber, Sam."

"Slick it back. And stop pissing Otis off."

"I didn't do anything."

"Margot thought you were going to leave a wet spot."

"Ruby can do better than Otis."

"I'm holding scissors, Muller."

"I'm just saying she could."

"Keep your fucking opinions to yourself."

"We're learning the sacada tonight."

"I need that like a head cold."

"You're getting better, Sam. You have to let yourself go."

"Last time I let myself go, I ended up with a paper bag over my face. Did you see Krupsky doing the twist?"

"I don't think he was doing the twist."

"Yes, he was."

"You're imagining things, Sam."

"He was doing the twist."

"If you say so."

It sure as hell wasn't a sacada.

# Chapter 44

*P*aint falls off the overhangs like corn chips. I'm scraping while Muller does the window frames. From my perch, I see manicured lawns and hydrangeas swinging in the breeze. It's one of those days when I don't feel rattled. Maybe it's the sun, or knowing this house will soon match its surroundings. Maybe I'm learning to appreciate careful maintenance and a good hedge trimmer.

Ruby comes outside with a cigarette going. I've cut back myself. Hauling a ladder the other day, I thought I was going to pass out. I've been making Muller do the heavy lifting. He huffs and puffs, complaining he's got a bad shoulder, but I caught him last night moving the oxygen tank closer to his cot. Now he's working the heat gun like a hair dryer.

Ruby comes and stands at the base of the ladder. She looks up with one hand shielding her eyes. "Good job, Sam," she says. "We'll be done in the bedrooms this afternoon. How about out here?"

"Everything's pretty much stripped."

Muller speeds up when he sees her watching. "You're in fine form today, Muller," she says.

"Anything to get the job done, Ruby."

"That's what I like to see."

When she goes back inside, Muller leans against the ladder. "What are you stopping for?" I say.

"I got something in my eye."

"Your eye was fine a minute ago."

"I should go wash it out."

"Use the garden hose."

"Sam, did you ever cheat on Mary?"

"No, I didn't, Muller."

"Did she ever cheat on you?"

"No."

"Is it possible?"

"Why are you asking?"

"Just want to know."

"You're a dummy, you know that?"

"It's a simple question, Sam."

"I haven't cheated because I don't want to cheat. Okay?"

"And Mary feels the same way?"

"How would I know?"

"Haven't you ever talked about it?"

"No, we haven't talked about it. Why, have you seen anyone slipping out of our house?"

"No."

"Then go wash your eye out, for chrissake."

He turns on the house and flushes his eye. Then he's lapping water like a dog.

# Chapter 45

**W**e're learning how to "walk between the woman's legs" tonight, which Muller says is based on the *caquero* style. He's been reading up on all this stuff in some book. Ruby loves hearing terms like *voleo* and *barrida*. How Muller remembers it all is beyond me.

"You're becoming quite the expert, Muller," Ruby says. "Maybe Otis and I should take up dancing. He could lose some weight."

"I ain't doing no tango," Otis says, suspenders dangling. "Neither are you, Ruby. No fucking tango."

"I'll bloody well tango if I want."

"You could use the exercise, old man," Max says. "Besides, Ruby hasn't been out in ages."

"Then we'll go to a movie," Otis says.

"When was the last time we went to a movie?" Ruby says.

"I don't like these modern films. Why can't they make movies like *Cool Hand Luke* anymore? There's an actor for you. Paul Newman. What ever happened to him?"

"What are you talking about, old man?" Max says. "*The Verdict?* *Butch Cassidy and the Sundance Kid?* *The Color of Money?*"

"Those sucked," Otis says. "Bunch of wussies now, anyway. What ever happened to that feller, George Kennedy? *Luke, where you at, boy?* That's acting. Whatever happened to him?"

"*Naked Gun?*" Max says.

Otis gets up and hikes his pants. "Ruby doesn't need to see anyone naked, Max. Least of all George Kennedy."

"I'd like to see Paul Newman naked," Ruby says.

Margot comes upstairs for more milk. "Who do you want to see naked?" she asks.

"Paul Newman."

"He turns me on like a four stroke engine." She opens the fridge. "We have any brownies left?" she says.

"There's one on top of the fridge," Ruby says.

"What the hell, Ruby," Otis says. "You told me we were out."

"You've had enough," Max says.

Otis jumps up but Margot elbows him in the stomach. "Ouch! Jesus, Margot!" he says.

"I need this brownie more than you," she says, pouring a glass of milk and taking the brownie downstairs.

"Woman's a menace," Otis says, watching Muller put one of Ruby's gold studs in his ear. "What the hell are you doing?" Otis says. "Big man like you. George Kennedy would never be caught dead wearing a God damn earring." He goes off scratching himself.

Actually, George Kennedy wore a loincloth in Spartacus.

# Chapter 46

Silvio has us out on the dance floor, showing us a new step. Every move he makes is so slick and effortless. Tonight, he has his wife with him. Her name is Carmen, a former tango champion with the build to go with it. He leads her out on the floor like a prize hen. "My lovely wife will now demonstrate a proper *gancho*," he says. She puts one hand on his shoulder, holding the other hand back. Then she hooks her sculptured leg around Silvio's thigh, leans back, then straightens, all in one fluid motion. Everyone applauds. "Now, please, everybody" Silvio says. "This is a dance of love. Every move you make is a suggestion—an invitation. *Invite* your partner between your legs, ladies. And you, gentlemen, accept the invitation. Do it with authority. Remember, *machismo*." Mary steps towards me and thrusts her hip into my side.

"That's pretty hard, Mary."

"I'm inviting you in, Sam."

"That's still pretty hard."

"*Me siento*, Sam."

"*Me siento*, yourself."

She gives me a glazed look.

"Begin," Silvio says. "Come this way towards me. Yes, very good. Now caress. *Caress*." He slaps his hands together. "Everybody," he says. "Stand at ease, please. Watch our friend, Muller. See how he takes his lovely lady in his arms?" Muller executes what Silvio calls a *barrida*. "Very good," Silvio says, crouching down beside them and takes Muller's foot. "When you tap her ankle," he says, "be very gentle. Tap both sides of her foot. You must always do it affection-ately. Now, the rest of you, see if you can do the same."

We try following Muller's example, looking stiff, bumping hips. "*Woo* her, Sam," Silvio says to me. "Tango must come from the heart. It must be passionate." Mary reaches down and pinches my ass. I yelp and Silvio looks over. "Your wife has the idea, Sam," he says. "Let us not forget the female *machismo*." Mary really dug in her nails. She's got enough machismo for both of us. No wonder I don't want to wear silk. "Come on, Sam, woo her," Silvio says. "Machismo must be met with machismo." Other yelps go up across the room.

See what you started, you crazy Argentine?

# Chapter 47

*O*ne night of tango and Mary's ready to jump on a banana boat to Santa Cruz. I try pushing her hand away, but she's got a strong forefinger hooked on my belt and a lion in her eyes. "Goodnight, kids," she calls to Judy and Muller. Once we're in our room, she gets me against the wall. One leg goes around my waist. "Let yourself go, Sam," she says.

"Let what go?"

"Everything," she says. "*Sólo lo hacen.*"

"You've lost me."

I'm forced down on the bed, suddenly having flashbacks of my youth, while she is trying to unzip my pants. "That's the way, Sam," Mary cries. "Let yourself go." Her hair is in my face, swishing back and forth, knees digging into my sides. Mary lets out a *voleo*, throwing her head back. The shower starts in the washroom. "They can hear us," I say.

"Shut up, Sam. *Como quieras.*"

"What?"

"*Como quieras.*"

"No idea what that means."

"Push, Sam, push."

She twitches and squirms, making more faces than she did at Judy's birth. "*Ya voy! Ya voy!*"

"Again, no savvy."

"*Ya voy! Ya voy! Ya voy!*"

Mary shudders, says, "*uch,*" and then rolls off me. Air suddenly bursts into my lungs. The woman's not as light as she used to be. I hope she realizes I've gone the extra mile here. "I can't paint houses all day and do this sort of thing," I gasp.

"Then give up painting."

"I haven't finished the overhangs yet."

"Ruby can find someone else."

"It's too short notice."

"Sam, this is the hottest I've been in years. Maybe the hottest I've *ever* been. Don't spoil it." She gives me a crazy smile.

"Don't even think about it, Mary."

"What was I thinking?"

"I have to work tomorrow."

"Screw work."

"Those soffits aren't going to paint themselves."

She's holding my shoulders down, swishing her hair against my cheek. "Come on, Sam," she says. *"Como quieras."*

"This is just cruel, Mary,"

*"Como quieras."*

"Judy and Muller can hear us, for chrissake."

*"Sólo lo hacen."*

I can see Muller nodding away in the hall, telling Judy it's the language of love, as long as you're Spanish or south of the Equator.

# Chapter 48

*I*t's Tuesday and hot as hell up on the ladder. My legs are chafed from the scrapers in my pockets and rubbing against the metal rungs. Muller looks all depressed again. Krupsky told him his sperm count wouldn't impress an eighty year old. He's got Muller wearing underwear with an ice pack in the crotch. Muller brought two spare pairs. Ruby put them in the cooler next to the Gatorade, saying, "Let me know when you need a change." Muller stands there pulling at his crotch, grateful for Ruby's concern, probably fantasizing a little bit.

"I won't be much good today, Sam," Muller says.

"It's just a goddamn ice pack."

"It hurts."

"Go inside then, you big baby." I still have gutters on the west side to do. That's the hottest spot right now. All the shade is on the east side. There's some shade under the eaves, but I'm still sweating like crazy, feeling the weight of some oncoming doom, sensing, like so many others, that I'm a fraud on the dance floor and possibly a failure as a father.

There's a dance contest at the end of the month. Silvio wants us all to participate. It scares me to death, knowing I could be laughed out of the room by my peers and possibly the janitor. "You're doing this, Sam," Mary warned me this morning. She bought me a silk shirt yesterday. All the couples have new outfits. Mary and Judy are both wearing bright red dresses. The red flares out the corner of my eye, and I understand what gets bulls all worked up. Muller's calm as can be. He's been in dance contests before. I can't imagine Seattle being a hot spot for salsa and flamenco, but Muller says he's been up against a few ringers.

I finish the west side soffits before the sun fries me to a crisp. I tell Ruby I'm knocking off for the afternoon and hand her my scraper. "No problem, Sam," she says. "You've made good progress. Are you dancing tonight?" I tell her we're rehearsing for the dance contest. "Well, go on," she says. "Take the big lug with you."

Muller can't wait to get in the car and start pulling at his crotch. He's a miserable sight. Muller says his balls are too cold most nights to make anything happen. "I'm trying, Sam," he says. I've hardly had time to think about his baby-making. Mary keeps calling me her *caballero*, a chilling prospect for me and all the caballeros out there. She and Judy have been dressing up more now, wearing these skirts with long slits up the sides. I'm sure they're copying Carmen. The woman's an erotic heartthrob, doing her cavallas with flecks of silver around her eyes. We practice our steps while Silvio walks around with the tips of his fingers pressed against his lips. We're learning Modern Tango. It's been modernized so young people will get on the bandwagon. Silvio says all young Argentines know how to tango. "In my country," he says, "people would rather dance than eat. And we *love* to eat."

"Is that all they do in Buenos Aires?" I say to Mary. "Dance, eat and screw their brains out?"

She keeps watching Muller and Judy dancing across to the room. "Look at them," she says. "Why can't you do that with me, Sam?"

"People die that way, Mary."

"They do not."

"How do you know?"

"Why don't you let Muller help you?" she says. "He said he would. You have to learn to be more graceful."

"I'm trying, for chrissake."

"Try harder," she says, thrusting her hip into my side.

"How's that supposed to make me try harder?"

"You need to be more mucho machismo."

"I'm as mucho machismo as Muller."

"I think he's very mucho machismo."

She didn't see him trying on Ruby's earring the other day.

# Chapter 49

*W*hen we get home, I head for the washroom and run a bath. Lying there with *The Road Less Traveled*, I consider those holes again. Mary and I must manage our holes pretty well. We wouldn't be married this long if we didn't keep them in check. Then I look at Max and Margot, no commitments, no voleos when you least expect them. They don't get dragged off to dance contests or into the bedroom, saying, "Let's go, amigo." They do what they want, when they want. Does that make their holes bigger or smaller?

I hear Mary and Judy practicing Spanish. They're taking lessons. They sit at the table, asking Muller, "*Querría bailar conmigo?*" and he responds with something that sounds vaguely Spanish. He never ceases to amaze me. He meringues like a Cuban, but can't even touch his toes. The other morning, I found him drying his private parts with his oxygen. Silvio had him do a tango with Carmen last night. It was pretty hot stuff. You didn't hear him complaining about his nutsack then. Carmen's a real grinder. If Muller was wearing his ice pack, there'd be steam coming out his waistband.

Muller gave a good account of himself, and you look at Judy beaming, and you wonder how he does it. The thing with Ruby seems to be tapering off, although Otis practically swallows his teeth when Muller and Ruby dance. He blubbers away, saying, "Get your pudding pop away from Ruby." Bisquick takes that as a call to attack Otis's gibblies, and pretty soon Otis goes off downstairs to do *Otis Cries for You*. Someone asked him on his show the other day what he's paying in royalties for the music. Otis said, "Zippo," and Margot practically tackled him out of his chair. She says he's a stone's throw from a serious judicial inquiry.

Mary's banging on the door now telling me she's got to pee. "Some of us have small bladders, Sam."

I get up and towel off. Muller and Judy are dancing in the living room. After a while, the music starts sounding the same. I open the bathroom door and Mary rushes past me, saying, "I don't know who's worse, you or Muller. Close the door behind you."

Muller has jambalaya with tiger shrimp and Andouille sausages simmering on the stove. We eat and I wash the dishes. Mary and Judy study their Spanish while Muller goes through some cookbooks. I'm so bushed from work—and Mary's midnight rambling—I head off to bed with the girls going, "*Buenas noches, viejo amigo.*"

During the night, I dream of Frank and this stupid idea he had back in the seventies. He wanted to create a fleet of wiener vans, each with a big plastic hot dog on top. He thought it would revolutionize the industry. He even had Nelson, our janitor, drive around to hockey arenas and baseball diamonds with the first prototype. It was a hit, but the van didn't meet city specifications. The inspectors sent Frank a cease and desist order. Frank told them to fuck off. The city told him to fuck off right back. Then came an injunction.

The wiener van sat behind the office until Frank's car broke down at the cottage. He called Nelson. Nelson didn't have a car so he had to use the wiener van. On the way home, they all got sick from gas fumes and ended up puking by the side of 47. After that, the wiener van went back behind the office where it sits now.

The night Max got mugged and tied up, he was staring at the wiener van for hours. "I was starving," Max said. "All I could think about was hot dogs."

Mary elbowed me at some point during the night. "What's so funny?" she said, and I told her I was dreaming about the wiener van. "That stupid thing?" she said, then put her head on my chest. "Forget about the wiener van." Her hand started wandering. "*Listo ir de nuevo?*" I told her to knock off the Spanish. I was too tired for *Listo ir de nuevo,* whatever that means.

This morning, I'm up and about, ready to face a new day. "What time's this thing tonight?" I say, searching for my underwear under the sheets. "Don't say it's early. I'll be fighting traffic as it is."

"It's seven o'clock," she says. "Can't you knock off early?"

"I still have the east side soffits to paint over on Cedar."

"Are you worried about this contest tonight?"

"Of course I'm worried. I'm afraid I'll break my neck."

"Silvio says you're getting better."

"I'm comic relief."

"I think you cut quite a dashing figure," she says. "Especially"— grabbing my hand—"with that swarthy tan of yours."

"Krupsky thinks I'm burning to a crisp."

"Forget Krupsky," she says, pulling me down. "*Dámelo, Sam.*"

"Dámelo to you, too, Mary."

"You don't even know what that means."

"I'm betting Muller doesn't, either."

# Chapter 50

The foyer of the dance studio is filled with intermediate and senior dancers. They've come to help judge our progress. A few of the intermediates offer words of encouragement, while the seniors seem to be happier checking their posture and tummies in the studio mirrors. Silvio claps his hands, telling us to line up along one wall. More people arrive. They watch us take our positions. "We will start with the rumba," Silvio says, and Carmen, dressed in a leotard and skirt, puts on the music.

"Just relax, Sam," Mary whispers.

We dance and Silvio observes, nodding when he sees something he likes. The seniors watch Muller and Judy the most. Judy's got a smile as big as an ocean. When the music ends, Silvio says, "Very good. Now the salsa." We take our positions with me counting under my breath. Muller and Judy are the only ones who don't look stiff. The rest of us are obvious beginners, missing the beat, crunching a toe here and there. I spin Mary and get my sleeve caught on her hairclip. Silvio walks towards us and gives me a critical eye. "Now you've done it," Mary whispers in my ear. He continues past and stands right behind us. I miss the beat again and get all gimpy. "Stop pushing me," Mary says. "He's right *there*." Silvio goes off with fingers pressed to his lips. I feel like I'm in public school, catching my nuts on the box horse. "What happened, Sam?" Mary says.

"I lost count. The man makes me nervous."

"We have to do better with the tango."

"That's the hardest one."

"Just remember what Silvio taught you."

"He taught me a lot of things."

"Be *mucho machismo*."

"*You* be mucho machismo. I'm busy counting."

We get through it somehow, and everyone applauds. Muller's grinning like a chimp. All the couples come out on the floor to do a final merengue. It's easier than the tango, more hips than feet.

We take our positions with knees slightly bent. "Don't wiggle, Sam," Mary warns, which I forget as soon as we start. She digs in her nails. I keep expecting Silvio's hands on my back. Then I see him over at the trophy table with Carmen. The song ends, and he walks to the middle of the floor with Carmen holding the first trophy.

"Very good everyone," Silvio says. "I am proud of you all. I would now like to announce the winners of the dance contest. First place goes to the very talented couple off to my right. Please applaud Muller and his lovely wife, Judy." Everyone claps and Muller gives a little bow. Then Silvio hands out the second and third place trophies.

"Lastly,"—Silvio takes a gold medal on a ribbon out of his pocket— "we always give something to the most improved." He walks slowly around the room, pausing at one point, then suddenly walks over to me. "To our most improved dancer," he says, "Sam Bennett."

A bigger round of applause fills the studio. People are clapping like mad. Silvio puts the ribbon around my neck.

"Congratulations everybody," he says. "My wife is bringing out refreshments. Our beginners will now move up to the intermediate level. Tomorrow, the seniors will graduate. I hope you will all attend." He goes and helps Carmen put out the drinks and glasses.

Judy and Muller come and join us. "You see, Sam," Mary says, "Silvio doesn't hate you."

"Well done, Sam," Muller says.

"You won the damn contest, for chrissake."

"Daddy," Judy says, "it's not who wins."

"Can't you take a compliment, Sam?" Mary says. "Go over and thank Silvio. Show some appreciation."

"He's talking to some people," I say, but Mary pushes me and I go stand with the others waiting to talk to him.

"Thanks, Silvio," I say when it's my turn. "I appreciate it." He smiles and makes a little bow. Then I thank Carmen, adding I hope I'll be good enough to dance with her someday. She stands like a commodore with her hands behind her back. She's all smiles and glitter. I excuse myself and join Mary, Judy and Muller. "Let's go," I say.

"What's your hurry?" Judy says.

"Where's your metal, Sam?" Mary says.

"It's in my pocket."

"You're supposed to wear it, Daddy."

"Okay, fine, I'll wear it to the car. Now let's vamoose."

# Chapter 51

*M*ax's dealer got busted last week in a sweep that cut off supply as far south as the University of Illinois. It left an uncomfortable void, making everyone listless and combative. Otis keeps throwing paper clips at Bisquick when he thinks Margot isn't looking. "Leave my bird alone," Margot yells, over her newspaper. The she goes and dumps him out of his chair. "When was the last time you cleaned this seat, Otis? Is this a French fry?"

On the drive over to Cedar Avenue today. Muller rides with Ruby and I follow behind. The house still needs another coat of paint. All of us are outside, Ruby and me up the ladders, Muller working on the concrete blocks below us. We finish the back portion of the house, then take off to shower and change. Mary and Judy are waiting. This is a big night for them. Dancing with the senior group is supposed to help build our confidence. I don't know how that works. We dance until ten o'clock and head home.

Muller cooks up a bunch of enchiladas and we eat out on the back deck. There's a party going on next door. Riley sticks his head over the fence. "Come have a swim," he says. We put on our bathing suits and join the crowd.

"Good to see you again, Sam," Pam says. Thankfully nobody's in the buff. I introduce her to Mary, Muller and Judy. "So we finally meet you and the kids," she says. "Ours are at some shindig down the street. Grab a drink and make yourselves comfortable."

Muller and Judy start playing volleyball. Pam wants to show Mary what they've done to the house. They disappear inside. Then Muller dives for the ball, practically emptying the pool.

"That son-in-law of yours is some character," Riley says, swirling a margarita around on the pool steps. I smell something in the air. A group of people are over behind the cabana in a huddle. "Don't mind them," he says. "Just a little ganja. You toke at all, Sam? Help yourself if you want. There's plenty available."

"Where are you getting it?"

Riley gives me a cock-eyed stare.

"See that hedge along the back there?"

"What about it?"

"Come look."

Riley takes me over and pulls off some leaves. "It's all marijuana, Sam," he says. "I brought four plants over when we moved. Stuff grows like crazy. So you're into this sort of thing, eh? Feel free to take some home. Like I say, it grows like weeds. Must be the exposure."

"I wouldn't mind doing that, Riley," I say. "How much can I have?"

"Take all you want."

I pull Riley over to the back of the cabana. "Thing is," I say to him. "Muller and I like the occasional stone. Only the girls, Mary and Judy, they don't know. We'd like to keep it that way. See what I'm saying?"

"No problem, Sam."

"We don't even smoke it, to tell you the truth."

"What do you do with it?"

"Brownies."

"That's a good stone."

"It's just recreational. A few co-workers, that sort of thing." Muller does a belly flop and everyone moves back.

"How much can you sell me?" I say.

"I'm not a dealer, Sam," he says. "Like I said, help yourself. Any chance of tasting those brownies?"

"I'll see what I can do."

He goes inside to get more margaritas. I find Muller tugging at the back of his swimsuit. I pull him over by the hedge. "You know what that is?"

"It's grass, Sam."

"Riley says we can take whatever we need." Muller keeps sticking his finger in his stupid ear. "Look, I'll grab some after the party's over. That should keep everyone happy over at Otis's. What the hell's wrong now?"

"My ear's plugged up." He kicks his leg out to the side.

"I told Riley the girls don't know about this, okay?" I say. "He's agreed to keep quiet. There's one catch."

"What's that?"

"He'd like to try your brownies."

"Okay."

"Lean over, for chrissake. Stop kicking. Someone's going to get it in the shins. Tilt your head more." I have my hand on the back his neck. People must think he's about to be sick. They move further away. "Wiggle your finger around in there," I say. "You probably have wax or something. Stop smacking your head, for chrissake."

"I think I got it," he says. He straightens up, looking all pleased with himself.

"Okay, we clear?" I say. "I grab some grass later, we bake at Otis's tomorrow, then bring some brownies back for Riley."

"It has to dry out first, Sam."

"What does?"

"The grass. It has to cure or it won't be any good."

"We'll throw it in Ruby's dryer."

"That won't work, Sam."

"So what do you suggest?"

"I've dried it in the microwave before. Not as good as letting it cure for a month. Up to you."

"Otis isn't going to wait a month."

Muller starts pulling at his nutsack. "I used to dry it on the roof," Muller says.

"On the roof, for chrissake?"

"Grass has to cure, Sam. It's like tobacco."

"Well, we not curing it on our roof."

"Over at Otis's, then."

"I don't trust him. I'll talk to Max."

When we get home, I call Max and tell him about the grass. "How much you got?" he says.

"Not a lot, Max. Just enough to get us over the hump."

"Can Muller come over tomorrow and bake?"

"It still needs to cure. Muller suggests we microwave for immediate use. Then dry the rest out on the roof."

"On the roof?"

"Nice and hot up there."

"Ruby's not going to like us drying pot on her roof."

"What do you suggest?"

"Maybe in the oven on low heat. I'll figure it out."

"Don't let Otis know where I'm getting the grass, Max."

"I'll tell him you took it off some teenagers."

"Not funny, Max." All I need is Otis going around shaking down teenagers.

# Chapter 52

The new grass supply sends everyone into overdrive; pans are greased, Muller's in an apron. Max puts the grass in the oven, while Otis crouches, looking through the oven window like it's a television. "How do you know when it's done, Max?" he says, and Max tells him he's not particularly versed in drying pot. "I know as much as you do," he says, and Otis crouches nervously, worried the grass is going to burn up and disappear. When the grass is suitably dry, Muller stirs the ingredients together, dumping the batter out in big brown globs. Otis keeps trying to lick the batter bowl. Bisquick flies about, jumping from head to head, grabbing a nipple here and there.

Down in the basement, Margot rants away, telling listeners to grow up. "Clean up your act, for God's sake," she says to one person. "The world doesn't owe you any favors. Tina who texted earlier? You want a baby? Get married first. I don't care who the hell you marry. Just stop saying your mother will help you out. What if she drops dead tomorrow? Where will you be then, young lady?"

The more Margot gives people shit, the more her message board fills up. She's got three computer screens going now. Radio and television stations have to screen their callers. Margot takes all calls, telling the slackers they're either a nincompoop or a tire biter. Some even send notes of appreciation. Maybe it's Margot's voice. When she says, "Get your act in gear," people pull up their socks. One of her latest inventions is the "I Cleaned Up My Act" board. People blog and tell others how they changed their lives. The numbers keep growing. These people are proud of themselves, and Margot's proud of them.

The rest are still nincompoops.

# Chapter 53

The Feminist Mothers for Breastfeeding wants Margot speaking at an outdoor protest this Thursday. Someone in the mayor's office took exception to a woman nursing her baby in one of the corridors. It's an outrage, as far as the feminists are concerned. Over Margot's speakerphone, you can hear the women using words like "subjugation" and "alienation", which drives Margot nuts. "Listen, Lilly," she says to one of them, "how you can use subjugation and alienation in the same sentence is beyond me. I got my own thoughts on breastfeeding in public. They may not be the same as yours. Keep that in mind. When is this hootenanny?"

Lilly gives her the time and says she needs an answer as soon as possible. Margot says she'll get back to her. She hangs up and says, "You can't sneeze without those girls getting on their high horse."

"You should tell them that, Margot," Ruby says. She's folding towels on the couch.

"They'll probably string me up."

"No they won't," Max says. "You'll have them eating out of your hand. Take Ruby with you. She can be your bodyguard."

"When did I become the muscle around here?" Ruby says.

Otis is starting another song. "Here's one from The Velvet Bulldozer, Albert King, doing "Don't Throw Your Love on Me So Strong." It's from *The Big Blues* album, 1961. I'm sending this out to Ruby, my wife and bodyguard."

"Ass kisser," Max says from the couch.

Ruby pushes his legs out of the way. "Move it, Max," she says. "I got a big load of towels and duvet covers."

"What do you think, Ruby?" Margot says.

"Sure, I'll go with you. Should be a hoot."

"Hey, Otis," Margot says. "Turn down the music. I gotta make a call." She gets back on the phone to Lilly. "I don't mind showing up," she says, "but don't expect any party line. You want my opinion, that's what you're going to get."

"You tell her, Margot," Max says. He's trying to get Bisquick to open a peanut shell. After a few tries, he does it himself and eats the peanut. Bisquick gives him the skunk eye. "It's your own damn fault, Bisquick. I gave you a chance."

Ruby has our painter pants fresh out of the dryer. "We'll be rooting for you on Thursday," I say to Margot. "Mary might have gone along if we didn't have our dance class."

"How's the dancing working for you?" Margot says.

"I still can't tango worth a shit."

"You're doing okay, Sam," Muller says.

"Thanks," I say. "Don't forget the brownies."

Otis swings around in his chair. "What about the brownies?"

"We have to take some back for my neighbor."

"Tell him to make his own brownies."

"He's our only source for grass right now."

"Your neighbor's our source?"

"Open your mouth on air and I'll brain you."

"How many you giving him?"

"Never mind how many he's giving him," Ruby says.

"I asked a simple question." Bisquick starts pecking at the record on the turntable.

"That's a mint album," Otis yells, and Margot blasts him with the cattle caller. "Fucking hell, Margot! Not so close."

Max laughs, saying, "Serves you right, old man."

"You see where my dentures went?" Bisquick flies upstairs with a set of uppers in his beak. "Grab that bird," Otis yells.

We head for the door as Otis chases Bisquick behind the couch.

# Chapter 54

The house on Cedar is almost done, except for the garage, which needs a second coat of paint. On the way home, Muller sits with the brownies on his lap. "Are we working tomorrow?" he asks, and I tell him it'll just be the morning. Ruby has a dental appointment. Max is meeting with another potential supplier up on Western. Every so often, Muller lifts the tin foil, smelling the brownies. I never saw the allure of grass before now. I was always more of a drinker. Frank could put away half a fifth of whiskey before a meeting. Some of them were hellish affairs, with Frank dragging me out afterwards to a bar. I'd arrive home in a taxi with Mary waiting, arms crossed.

I'd always be up in the morning, slipping out before Mary could say anything. On the upside, I kept bringing home a paycheck. The braces were paid for, the car, the new stove, the riding lawnmower. I don't have it anymore. I'd rather walk around, getting some exercise.

Muller's been taking over the lawn duties lately. He misses spots and scalps the garden edges. Judy thinks it's cute the way his tongue sticks out the side of his mouth. Mary thinks Muller's low sperm count is just an excuse for not performing. "It's all in his head," she says. I tell her Muller isn't that brainy. "Well, it's something," she says. She gave Muller *The Road Less Traveled* and *The Power of Thought and Your Body*. Scott Peck's okay, but the other guy is one of those "can do" types. I hate people who write books saying you can do anything. Some people can, some can't. I don't think Frank ever thought he *couldn't* do anything. Even when it was obvious he couldn't, he'd just say, "Screw it, I didn't want that account, anyway."

With Muller, you put a fry pan in his hand and he's off to the races. Tell him to have a baby and he's a shrinking violet. "He tends to fizzle," Mary says.

"What do you expect me to do about it?" I say.

"Talk to him, Sam. Give him some encouragement. And do it before he runs the lawnmower into that hedgerow."

I go outside for a cigarette. Muller finishes, rolls up the cord, slams the garage door behind him. "My balls hurt," Muller says.

"What does Krupsky say?"

Muller shrugs, blowing smoke out his nose. "He's says it takes time, Sam. It could be a couple of months. Maybe years."

"Years? We'll be in a senior's home. Fucking Krupsky."

"He's a nice man."

"He's a horse's ass. And he can't twist worth a shit."

# Chapter 55

*I*ris started her treatments this week. Mary says she's doing well so far, but it's early. She and Judy are going over there tonight with some of Muller's squash and coconut soup. Muller and I do the dishes, then go out back. The lights are on in Riley's cabana. As soon as the girls leave, we take the brownies over to Riley's fence. I give the only birdcall I know. I think it's a swallow.

Riley's head pops up. We pass the tray over and hear him and Pam munching away. "Delicious, Muller," Pam says. "Come over for a swim." We get our trunks and end up in the shallow end, drinking daiquiris. Pam does lengths while Riley sips away. Muller's bathing suit keeps inflating.

"I had a thought," Riley says. "We're throwing a party on the twenty-fifth. You interested in catering, Muller?"

"Catering or making brownies?" I say.

"Straight catering, Sam. I wouldn't be opposed to some brownies. We all smoke pot. What do you think, Muller? Ever do any catering?"

"A few small functions." He pushes the air out of his bathing suit leg.

"Can you handle forty or fifty people?"

"What sort of menu?"

"Up to you."

"I could do Mexican. Quesadillas, that sort of thing."

Pam swims over. "What are you guys talking about?"

"Muller's going to cater our party," Riley says. "He's thinking Mexican."

"Wonderful. We'll give everyone sombreros."

"That's a lot of people, Muller," I say.

"Nonsense," Riley says.

"I'm going to start the guest list," Pam says. She gets out of the pool, pulling at the seat of her bathing suit.

"Don't forget that couple we met in Cancun," Riley says. "Craziest bastards you've ever met. Drank half the bar, then supercharged three joints. Oh, and the Andretti's, Pam."

"Sam," she says. "Make sure Mary knows it's the twenty-fifth."

Going back to the house later, I grab Muller, "I got a bad feeling about this. Forty people stoned out of their gourds?"

"So?"

"What if Riley blabs to Mary about the brownies? You saw what she was like when she found the whiskey."

"What if I make the brownies without grass?"

"I've already stripped two of his plants, for chrissake."

Muller starts banging his ear again.

"You're going to give yourself a concussion."

"I think I got it out."

"Terrific. Bully for you."

# Chapter 56

*M*uller begs off sick again, the big baby. Judy puts him to bed with some hot lemon juice. I drive to Otis's place on my own, letting myself in the back door. They're all in the kitchen having coffee. "Muller's not feeling well," I say.

My cell phone rings. It's Mary on the other end. "Muller just told us about the catering job," she says. "This so exciting. It's exactly what he needs right now."

I can hear Judy in the background, asking Muller why he didn't tell them before. "You've got a gig! You've got a gig!"

"Nice going, Sam," Mary says. "We're sorting the menu out now."

"I thought he was sick?"

"He's feeling better. What do you want for dinner?"

"Anything but Mexican."

"Judy and Muller are starting a catering business."

"Where?"

"Here, of course."

"Why can't they do it back in Seattle?"

"This is the first time we've seen Judy in five years."

"They live in Seattle, Mary. That's all I'm saying. What about their house? Aren't Meek and Beek going to miss the Space Needle?"

"I think you're seriously regressing, Sam." She hangs up. I help Max take paint cans to the truck.

All the way over to Cedar Avenue, I'm thinking about Judy and Muller. What if they stay in Chicago? Then there's this stupid party coming up on the twenty-fifth. Margot was practically catatonic on her first brownie. She tried scrambling eggs on the heat register.

I start thinking of different scenarios in my mind. I could take out Muller. Maybe push him off a ladder. It's extreme, and he's already survived one fall, but that could stop the brownies. The only other option is to get rid of Riley's plants. Chicago's short on grass right now. Where are they going to get more on such short notice?

We work until noon, then head home. On the way, we stop by the video store and pick up a movie. I grab *The Pink Panther*. Muller says he hasn't seen it. I don't know what they do in Seattle. Who hasn't seen *The Pink Panther*? Later that night, I put it on, and we all curl up on the couch. Muller starts to fade around ten o'clock. Judy finally puts him to bed. I do a lot of yawning, hoping it'll put Mary to sleep. She finally stands up. "I'm turning in," she says. "Are you coming?"

"I'm not tired," I say. "I think I'll watch the news."

"Okay," she says. "Don't stay up too late."

I wait until everyone's asleep, then I grab some garbage bags. The pool lights are off next door. I climb over the fence. The pot leaves stick out like scissor blades in the moonlight. I start pulling them out by the roots, getting my hands all sticky. It's a messy job pulling up pot plants. The stems punch holes in the bags and the leaves stick out in all directions.

As soon as the plants are bagged, I climb back over the fence. A shadow comes out from behind a tree. "What are you doing?" Muller says.

"Damn it, Muller, you scared the shit out of me."

"Why are you stealing Riley's pot plants?"

"Just shut up and help me get these bags in the car." We drag the garbage bags across the back yard to the garage. The smell is terrible. As soon as we get them in my trunk, we slip back across the lawn, making sure we haven't left a trail of leaves.

"Now get in the car," I say to Muller. We start driving towards the Lakeshore. "It's the only way I could think of," I say. "No grass, no grass brownies. Makes sense, right?"

"Why didn't you ask me to help you earlier?"

"Because you'd probably fall in the pool."

"I'm not an idiot, Sam."

"What were you doing up, anyway?"

"I was hungry. You left the back door open."

"I thought I closed it."

"Where are you dumping the plants?"

"I haven't figure that out yet."

"There's a garbage bin behind Krupsky's office."

"You remember that, but not him twisting?"

"I don't think he was twisting, Sam." Muller rubs his eyes.

Then it hits me. "Hold on a second," I say.

"What?"

"Look, Riley's party is the problem, right?"

"I guess so."

"But we still need the grass. I mean, we don't have to get rid of it. We just need to stash it somewhere."

"Otis's?"

"That'd start a feeding frenzy. No, somewhere else."

"I feel bad about this, Sam. Aren't we stealing?"

"Look, Max will have a new supplier in a couple of weeks. We'll give Riley a bunch of brownies, everyone's happy."

"So where are we stashing the bags?"

"I know a spot."

I drive down Kingsbury, looking in my rearview, imagining sirens and flashing lights. When we get to the office, I pull around to the alley, park near the loading dock and open the trunk.

I point to the wiener van parked by the far wall. "There."

"It's a giant hot dog, Sam."

"I know what it is."

# Chapter 57

*W*e're learning *Tango Nuevo* tonight. Silvio told us last week it combines the Argentine embrace with American hip-rubbing. All Mary needs is more hip-rubbing. She called Margot earlier, wishing her luck at the protest rally. Ruby's taking a video camera.

We get to the dance studio early, practicing our steps. Then everyone arrives and we start to *Tango Nuevo*. It's all grinding as far as I'm concerned. Muller finds it easy. The steps come naturally to him, the step, the glide, and the dip. By the time Silvio claps his hands, telling us that's it for the night, I'm sweating like a bastard.

Mary calls Margot when we get home. "Turn on the television," Mary calls out. "Margot's on the news."

The announcer is describing the scene of mayhem earlier. "Things got out of hand outside City Hall earlier this evening when Margot Simmons, star of *Reality Check*, a big hit on the web, showed up as a main speaker. Known for her 'take no prisoners' style, Simmons wasted little time giving everybody a healthy dose of reality."

The camera zooms in on Margot standing at a podium. "I'm not supporting anybody here," Margot says. "As far as I'm concerned, you're all a bunch of ninnies. In my day, you took your baby in the washroom if you wanted to breastfeed. Why are you dangling your knockers out in the open, anyway?" Boos erupt. Placards bump into each other.

"Oh, get off your high horses," Margot says. One of the feminists starts shouting, "Subjugation! Subjugation! We won't be denied our rights!"

"Young lady," Margot shouts back, "someone needs to subjugate *you*. Tits belong in your blouses, girls. That's not subjugation; it's called decency. Why don't you fight for something worthwhile? Like daycare. The mayor's doing diddley in that department."

They cut back to the announcer, a stiff little blonde. "Well, you can't say Margot Simmons doesn't speak her mind."

Mary's still on the phone. Muller goes around the channels, finding similar updates. Then there's the mayor, caught walking to his car. "What do you think of Margot Simmons?" the reporter asks. "Have you seen or heard her show?"

"Haven't, no."

He's whisked away as the feminists chant in the background. A woman keeps asking Margot what she knows about breastfeeding. "For goodness sake," Margot says. "You feed, you burp, you check for a pantful. Stop making a production out of it."

"Margot's right," Mary says.

"You can't win with that bunch," I say. "What's Margot doing now?"

"She's going on in a minute."

We crowd around Mary's computer in the sunroom. Otis is spinning records, slurping a milkshake. Bisquick pecks at the remains of Otis's hamburger. Margot appears in frame. She shoves Otis out of the chair and pulls the stylus off with one motion.

"Don't scratch my records," Otis yells.

"Stick it up your arse, Otis." She pushes Otis again and Bisquick goes after him.

"Fuck off, Bisquick."

Now," Margot says, adjusting herself in the seat. "I've got a few choice words for all of you out there. First,"—she lets out a raspberry—"that's for the idiots sending me hate mail. And for those of you supporting me, learn to spell, for God's sake. I've read about fifty different spellings of *inalienable rights*. It's spelt the way it sounds. Mothers, feed your babies in private. You're just begging for attention. And as for the people at City Hall? Set up feeding areas. All it takes is a partition. Isn't that better than the shit you caused today?"

The screen fills with blogs and emails. Bisquick flies back and pecks at the monitor. Margot puts on her bifocals. "For heaven's sake," Margot says, "Nobody's *subjugating* anybody, Lilly. Does anyone have anything constructive to say, or are you all—wait, here's something. A woman in Rockford designed a shirt with vents just for breastfeeding.

Slip the baby through the vent, let him feed. That's a wonderful idea. These shirts are available on the web."

Ping.

"Not here, on the web."

Ping.

"What did I just say?"

Ping, ping, ping, ping.

"Look, all of you, go to Babyshirts—one word—dot com. I said, *one* word. Don't you people listen? Here, I'm writing it down . . . see?"—She holds up a piece of paper—"For Pete's sake, people. Mavis, if you're watching, I got twenty orders. I'll forward them in a minute. One last time. Send your orders to Babyshirts.com. Attention, Mavis Doolittle.

The pings continue and Bisquick keeps pecking the monitor. Margot lets out another raspberry and Otis farts.

Fifty thousand views.

# Chapter 58

"I don't get it," Riley is saying. He and Pam are there by the cabana, looking at the bald spot in their hedge. "Why would they pull all the plants out by their roots?"

"Probably teenagers," I say.

"I thought it was you at first, Sam."

"No, I was out like a light last night."

"Still seems strange."

"Who knows what goes on in the minds of teenagers? Probably pool hoppers. Sorry, folks. I guess that kills the grass brownies idea. I'm sure Muller can do something else."

"We were really looking forward to grass brownies," Pam says.

"How about bunuelos?" Muller suggests. "It's kind of a fritter."

"Bunuelos?" Riley says.

"With raisin sauce and chilies," Muller says.

"It sounds delicious," Pam says.

"Give it some thought," I say. "Nice raisin sauce on top. Trust me, your guests will be over the moon."

Riley's still staring at the holes in the ground. "Probably a professional job," I say. "Some of these teenagers are devious little pricks." Muller digs his toe in the grass.

"Damn shame," Riley says.

In the car, going across West North Avenue, Muller sits there, looking all glum. His hair sticks out in wild tangles around the rim of his baseball cap. "I still feel bad," Muller says.

"Why?"

"I feel like a thief."

"It's grass. It's not a riding mower."

"If you say so."

"Stop saying, *if you say so*. And stop looking so guilty. We're saving Riley from a big insurance risk. Stoned people don't float."

"That's not true."

"Okay then, picture Judy and Mary face down in the pool."

"It wouldn't come to that."

"It could."

"I think you're exaggerating, Sam."

"Am not."

# Chapter 59

"*D*egenerate bastards," Margot screams. "Is nothing sacred anymore?" She thinks the whole universe needs a good spanking. "What's the world coming to? It's like stealing a farmer's corn, for God's sake."

Max wants to scout the neighborhood, looking for kids riding erratically. Otis thinks Riley should call the cops.

"You've got the brain of a flea, Otis," Margot says. Margot goes downstairs and lambasts some guy who just came out of the closet. "So you're out," she says to him. "Whatdya want? A float?"

Ruby's not too bothered about the grass. She's more worried about getting our latest house painted. As soon as she's finished her coffee, we head out. She has to pick up some paint, so Muller and I go straight to the house. Along the way, Muller starts whining about stealing the grass. "Cut the crap," I say.

"I still feel lousy, Sam."

"Look, you make a bunch of great food. Add some pitchers of margaritas, salt the rims, everybody's happy."

"I guess so."

"Let's give the car another wash on the way home."

"Why?"

"Because, it still smells like a bloody grow-op. Mary's not an idiot. She already suspects something. Let's just hope Riley doesn't go blabbing about those stupid pot plants."

"Maybe you should just tell Mary."

"Tell her what? That we've been getting stoned all this time?"

"Judy's done pot before."

"Well, Mary hasn't. Latin dancing's bad enough. I don't want her any more stimulated. She's been eyeing me like I'm a squeeze toy."

"Judy's been wonderful lately."

"Glad to hear you're back on good terms."

"I mean wonderful in bed."

"Shut up!"

We give the garage over on Cedar another coat of paint. Then we stop at the car wash on the way home, wash out the trunk and the mats. Muller starts telling me his plans for a themed catering business. "You choose your country," he says. "Everything's authentic. Fixed pricing, too."

Mary and Judy are meditating in the sunroom when we get home. Spaghetti sauce bubbles on the stove. Muller lifts the lid, takes a long sniff, and adds some pepper. We eat dinner and watch the news.

Before going to bed, I check the sliding doors in the kitchen. Riley's standing there in his shorts and flip-flops. "What's up?" I say to him.

"Here," he says, handing me a baggie. "I remembered I had some drying in the cabana. Tell Muller to work his magic." He disappears around the side of the house.

"Who was that?" Mary asks when I come in the bedroom.

"Riley. He dropped off some ingredients for the party."

"What ingredients?"

"Oregano and tarragon."

"He's bringing over spices at midnight?"

"I've decided to stop judging people, Mary."

"When did this start?"

"When I realized life's a carnival and I'm a piñata."

"*Carnaval.* Why don't you take Spanish lessons with us?"

"Two Spanish speaking people in this house are plenty."

"*Un español llamado.*" Mary's hand snakes across under the covers. "Sam, you're enormous."

I realize the baggie's stuffed down my underwear. "I have to pee."

"Hurry back."

I run to the washroom and put the baggie behind the toilet. Be prepared for major shrinkage, Mary.

# Chapter 60

*I* wake up with a sinking feeling. Meek and Beek come flying down the hall in a state of confusion. Then a cupboard door slams. I lie there taking inventory of all the things I've done these past few months. Any one of them could put me up shit creek. I go to the washroom and hear Mary say, "I *will* talk to him . . ." and then she's standing at the washroom door. "Sam," she says "Get in the kitchen this minute."

Muller's sitting at the kitchen table, looking like he has friction burn. Judy's next to him. Mary's standing by the sliding doors leading to the deck. There's a baggie in her hand.

"Riley just dropped *this* off," she says, tossing it on the counter. "He said to add it to the pile. What pile is that, Sam? Maybe it has something to do with this?" She takes the brownie out of her dressing gown pocket and bangs it down on the counter. "Are you going to say anything, Sam?" Then she storms down the hall, slamming the bedroom door. Meek and Beek zoom past me. Then the door opens again, and Mary says, "Sam, get in here."

She's standing by the bedroom window with her arms crossed. "Now, explain yourself," she says, "and don't give me any more lies. What were you doing the other night when you said you were going for burgers? Was it a drug run? Is Riley some big dealer? Are you a *mule*?" She picks up a hairbrush. "The truth, Sam, I mean it."

"I'm not a mule, Mary."

"What are you then?"

I sit down and rub my head. There's no point lying anymore. She has the hairbrush in a throwing position. I describe how it started, Max offered me a joint the last day at work, Muller baked grass brownies. "It's just been recreational," I say. "A brownie here and there after work. Nothing serious."

"And everyone's stoned over at Otis's house?"

"Not all the time."

"What does that mean?"

"I stole Riley's plants to stop the supply."

"You *stole* his pot plants?"

"I had to, Mary. Riley wants grass brownies for his party."

"Why do you care?"

"I was worried about you and Judy."

"You stole the plants so Judy and I wouldn't get stoned?"

"Exactly."

"And Riley isn't a drug dealer?"

"Not to my knowledge."

"What about Margot? Is she stoned, too?"

"Out of her gourd."

She takes the baggie out of her dressing gown. "Is this the last of it?"

"There's another ounce behind the toilet."

"For God's sake, Sam."

"I can't destroy it, Mary. I already stole Riley's plants. He's going to figure something's up."

"So what are you going to do?"

"I don't know. I'm out of ideas."

Mary sits down on the bed beside me. She squeezes the baggie between her fingers. "I need you to level with me, Sam," she says. "I want the truth."

"Sure."

"How good are Muller's brownies?"

"On a scale of one to ten? Probably ten."

"You'd better give this to Muller, then," she says, handing me the baggie. "This party's the last?"

"It is for me."

"And you'll wear your silk shirt when we dance?"

"Every night."

"No complaining? No more snide remarks?" I try to pull the baggie gently away, but she hangs on. "Promise, Sam. I'm not kidding."

"I promise, Mary. Scout's honor."

I was never a scout.

# Chapter 61

*M*uller stirs in time to The Rec Room of Sound. Everything's there on the counter: flour, corn meal, more peppers than a salsa factory. Pam's over every hour. "You're a wonder, Muller," she says

Mary and Judy give Muller the ingredients, reading off measurements from the cookbooks. A teaspoon of this, a dab of that. Muller doubles and quadruples, sometimes grabbing fistfuls of things. Everything smells like a *cocina*, as Mary would say. I didn't know so many ingredients went into Mexican food. With a ladle to his lips Muller tastes, shakes his head, then adds something else. It's a marvel to watch, even if it is Muller. Recipes are made, plates are covered with cellophane. Some are put in coolers while others go next door.

The phone rings. Max is calling. "I'm having no luck," he says. "I can't find grass anywhere." It's a nervous bunch over there at Otis's place. Margot's turned her show into a one-sided shouting match. Otis is strung too tight for words. Tears flow without any feeling.

Meanwhile, Muller sweats, steam rises from pots on the stove. The brownies are left until last. I'm working on the margaritas downstairs. The icemaker on the fridge is turning ice into slivers that I put in freezer bags and hustle next door to Riley's bamboo bar. A stack of sombreros sits on a chair, tilting in the wind, while mariachi music plays through outside speakers. At the bottom of the pool, the vacuum goes back and forth in methodical lines.

The phone rings again. I take it in the bedroom while I put on my new Hawaiian shirt. Max is on the other end, telling me Margot's got her head in the toilet. "It's not pretty here," he says.

"Can't talk right now, Max," I say. "We're catering a party next door. Guests are starting to arrive."

"I think Margot's going to do something drastic."

"Like what?"

"I don't know. She keeps eying the deodorizer puck in the toilet. We have to do something. Otis is threatening to put a call out for grass on his show. Doesn't Riley have any connections?"

"Christ, no."

"I don't know how long I can keep Otis off the air."

"Okay," I say. "Listen carefully. And don't repeat this to anyone else, okay? Not even Ruby, understand? You know the old wiener van at the office?"

"Yeah."

"I stashed some pot plants in the back."

"You have pot plants?"

"They're Riley's. I stole them."

"You stole a guy's pot plants?"

"I'll explain some other time, Max."

"Can Muller come over later?"

"We have to stay at the party. Hold on until tomorrow."

"Easier said than done."

I hang up, grab stuff out of the freezer, and run out the door. Voices come from the side of the house. Car doors slam. People are standing around the pool drinking margaritas and eating tamales. It's like they've never seen a Mexican staple before. I put ice behind the bar and go back for more tequila. Muller's in the kitchen, dumping brownies out onto plates. We carry the brownies over to the fence, handing them to Pam. Orange and yellow cloths cover the tables. Drinks are consumed. Salt builds up in the corners of peoples' mouths.

"Come have a swim, Sam," Riley says. "Everything's going great. Muller's an artist. You taste these tamales?"

"I'll be back in a minute," I say.

Mary and Judy appear at the pool gate wearing bathing suits with sarongs tied around their waists. Mary gives me a pinch as I go past. Back at the house, Muller's dumping more brownies on the counter. It's his last dish of the night. The man's a sweat machine. "They're going through the food like bandits," I say.

"*Banditos*," Muller says.

I go down to the basement for more ice. My cell phone rings. Max on the other end. He's over at the wiener van. "Jesus, Sam. There's enough for a hundred brownies here."

"Couldn't you have waited until dark?"

"I know the security guard. We're having a toke while I speak."

"Damn it, Max."

"Relax. Zack's helping me get the plants."

"Don't let anyone see you, for chrissake."

"It's the weekend. Nobody's around."

"I gotta go."

"How's the party?"

"Everyone's wearing sombreros."

"Don't do any pressed hams."

I hang up and run upstairs. The kitchen is empty. Pots and pans fill the sink. Sombreros bob up and down on the other side of the fence. I go around to the gate and find piles of clothes, chairs overturned, people in all stages of undress. A splash sends water up into people's drinks. Muller come to the surface with a wild mass of hair in his eyes. Streamers cover the water, wiggling towards the filter.

"Join us, Sam," I hear Riley say. He's sitting on the pool steps, naked. Mary's next to him. She's munching away on a piece of brownie.

"Mary, what the hell are you doing?"

"Get those stupid things off," Mary says, pulling my shorts. "*Quiero cierto libro.*"

"I don't know what she's saying," Riley says, "but I like it." Mary's beyond giddy. I sit down and watch my shorts inflate. "So, Sam," Riley says. "Mary tells me you're an advertising guy."

"*Was* an advertising guy, Riley."

"Anything I might have seen on TV?"

"Q-tips."

"That one's funny."

"What line are you in, Riley?"

"Law."

"Criminal or civil?"

"Criminal."

"And you grow pot?"

"Who watches lawyers?"

"Other lawyers?"

"That's actually true, Sam. Very good."

"How many infractions have we committed here?"

"Many, Sam, many."

"Sam is *no es gracioso*," Mary laughs and slips underwater.

"Is she coming up?" Riley asks.

We both look at Mary's hair floating. We reach down and haul Mary up by her elbows. She bursts out laughing again. "*Fantásticas,*" she howls.

"I take it that's good," Riley says.

It is if you're an Argentine.

# Chapter 62

*A* gunshot goes off out front. Hands rise instinctively in the air. I grab a towel and rush past two people doing a merengue. Not a good caza between them. A small crowd is standing in the driveway in soggy sombreros and sarongs with donkey prints. Under the streetlight, I see Frank's one entrepreneurial failure. It's the wiener van.

Max and a security guard come across the lawn. It must be Max's friend, Zack. Two people immediately assume the position up against the fence. Max and Zack are obviously stoned. I cut them off at the front of the house. "Hey, Sam," Max says. "We got the wiener van started."

"How?"

"Zack made a call. His brother's a mechanic. It only cost us an ounce. Pretty cheap, considering. Even got a license plate—"

"Where the hell's your car?"

"Ruby's got it. Zack doesn't drive, so we had to make do."

A line is forming by the wiener van. People want hot dogs. They've already eaten ten platters of tamales and enchiladas.

"Why did you bring it here, Max?"

"I thought I'd see if Muller had any brownies left."

"Not now, for chrissake."

Muller comes out in a Mexican towel. "Everyone's hiding behind the cabana, Sam," he says.

"Why?"

"Someone saw a cop. Is that the wiener van?"

"Are there any more brownies, Muller?" Max says.

"I've got another pan in the oven."

"Give me enough for Otis and Margot at least, Sam," Max says.

"Then you're clearing out, right?"

"No problem. We'll be off in a jiffy." Max and Zack follow Muller over to my place.

I return to the pool. Everyone's slowly coming out from behind the cabana. Judy and Mary have disappeared. Riley's on the pool steps with a margarita in each hand. "Where's Mary and Judy?" I ask.

"Inside with Pam."

I go inside, stepping over people, seeing a piñata open and dis-emboweled on the floor. Candies are everywhere. Someone's already slipped, leaving skid marks across the linoleum. The living room's full of women dancing in Mexican blankets. "Hey, Sam," Pam waves, boobs bouncing.

"Where's Mary and Judy?"

"They were here a minute ago. Check the bedrooms."

I find them in in the master bedroom looking out the window. "There's a giant wiener out there, Daddy."

"*Eso es un gran pedazo de carne,*" Mary giggles.

"It's the wiener van," I say.

"That old thing," Mary laughs. "I've seen better."

"Mom! God, you're blitzed. Look at your eyes."

"Look at *your* eyes. Look at everybody's eyes. Your father has beady little eyes. Beady, beady, beady."

Judy looks at me. "They are beady."

"That's cause he's a fibber."

"I thought you said *Flipper,*" Judy laughs.

"You can't lie to me, Sam."

"I'm not trying to lie to you, Mary."

"Make sure you don't."

"Absolutely," Judy giggles

"Watch him," Mary says. "I'm going for another drink."

"We're coming with you," Judy says.

Out in the hall, Pam pulls us into a rumba chain. Blankets drop, feet stumble over toppled margarita glasses. Someone's thrown down a sombrero and they're dancing around it. I inch along the wall, checking the front window. People are banging on the side of the wiener van. "Damn you, Max," I say.

Someone does a header into the fridge. Outside, the yard is complete pandemonium. Naked bodies wander around in a daze, Tiki lights wobble. Next to the pool, a line of people is spread-eagled against the fence. Zack's patting down Riley. "Hey, Sam," Riley says. "How's it going?"

"He's not a cop, you know," I say.

"I don't mind."

Someone squeals and bumps into me. I feel myself going back, lanterns and red crepe streamers pass before my eyes, water rushes into my ears. A body lands on top of me with a familiar voice saying, "Urumph!"

When I open my eyes again, I'm lying next to the pool with people staring down at me. Then I see a pair of big lips surrounded by dripping black curls coming towards me. Muller's giving me mouth to mouth.

# Chapter 63

*A* green curtain surrounds me. The doctor looks at my chart. "We'll keep him here until tomorrow just to be sure," he says. Muller has tears in his eyes. The bastard took me out with a cannon-ball and gave me the breath of life. In some cultures, that would make me his bitch.

A nurse comes by later, takes my temperature, then leaves. I have no sense of time. Mary and Judy are fast asleep in chairs. Muller continues to weep over my sanitized sheets. I can still taste chlorine. "Sam," Muller says, "Are you awake?"

"I can't feel my hand."

"Sorry," Muller says. "I was sitting on it."

Mary and Judy wake up. "How's he doing?" Mary says.

"He can't feel his hand," Muller says.

Mary jumps up. "My, God, you're paralyzed?"

"Relax," I say. "Muller was sitting on it."

"He certainly sounds okay," Mary says.

"You still look a bit green, Daddy."

"I cleaned the bottom of the pool with my face, sweetheart. Thanks to your husband."

We check out the following morning. Mary makes up a bed in the sunroom. Light reflects off my forehead, the lovebirds coo, Muller makes mulligatawny soup. Just before dinner, Riley and Pam drop by with confetti in their hair. They're still tidying up the mess. "You gave us a hell of a scare, Sam," Riley says.

I see the pool skimmer handle going back and forth across the yard. A sombrero sits on top. The kids must be helping out. "We'd better get back," Pam says.

I eat soup and watch The Rec Room of Sound. Otis is crying for a woman whose son shot off his big toe. He was trying to take out a rat with a twelve gauge. "Your son's toe is in a better place," Otis cries.

Margot rolls her eyes while Ruby goes back and forth with laundry. "What did he do now?" she asks Margot.

"Just told a woman her son's toe is in a better place."

"His toe?"

"He shot it off with a twelve gauge."

"Shut up," Otis says. "I'm trying to comfort this woman."

Margot comes over and pushes Otis out of his chair. "Look, ma'am," Margot says. "The toe's gone. Your son's a twit. He's obviously no match for a rat. Take the gun away from him before he shoots himself in the nuts."

"And with that," Otis says, "we end today's show."

"You've only been on an hour, Otis."

"Oh . . . Here's Booker T. and the MGs doing, 'Time is Tight,' which should give *me* time to use the little boy's room. Be back soon, folks, with more *Otis Cries for You*. To our last caller,"—his hand goes to his mouth—"your son's still got other toes, ma'am."

I close my eyes, drifting off as the needle skips on Otis's record. In my dreams, I see the wiener van, all shiny and new, leading children into Lake Michigan. Mary wakes me up, saying I'm talking in my sleep. "You were calling to Frank," she says.

"What was I saying?"

"You wanted to know if hot dogs float."

Judy and Muller are playing Scrabble. Muller's tapping a tile against his lips, probably trying to spell, "cat." Across the yard, Mexican blankets hang over the fence. Riley's youngest, Lisa, is up on the diving board, hands above her head. A light breeze brings the smell of chlorine through the window. It reminds me of deodorizer pucks and Margot. She's on the air, giving shit to some blogger with a foot fetish.

"How can you stick something like that in your mouth?" she says. "Honestly, I think you people say stuff just to bug me. Did you know you're playing tonsil hockey with athlete's foot? Not to mention Plantar Warts? You might as well be kissing a shower floor."

It hurts to laugh. I cough and sputter and Mary brings me tissues. "Pam came by a little while ago."

"Why?"

She holds up Zack's security guard hat. "They found it in the shallow end."

"I'll let Max know."

"He called earlier to see how you're doing."

"That's nice."

"Ruby says to get plenty of rest. Muller is going with them tomorrow. That'll be his last day."

"Why?"

"He can't paint and cater, Sam. The phone's been ringing all day."

"Who's calling?"

"People from the party. They love Muller's cooking."

"He and Judy are never going back to Seattle, are they?"

"Be happy for them. They've found something they can do together. Who knows? Maybe we'll be hearing a baby soon."

"This is supposed to make me feel better?"

"You'll be a grandfather."

"Seattle's ranked one of the best places to raise a kid."

"Where did you read that? Is that true, Judy?"

"Just a sec, Mom. I think I've got a ten point word."

"It isn't aggravation, is it?"

"Stop being so obtuse, Sam."

"That's a word I haven't heard in ages."

# Chapter 64

*M*ary called Iris this morning and Frank answered the phone. He's back from Los Angeles for a few days. The media's been calling wanting to know if the deal's official. Frank can't say anything because of some unexpected snags. He's probably asking for more money. Frank loves to fuck around with contracts. I remember him asking a client for a contract of *civility* once. The client didn't know what the hell he was talking about. So Frank sends over a simple explanation: "I agree not to piss the agency off, and vice versa."

The client said it wasn't legal. Frank sent it to them again, and again, they returned it with the same comments. Frank finally went over and said he wasn't leaving until they signed it. The president finally signed, telling Frank he'd already broken the contract ten times over. "You've pissed me off that many times today alone."

Frank always gets his way, usually by exhausting people. Surprisingly, it never seemed to hurt our business. The agency grew, we took on more people, we won major awards. *Advertising Age* called Frank the last of the Mad Men, a term coined on Madison Avenue in the forties.

Frank remembered a gang in Belfast called The Mad Men. He said they were the worst motherfuckers on the planet. "Now they're calling *me* a Mad Man," he laughed, and sent the article over to Ireland.

I got a note from him yesterday, saying things are good with Iris. His schedule is crazy, but he sees an end in sight. A few months more and he'll be back home to stay. He also added something of interest, which, knowing Frank, was just weird enough for his taste.

*Sam,*

*We had a little incident at the office over the weekend. Somebody stole the wiener van. We're talking to the security guard now. He says he lost his hat giving chase. Little fucker's involved, I can feel it. Crazy thing, they brought it back with the tank full and a new license plate. Still wondering what to do with the wiener van, Sam. Any ideas?*

*Frank*

Knowing Max, he'll probably steal it again. I write back to Frank, telling him he's a lucky man: Iris is up and about, he's rich. That's got to make him happy. I'm sure he's doting on her, ordering from some exclusive restaurants. Everything's probably delivered on silver plates. Anyway, I end the note by telling him:

*Again, glad to hear Iris is doing well. We're very excited by the news. Hope we can get together soon (your schedule allowing) and drink to her good health. In terms of the wiener van, here's my final thought. Have it gold-plated. Everyone should know that even you, the great man himself, failed occasionally.*

*Sam*

Muller has a catering job coming up on the fifth. This one's a French theme, so he's making quiche. Judy loves to watch him work. He's a bait-and-switch kind of cook, substituting one ingredient for another. I don't know whether it's inspired or he simply forgets the recipe. In any event, he's whisking away, singing codas off key. Once the quiches are cooling on the counter, he launches into a chocolate mousse. The man sweats like a pig. We'll have to cover him with cornstarch, or put him in an absorbent body stocking.

It's only a matter of time before his hair ends up in something. The man's an ape. Mary bought him a hairnet, but he says it irritates his forehead. Margot gave a girl a stern lecture the other day about pubic hair. The girl was complaining about getting them caught in her throat. "If you think that's your claim to fame, young lady, I don't feel sorry for you. As far as I'm concerned, you deserve polyps."

That's cold, Margot, even for you.

# Chapter 65

*M*uller stopped wearing his frozen underwear, complaining of chaffing and dreams of polar expeditions. As for his crush on Ruby, it's waned. There's still the occasional puppyish look, but I think we're past the goofy part. Ruby's been so busy lately, I doubt she's even noticed. Three new contracts came in last week. It'll be tough getting them finished before the cold weather comes, but one of them is interior work, so that's a blessing. In any event, Ruby's been so stressed, she started sounding like Margot the other day. "Stick your finger in his eye or something," she said. Otis was crying for a woman over in Kenosha. "She's getting a small cyst removed," Ruby said, "not her lung."

Margot has one of those big foam fingers you get at baseball games. She stenciled *Idiot* across it. Whenever Ruby tells her to shut Otis up, she sticks it in his ear. Then she pushes him out of his chair. Bisquick loves the finger. He likes to peck at it. "Listen, honey," Margot said to the woman, "it's minor surgery. You'll be home the same day. Don't listen to Otis."

Margot's officially moved into the downstairs bedroom. I think she just wants the company, even if it does include Otis. The brownies keep everyone on a certain level of tolerance. We've been drying Riley's plants on the garage roof, gathering the crisp leaves.

I got a shocker the other day. Mary came and asked for some grass brownies. "They're for Iris," she said. Iris has insomnia. Mary saw something on Dateline about marijuana helping cancer patients sleep. Now Iris sleeps like a log and laughs at everything Frank says. I'm feeling a lot better myself. Maybe the occasional near drowning does a body good.

In a few weeks, I'll be up at Oshkosh, fishing with Dewey and Nick. Dewey's bought into his brother's framing business. Nick's been renting hockey arenas in small towns, putting on craft shows. This could be our last fishing trip for a while. Judy still wants me to take Muller along. The catering jobs are spread out, so she doesn't see a problem. I keep thinking of excuses, but Judy wants us to bond. "We bond every day," I tell her. She's got this image of us out in a boat, Muller with hooks in his hat. I tell her they're flies. "Fishing flies," I say, but she keeps calling them hooks. It took her years to stop calling any button or dial a *thingy*.

Max has a new sideline business. One day, a few weeks ago, he got this idea. People were coming home to a new painted house, but a lot of mess as well. He figured he could start up a cleaning service. Three of our customers have signed up so far. You have to hand it to Max. He's come a long way from being fodder for muggers. When I think about it—and I've been doing a lot of thinking lately—I'm the only one without a business. In a sense, I'm flapping away in everyone else's jet streams. We're between jobs at the moment so I decide to give Margot a call. We haven't really talked since she started her show. I call and suggest breakfast. "Why not?" she says. "Otis is giving me cramps."

Muller, Judy and Mary are carrying platters to the car. They hop over the boxwoods like cartoon characters. Mary comes back for her keys. "Sam," she calls out. "I've left you a list. Muller needs chick peas, pimentos, and a few other things."

I drive to the supermarket on my way to meet Margot. The place is teeming with families. Little kids race down the aisles, nailing old ladies in the legs. I pick up everything and go to the cash. My heart starts pounding. I feel dizzy. "Could you hurry?" I say to the cashier.

I pay for the groceries, grab the bags and go outside. It's hot in the parking lot, heat rising, people walking around in a daze. I put the groceries in a cooler behind the seat. Next, I drive over to pick up Margot. "I hope you've got a credit card," she says when she gets in the car. "My invoices are piling up with no payments." We drive to a local pub over on Winchester. "You look pale," she says. "Drowning doesn't agree with you."

"No kidding."

"What are you having? I could eat a horse." She puts on her bifocals and flips through the menu.

"Coffee's fine," I say.

"You're not eating? What's gotten into you?"

"I just about collapsed at the supermarket."

"Try home delivery."

"I mean it, Margot. It scared the crap out of me."

"What does your doctor say?"

"I should dance" I look out the window. Down the street, a dog's running around a lamppost on a leash. I feel like I'm on a similar trajectory. "I was thinking about Don Conroy the other night," I say.

"What made you think of him?"

"I don't want to end up like that."

"He's dead, isn't he?"

"You know what I mean."

"What brought this on?"

"I don't know. I'm feeling useless. Everyone's making something of themselves. You, Ruby, Max, Otis—even Muller."

"That's what's bugging you? We took a shot, Sam. No big deal. What does Mary say?"

"I haven't talked to her."

The waitress brings our coffees. "I'll have the all-day breakfast," Margot says, "an extra order of toast and a Caesar salad on the side."

"I'm fine with my coffee," I say.

"So you're saying it's us? We're having all the fun?"

"Something like that."

"Want my show? Take it, Sam. Those idiots would schtup a bus."

"I don't want your show."

"What do you want?"

"I don't know. What do you think I should do?"

The waitress brings the food and Margot starts wolfing. "I'm only good where there's a clear case of stupidity," she says, licking jam off her fingers. "Listen, Sam, you're doing better than most of us. You've got a wife, a kid, a son-in-law, hopefully, grandkids. My closest relative is a cousin who bottles tap water."

"Have you ever had a panic attack?"

"Can't say I have, Sam. Why?"

"I'm wondering why it's happening to me."

"How should I know? Stop thinking so much. It's a headache waiting to happen. Look on the bright side, Sam. You're not dead. Wasn't Conroy in his mid-fifties? You smoked and drank more than he did. Be thankful you're just dizzy. You could be a wormy corpse. Want some of my salad?"

"Not if I'm going to be worm food."

# Chapter 66

The phone rings while I'm shaving. Dewey's calling about the fishing trip. Everything's set, we've got a cabin near the lodge. I tell Dewey I have to bring my son-in-law along. "He's from Seattle," I say.

"Nothing wrong with Seattle," Dewey says. "What's his name?"

"Muller," I say. "I hope your boat can hold him."

Dewey laughs and says he has to go. Business is crazy right now. "Talk to you in a couple of days," he says. "Heard from Frank?"

"Iris is ill."

"Sorry to hear that. I always liked Iris."

"Me, too."

"What was it—or is it?"

"Early lymphoma."

"Not good. Anyway, see you on the tenth."

He hangs up and I check the mail. Someone's on the diving board next door. Riley's girls are walking around the pool, tugging at their bikini tops. Judy never wore bikinis. She was always a plump kid, shy, self-conscious. When the Andersons lived next door, I'd take Judy over swimming. As soon as she'd get out of the water, she'd huddle in a towel. I worried myself sick about her. She didn't go to her prom; nobody asked. Then Mary's sister Florence called from Seattle. She asked if Judy wanted to go out for a visit. Judy left after graduation and started working in their florist's shop. They have three: two in Seattle, one in Portland.

A month later, Judy called saying she was dating. "His name's Muller," she told us on the phone. Six months after that, they were getting married. Florence was taking care of everything. We flew out on the twelfth. It was a nice wedding, lots of flowers, obviously. We stayed a week and Al, my brother-in-law, took us around the shops. "Sixty percent of our trade comes from funerals, Sam," he said. "Stay close to funeral homes, that's my motto."

He had a map on his wall with green pins showing all the funeral homes in Seattle and Portland. Any location where three pins was close together, that's where Al planted his next shop. "Easy as pie," he said. "Judy's getting to be quite the little flower arranger. Takes after Florence."

"What are your thoughts on Muller?"

"What about him?"

"You known him long?"

"About as long as Judy. He videoed a few weddings for us. Nice guy. A bit clumsy. Good heart, though."

Muller was videotaping weddings on the side, that and selling discount vacation packages at Mayan resorts. Some of the hotels disappeared during hurricane season. The travel agency told him to keep selling. Then he got fired for telling people to pack rain gear. It's hard not to feel sorry for the guy.

I still don't know what they were living on out there. Judy couldn't' have been making much. They have a small bungalow out in East Queen Anne. Florence called the other night to see when Judy would be coming back. Judy told her about Muller's catering, the dance classes, her trying to get pregnant. Florence had a bit of a wobble. Judy's the girl she never had. She wished Judy well, saying there would always a job waiting. "Thank you, Aunt Florence," Judy said.

Al got on the phone and asked if I wanted to do a little franchise operation. They've been importing these vases from China containing a computer chip in the base. When it's delivered, it starts singing, "Happy Birthday" or "Happy Anniversary". Customers love them. Al plans to market the things right across the country. "You could be in on the ground floor," he said. "What do you think?"

"Who doesn't like singing flowers?"

"Give it some thought."

I hung up, imagining a floral bouquet singing, *"So you dying, don't feel bad. Here's a song. Enjoy the glads."* Al will probably make a killing on the vases. It's just stupid enough to work. People love stupid things.

I get a beer out of the fridge and take it outside. Cassidy is doing cartwheels off the diving board. I hear her say, "I think there's a taco on the bottom." Then she goes for the skimmer.

# Chapter 67

The kitchen counter is covered with platters wrapped in cellophane. Three contracts have come in this week. I keep saying, "Are you sure you want to come fishing, Muller?" Judy tells me there's one week free. "It's meant to be, Daddy," she says, and then shows me a brochure she made on the computer. It's full of floral arrangements. "What do you think?"

"Is this for Florence and Al?" I say.

"No, Daddy," she says. "Muller and I are expanding. Every time someone calls about I function, I ask if they need flowers. People call florists right after they call the caterers. Uncle Al told me that."

"Very clever."

"Look," she says. "Different flowers for each country."

"She's doing tulips for a Dutch job next week," Mary says.

"That's great, sweetheart," I say. "I'm very proud of you. Now Daddy wants to take a long bath with my head underwater."

"What's wrong, Daddy?"

"Your father's been moping around all week," Mary says. "He thinks he's wasting away."

"You can help Muller make *papas bravas*."

"No thanks, sweetie."

"They're good," Muller says.

"I could teach you to arrange flowers," Judy says.

"One flower arranger in the family's enough."

"Margot says Daddy's jealous of everyone's success," Mary says.

"That's not what I said."

"What about those singing vases of Al's? Florence says he's going to make a killing. Maybe that could be your *raison d'être*."

"Is that like a vision quest?" Judy says.

"No, sweetie, it's not like a vision quest."

"We know a shaman, Sam," Muller says.

"That's nice. Shaman's are good to have around."

"Want his number?"

"You keep his number?"

"I got it somewhere."

"Why not?"

He can't be any worse than Krupsky.

# Chapter 68

_T_raffic is heavy on Western right up to Pratt. Cars come out of side streets without looking. Honking your horn doesn't make any difference. It's a sleepy procession with the occasional finger or fist tossed out the window. At Otis's place, I let myself in the back door and hear retching upstairs. Same thing when I go to the rec room. Margot's saying, "Oh, God," and the toilet flushes. I look at her computer screen and see myself. "You've got dead air, Margot," I say. The bathroom door opens slightly. "Put on some music or something," she croaks. "I'm dying in here. Max brought home some clams last night. Damn things have been coming up ever since. Where's Otis?"

I find him in the laundry room sitting on a bucket. I call upstairs to Max. No answer. I call to Ruby. "He's out back," Ruby yells from the bathroom. I find Max throwing up behind some Virginia Creepers.

"I'm really sick, Sam. Ruby's hogging the toilet."

"What happened?"

"Zack's been selling clams out of his truck." He starts to heave again. "Can you get me a roll of toilet paper?"

"Sure, Max." I go back in the house and search the hall closet. "Where's the toilet paper, Ruby?"

"We ran out three hours ago. Use magazines."

"It's for Max. He's out behind the garage."

"Tell him I'm going to brain him."

"Do you want me to go buy some toilet paper?

"Yes, please. Get Pepto Bismol, too."

At the store, I buy toilet paper, Pepto Bismol, and a mop. When I get back, they're all still retching. Otis is over the laundry tub. Even Bisquick's making horking sounds.

I put on some music, watching blogs multiply across the bottom of the screen. Half the sentences I can't understand. The others lack any grammar whatsoever. One blogger writes: "Can U tell me what to do wth my mther? 80 yrs old. Cnt wipe hrslf anymor. Need nurs. Redy to put her away. Any thghts?"

Other blogs appear with the same urgency. Some ask for Margot's advice, others want a big cry from Otis. "Listen, folks," I say. "Margot and Otis have food poisoning. Can you hold off on the blogs for a bit?"

A message pops up:

"Who R U?"

"A friend. Listen, they'll be back on the air later. I'll put on some more music, okay?"

"Wha about my mther?"

"Look, I can barely understand your messages."

"Hw old are U, man?"

"Same age as Margot and Otis. Why?"

"Ever hear of txting?"

"Ever hear of spelling?"

"Wht about my f#*# mthr?"

"What about your mother?"

"She nds a nurse."

"Then get her a nurse. Call one of those home care places."

"Got a #?"

"No, I don't have a number. Look it up."

"Im holding my mthr over tolet."

I grab a phone book off the floor. "Home care . . . home care. Try this one." I hold the book up to the screen.

"Thx, man."

Bisquick flies over and sits on my head. Margot retches again in the washroom. Otis lets out a leaden fart.

Another message:

"Do U knw a good ciropractor?"

"For God's sake, people. Your spelling is atrocious. It's c-h-i-r-o-p-r-a-c-t-o-r. Didn't your teachers ever explain phonetics?"

"I *am* a teacher."

"Ma'am, your spelling's disgraceful."

"Gimme a break. My back's killing me."

The bathroom door opens slightly. "You're pissing in the wind, Sam," Margot says.

"They can't even spell one syllable words."

"Talk to the hand." She retches again and slams the door.

Another message:

"I'm with you, Sam. Texting is destroying the English language. We embrace the latest technologies only to write like apes."

"Amen."

"Without sentence construction, all is lost. Communication becomes a series of babbles and non sequiturs."

"Couldn't agree with you more."

"We need to stress the importance of language, understanding the distinct meaning of each noun and verb. Otherwise we'll all be talking like darkies, calling each other 'Ace' and 'Busta' . . ."

"Look, lousy spelling and contractions are one thing . . ."

Another message:

"What's a contraxion?"

"It's contraction. C-o-n-t-r-a-c-t-i-o-n. It's where you join two words together. You get 'can't' from 'cannot', 'don't' from 'do not'. Don't you people understand simple grammar?"

Another message:

"Mr. Know-it-all."

"I know it's you, Ace."

"Don't call me 'Ace'."

"Racist prick."

The bathroom door opens again. "You can't win, Sam. They've got all the time in the world."

"Terrific," I say, trying to figure out Otis's turntable. "Here's something from Tyrone Davis." I make the mistake of putting the stylus down first. Tyrone does a slow drawl up to the beginning of "Can I Change My Mind."

The texts and emails keep coming, asking if I'm going to teach any more English today. When the song ends, I say, "To those last bloggers. No, I'm not teaching any more English today. Besides, it's not English; it's grammar. One is a language, the other is the *construction* of that language. Margot, how long are you going to be?"

Otis comes stumbling out of the laundry room, suspenders down, t-shirt all stained. He scratches his stomach and stares at the screen. "Take over here, will you?" I say to him.

"Why?"

"Some people want you to cry for them."

"Who does?"

"C'mon, Otis. I have to get Max out of the garden."

Ruby finally showers and dresses and starts loading the truck. "Come on, Max," she calls out the back door. "Washroom's free."

He goes upstairs while we get the last of the paint cans out of the laundry room. It smells like a sewer in there. Ruby sets off a roach bomb in the sink. The smell sends Ruby and Max out back, barfing in the bushes. Then we find out some of the paint is the wrong color so Ruby decides to call it a day. When I get home, Mary, Judy and Muller are standing there with smiles on their faces. Muller slaps me on the back, Judy gives me a big hug. Even Iris calls, telling me I'm right up there with Captain Kangaroo. "Delightful, Sam," she says. "We truly enjoyed your little sermon on grammar today." She and Frank are still laughing their asses off. Judy thinks I should get some puppets. Mary wants me to wear a button-down sweater. I don't know who's being serious.

Margot is back on air, talking to the man with the incontinent mother. "Whippity shit," Margot tells him. "I just spent five hours on the can today. Nobody was wiping my ass."

"Margot's been getting calls all afternoon about you, Daddy."

"That's nice, sweetheart."

"You should really do it. Have your own show, I mean."

"I wouldn't know where to start, pun'kin."

"Go shower and we'll start dinner," Mary says. "And don't go dropping any vowels, Sam. I'll have to come in and pick them up."

"You're a scream, Mary."

I shower and shave with a *bandoneon* playing on the stereo. It's a strange sort of flighty music. Muller says it goes back to when poor migrant workers used to tango for entertainment. It sounds like something a poor migrant worker would use. I run a Q-tip around in my ears and join the others for dinner. "It's a little loud," I say to Muller above the music. "Even for a penniless Spaniard."

I fall asleep on the couch after dinner, dreaming of miniature castles and a giraffe that sounds like Muller. "What time is it, Sam?" the giraffe asks and I wake up. Muller's head is on my shoulder. He stretches and yawns. "You make one ugly giraffe, Muller."

"You were really good today."

"Where are the girls?"

"They went to bed." Muller stands and stretches. I do the same.

"You want a whiskey?" I ask.

"Okay."

We take the drinks outside. The pool filter hums next door. Someone's left the lights on. We hear a giggle. "That you, Sam?" Pam calls over the fence.

"Evening, Pam."

"Riley and I are skinny dipping. Want to join us?"

"Might as well."

We take our drinks over, strip down, and sit in the shallow end. "The pot's growing again," Riley says. I look over and see a bit of growth next to the cabana. Riley slaps Muller on the back. "We'll be ready for brownies soon, won't we, Muller?"

"Muller's concentrating on his catering now, Riley," I say.

"A few brownies wouldn't be a problem, would it?"

"You'd better watch those plants," I say. "Dope thieves always return."

"I don't like the sound of that," Pam says.

We finish our drinks and decide to turn in for the night.

We go through the hedge. Muller says to me, "Pam's attractive."

"Shut it right now."

"I'm just saying—"

"Never mind what you're just saying. Keep your mind on Judy and your catering."

"You'll make a good grandfather."

"We'll see."

"Seriously, Sam. I watched you today. You're a natural teacher. Judy said the same thing."

"It only works on illiterates."

# Chapter 69

*Grammar for Gits* spikes, and then takes a sudden nosedive. To be honest, I'm a snore. Most of my listeners are either new arrivals to the country or Otis crossovers. One of them asked me the other day, "Do you do that crying bit as well?" I told him I didn't and he said he'd wait for Otis. I quit after the first week. 'Ace' sent condolences, spelt "con*dull*ences", and I sent back, "Haw, haw." Margot still gets the occasional question about "i" before "e", something she fields with, "Go buy a book. They're square. They have pages."

Sarcasm goes right over their heads, insults barely ruffle their feathers. I don't know how Margot puts up these people, or them with her. She's a marvel in many ways, brittle as a ginger snap one minute, soft as cooked macaroni the next. She doesn't waste words. What's the point? She's not trying to change the world. She just wants people to think before spraying their privates with deodorant.

Otis, on the other hand, weeps hysterically at the drop of a hat. It's pathetic. Nobody can blame him for anything—he hasn't *done* anything except sob like a big baby. He makes the occasional observation, but he's essentially innocuous, and, therefore, mildly therapeutic. You can't get upset at his logic because, frankly, he's illogical. Judging from the people who call, they're illogical, too. In other words, he's the friend you always wanted. Never judgmental, never saying anything. He's a pet rock.

# Chapter 70

*I* see the world as an organized place. People stop at stop signs. They drive the speed limit. All in all, things move in an orderly fashion. It feels good up here under the eaves. It's nice knowing I'm with the bees, not down with the bottom feeders. We're making good progress with the painting these days. Three houses are done, the contract on the fourth has been signed. Margot asks for twenty percent up front. She sends Ruby out with proper paper work, our official letterhead on top. It *looks* professional, anyway. People like the way we present ourselves. It also helps that we have the garb, the painter paints, and the bandanas. I've become weathered and paint-splotched, going home with more dirt under my nails than a gravedigger. When I shower and change, Mary calls me Crocodile Dundee. It's her way of bucking me up before we go to the dance studio. We're starting the intermediate dance classes tonight. Mary wants me ready to *voleo*.

The intermediate level—according to Silvio—takes us back over the original dances, practicing now the subtleties of each step. "You will now learn to be *graceful*," he says, and I'm sure he's looking at me.

We start out doing some simple moves, and I still step on Mary's toes, but we cut reasonable figures. Then Silvio takes Carmen out on the floor. "We will show you once again the promenade hold." To the sound of the bandoneon, they dance from one end of the room to the other, gliding away with Carmen smiling the whole time. Above, the disco ball glitters, throwing swarms of light squares across the floor and up Carmen's legs. The woman's a treat. "I wish we moved like that, Sam," Mary says.

"We'd need a gallon of Latin blood," I say

As they finish, everyone applauds, Silvio bows, and Carmen raises her hand. They walk off the floor and into the dressing room.

"I could dance every day of my life," Mary says.

"You'll have to settle for twice a week."

"We did wonderfully tonight, Sam."

"We shouldn't press our luck."

Coming up the driveway later, I see an elderly neighbor using her car remote. *Beep, beep, beep.* She's an ancient old thing, always hobbling about in her garden, trying to pick up the garden hose with her cane. She bought a new car last month. She's still trying to figure out the keyless entry system. "Having trouble?" I ask.

"I can't tell if it's locked or unlocked," she says.

I go over and check. "It's locked," I say. She goes inside. Five minutes later, *Beep, beep, beep.* Probably using it to turn on the television.

# Chapter 71

*I*t's the usual mayhem getting Muller up. If he doesn't see a hint of sunlight, he rolls over and goes back to sleep. Judy pushes from one side, I pull from the other. He stumbles off to the washroom. I start loading his stuff in the car. Muller travels with a bunch of old army surplus knapsacks, each with decals from God knows where. One even says, "Welcome to the Moon. Thanks for visiting".

We get on the road, driving north towards Oshkosh. Muller sleeps for the first hour, making a smacking sound with his lips. Just south of Lomira on 41, he sits up. "Can you pull over, Sam?" he asks. I stop near a stand of birches so Muller can have a piss. He comes from a state where trees are as wide as houses. A birch isn't much cover for someone his size, especially the way he pisses.

We're off again, cutting over on 45 to the lodge. We get there and start unloading our gear. Then Muller stands on the dock. He looks dumb as hell in his camouflage shorts with a t-shirt that says, "Big Bear", something I wouldn't do in this state. When Nick and Dewey arrive, we take our luggage to the lodge. Muller's carrying a tote bag full of herbs and spices. Nick and Dewey think he's kidding.

"Is he for real, Sam?" Nick says, and I tell him Muller's a cook *supreme*. "Let's see how he does on a shore fry," Nick says. He's put on weight. Both of them have. Of the two, Dewey seems to be carrying it better. Nick's gut looks like it could explode. Dewey's hat is covered in trout flies he's tied himself. Muller keeps looking at Dewey's hat. "I tie them myself," Dewey says to him. "Take a look." Dewey hands Muller his hat.

"Nice," Muller says.

The lodge itself is a barnlike structure, a throwback to the forties. The cabins are spread all over, some back in the woods, some closer to the water. Outboards float in a long line tied to the dock. They bounce up and down in unison. Once we've signed in, we take our rods and coolers to a cabin near the main dock. Nick and Dewey take one bedroom, Muller and I the other.

Muller makes dinner from stuff he brought up in assorted Baggies. "He certainly gets into his work," Nick says, but he's soon eating away, telling Muller he cooks like a dream.

We make an early night of it. The plan is to head out before sunrise. We're heading up the river to this place Dewey knows about. He's big on lures, but Nick prefers worms. Worms make Muller squeamish. I packed a rubber one for him. "Thanks, Sam," he says, taking it and clipping it to one of his leads.

We fish most of the morning, then Muller starts bringing food out of the cooler. Everything's wrapped in tin foil. Nick and Dewey scarf the burritos like crazy, asking what he puts in them.

"Monterrey Jack," Muller says and Nick says, "Your son-in-law is spoiling us, Sam." Then Dewey brings out a bottle of Wild Turkey, and we sip that, casting out our lines.

"So, Sam," Nick says, loosening his vest. "What's this I hear about you putting a pressed ham on Frank's partition?"

"Moment of whimsy," I say. "Max gave me a little going away present. A joint, actually. We did it in the washroom."

"Who's Max?" Nick says.

"Our night security guard."

"Skinny kid?" Nick says. "I remember him. He used to hang around your office. Gave you a joint, huh? Never figured you for the goofy stuff, Sam. How was it?"

"I mooned a liquor store."

"You do the wacky tobaccy, Muller?"

"A brownie here and there."

"Smokin' joints, eating brownies. You're making Dewy and me feel like old maids. Any chance you brought some with you?"

"I could make some brownies. Is that all right, Sam?"

"Is that"—Nick's big head goes all red—"is that okay? What the hell you askin' him for? You have the makings for grass brownies?"

"I thought we came up to fish, Nick," I say.

"We got four days, Sam. You saying we can't do both?" Nick and Dewey have their big bellies on their knees. "How much grass you got, Muller?" Nick says.

"An ounce, I guess."

"An—what's wrong with you two?" Nick says. "We come up here to have a good time and you're holding out on the goofy stuff?" Dewey laughs and pulls down the brim on his hat. "Hell," Nick says. "I'm ready to cut bait now."

"You sure it's okay, Sam?" Muller says.

"I told you, Muller," Nick says. "Stop askin' him what to do. The man paints houses, for chrissake. Who's this woman you work for?"

"Her name's Ruby," Muller says.

"What's gotten into you, Sam? Dewey's bought into three framing stores. I'm raking in fifty thou from the craft show circuit alone."

"Sam's trying to find his niche," Muller says.

"Trying to find his nuts is more like it," Nick says. "Nothing worse than a guy sitting on his thumbs. That's not like you, Sam. Hand me a worm, will you?"

We fish for a couple more hours, catching a bluegill and a crappie in the cabbage grass. Back in our cabin, Muller starts baking. The fish are out on the barbecue, wrapped in tinfoil, surrounded by lemons, garlic and leek. Dewey sets the table while Nick watches Muller dish out the food. We eat with a breeze coming in across the river, leaves rustling in the maples. Muller gets up and checks on the brownies. He brings the tray out of the oven, putting them in a wicker basket.

Nick and Dewey toss them between their hands. "That's what I'm talking about," Nick says, taking a bite, then grabbing a glass of milk. "Hot. Good, though."

"Watch yourself," I say. "They sneak up on you."

"I don't need a lesson in grass brownies." On the second brownie, his eyes go big as high beams. "Holy smoke," he says. Dewey's bifocals slide down his nose.

"Let me tell you about that pappy-in-law of yours there," Nick says to Muller. "He did some good stuff in his day. Least you had spunk then, Sam. Old age catching up to you, or what?" Nick is munching away.

"Slow down, Nick," I say. We've got two more days." Dewey starts examining his flies.

"Sam," Nick says, leaning over the table. "You got brains, for cryin' out loud. What the hell's the problem with you?"

"Who says there's a problem?"

"You lose your mojo? Tell your buddy the truth."

"I'm still working that out." Muller sits back, eyes half closed.

"What"—Nick's staring over— "What's Big Bear on your t-shirt for, Muller? That a local soft ball league or something?"

"Judy calls me her Big Bear. She had it made up."

"They're trying to get pregnant," I say.

"Not on this doggone stuff, you won't," Nick laughs. "It'll turn your wiggly into a raisin, Muller."

"That's what my doctor says." Nick and Dewey laugh.

"Krupsky's an asshole," I say.

"That your doctor?" Nick asks.

"He's the reason we took up dancing."

"You're dancing?" Dewey asks.

"He thinks it'll make me healthy," I say.

"Probably lose your wiggly altogether."

"You've obviously never done the tango," I say.

"*Tango*?" Nick says, "What's gotten into you two?"

"It's the dance of love," I say. "Muller's good at it."

"You're getting better, Sam."

"Painting houses *and* doing the tango?"

Dewey suddenly falls out of his chair. His white foam soles stick up in the air. We sit there staring at his shoes. "I landed on my hat," Dewey says. Muller helps him up and pulls a hook from Dewey's ass. Nick howls. "I think I just pissed myself," he says, lifting his belly. "Look at that. I pissed myself."

Muller takes a rod leaning again the wall. "I think I'll fish off the dock," he says.

He goes out and Nick leans across. "Listen, Sam," he says. "Dewey and me got a business proposition. We're taking on investors. Dewey's found some guy who carves his own frames. Really nice designs. We can get a bunch copied in Thailand. Maybe a buck a piece."

"What do you do with them?"

"Do with"—Nick bangs the table—"Do with them? Sell them, you moron. Out of Dewey's shops. Through my trade shows."

Dewey's up looking out the window. "Muller's dancing out there," Dewey says. We look out and see a small light above the gas pump shining on Muller. His arms are going all over the place. "Something's wrong," I say.

"Let him dance, Sam," Nick says.

"That's not the way he dances," I say.

We go down and find Muller's hand caught in a pike's mouth. "I was getting my hook out and it bit me," Muller says.

"Don't pull on it," I say. "Their teeth go inward." Dewey and I pull the pike's jaws back. Muller's hand is bleeding pretty badly. We take him up to the cabin and get out the first aid kit. He sits at the table holding his hand. He keeps asking if he can get rabies.

The grass runs out on the next batch of brownies. Nick gets on the phone, asking someone at the lodge if they have any. They hang up on him. Then Muller finds another small baggie in his knapsack. "Thank you, Jesus," Nick says, and ends up pissing himself again. "I'm gonna need a catheter one of these days. I'm already using sanitary nappies for my hemorrhoids."

Next morning, we pack up and take everything to the cars. "Keep in touch," Nick says. We shake hands. "And don't forget that idea we talked about, Sam. So long, Big Bear." Muller keeps checking his hand for signs of rabies.

# Chapter 72

There's a letter from Frank on the kitchen counter when we get home. The first thing I notice are all the exclamation points:

> Sam,
> You hit the fucking nail on the head the other week! People are going to the dogs grammatically. I had lunch with an old friend of mine earlier—textbook publisher. I pitched an idea over dessert. You're going to write grammar books, Sam—rules for texting, blogging, etc! Sort of a Dr. Seuss kind of thing. We'll find a cartoonist. You write some pithy rules, he illustrates. Get ready to boogie, Sam! We're fucking on our way!
>
> Frank

It's hard to know if he's kidding or not. I call his office and he says, "Just write what you said on air, Sam. Give'm hell, but do it in a Seuss kind of way. Get my drift?"

The next morning, I'm in the basement. My laptop is open on a rusty TV table. I've even taken a hit of oxygen for a little pick-me-up. Behind the furnace, there's a box filled with Judy's old Dr. Seuss books: The Lorax, Horton, Uncle Terwilliger. I drag them out, dust them off. In the words of Seuss, Frank wants me to plant a *truffula*.

I start reading this one book where it says you can swallow what's solid, but you have to spit out air. I yell upstairs to Judy, "Come down here, sweetheart. Daddy has a question."

She thumps down in a baggy tracksuit. "What is it, Daddy?" she says.

"You used to love this stuff. What does 'swallow what's solid and spit out air' mean?"

"Don't waste time on things that don't matter."

"Okay, sweetheart. Thanks. I'll call if I need you again."

"No problem," she says, running back upstairs

I pull out "Oh, the Places You'll Go!" It makes more sense than "Green Eggs and Ham." Most of them are crazy analogies, like a man who watches the lazy town bee, another who crosses t's. Just when I think I've got one character figured out, he introduces another and I'm back to square one. I finally type the first thing that comes into my head. Nothing looks or sounds right. When I was copywriting, if it didn't come naturally, I'd write a bunch of nonsense down. Now I can't even write nonsense. I walk around, banging my head against one of the pipes. Then I see a piece of paper sticking out of "Hop on Pop." It must be something Judy wrote back in public school:

*My daddy's tall*
*My mommy's small*
*I don't have a sister*
*Or a brother at all!*

I'm back at the typewriter: *Some things are easy, some things are hard. Don't make them harder by . . . fuck . . . . by . . .* I lie down on Muller's cot and turn off the light. Then I put on his earphones. It helps a bit and I start rhyming again: *Let's begin with a noun and work our way up. A noun's just—*something lands on top of me. "Dammit, Muller," I say. "Get off of me, for fuck's sake."

"Why's the light off?"

"Because I'm trying to concentrate. What are you doing?"

"Changing my socks."

"Well, get off me."

"Dinner's almost ready."

"Fine. Let's go." I push Muller upstairs. Everything's out on the table. The roast sits there in a cranberry glaze, with new potatoes and green beans.

"How's it going?" Mary says.

"It's a bitch."

"Did you read my Dr. Seuss books, Daddy?" Judy says.

"Yes, I did, sweetheart."

"They're good, aren't they?"

"He certainly has his own style."

"Are you going to have creatures?"

"It's a grammar book."

"How about a rhyming fish?" Muller says.

"Or a bird that spells," Judy says.

Look, for chrissake, let's not Hop on Pop.

# Chapter 73

*I*'m up on the ladder today, rhyming away. *A clown is a noun. Use a noun or sound like a clown.* Ruby stands below me. The ash on her cigarette droops towards the ground. She finally climbs up the ladder with a thermos of coffee. "What gives?" she says.

"I'm trying to write a children's book about grammar."

"When did you decide that?"

"Frank got the idea watching me on air."

"You told everybody they're illiterate."

"Frank wants me to do something about it."

"It'll never fly."

"Why not?"

"How did you learn grammar, Sam?"

"By getting my knuckles rapped every two minutes."

"Exactly."

"Frank's thinking something along the lines of Dr. Seuss. I'm still trying to figure out green eggs. Judy gets it, or I think she does."

"Want me to take over scraping?"

"Yeah, I should get going. I've got a tight deadline." I climb down and hand Ruby my scraper. She takes the rungs two at a time. Paint chips fall, the ladder shakes. She has six feet of eaves scraped by the time I reach my car.

The phone's ringing when I come through the door. It's Frank saying he's got two investors on board. "We're waiting on you now, Sam," he says.

I go downstairs and start typing again. I ignore the bird tweets, the washer going. By ten o'clock, I've got three poems. I take the first one upstairs along with the last load of laundry. Judy and Muller are back playing Scrabble. Mary's drawing red and green lines on a chart she's made up for Muller's catering jobs. The red ones indicate jobs done, the green, jobs coming up. "What do you think of this?" I say to them.

*Nouns can be proper*
*As proper as can be*
*They mean something special*
*So they're proper, you see*
*They could be a person, a place or a thing*
*They could be a song*
*Or a person who sings*
*It's really quite simple*
*Just learn from the start*
*A noun becomes proper*
*When art becomes Art.*

"I don't get the last part," Mary says.
"That's because I'm reading it."
"Oh."
"The A in Art is capitalized."
"So you turned Art into a proper name."
"Exactly."
"That's clever, Sam," Muller says.
"I like it, too, Daddy."
"I thought names are pronouns?"
"Nope. Proper nouns."
"What's a pronoun?"
"It supports a proper noun when they're in the same sentence."
"Now I'm confused, Sam."
"A pronoun is a word like 'he'. It's in the same sentence supporting the person's name."
"What if the sentence only has 'he'?"
"It's still supporting a person's name."

"Even if it's not there?"

"Yes, Muller."

"I'm still confused, Sam."

"Read the book, for chrissake."

# Chapter 74

*F*rank's been learning to use the computer. Iris has all their expenses on Quicken with charts and graphs. Frank loves that sort of thing. As soon as Iris showed him their capital earnings, he was on the keyboard trying to fiddle the numbers. He's also learned how to download files and edit, which could be a nightmare. I sent him over the poems this morning. While I wait for his comments, I try to tackle simple rules for blogging and texting. It's titled: "Don't Drop Those Vowels." This is how it goes:

*If you're writing or blogging*
*Spell the whole word*
*Dropping your vowels*
*Makes it absurd*
*One more letter won't hurt your hand*
*It's better than words*
*You can't understand.*

Judy gets a kick out of that one. "It's so true, Daddy," she says. "I can't understand Muller's texts half the time."

Muller's still working out pronouns while I send the poem to Frank. "If I start a sentence with your name," I say to Muller, "and in the next sentence I use 'he,' that's a pronoun. You're still the subject. Understand now?"

"I think so, Sam."

"You sure?"

"Not really."

The computer pings. Frank's sent an email. He likes where I'm going, especially the latest one on texting. "I laughed out loud, Sam," he writes, including *LOL* (something Iris must have shown him). Iris adds at the bottom that I'm a natural. "Loved the bit about not hurting your hand," she writes. "Cute."

Frank wants a central character for the book, something cute. The cartoonist draws up a man with a top hat holding a pointer. I think the he stole it from Monopoly. All the type is in yellow with white borders. It's a little hard on the eyes, but that's what Frank wants. He figures nobody reads anything unless it stands out like a sore thumb.

Frank's publisher wants hard copies on the shelves by the end of next month. The eBooks will follow. Frank's already sending dummy proofs over to the house. I forward the attachments to Margot. We always used to show our stuff to her. "You want my candid opinion?" she'd always say. "I wouldn't line Joey's cage with this crap."

Anyway, she sent the following email back:

*I like it, Sam*
*You might be a hit*
*Tell those fuckers*
*They can't spell worth shit.*

Muller's reading Margot's email over my shoulder. "She's pretty good, Sam," Muller says.

"Profound as ever."

"'They' is a pronoun, right?"

"Yes, Muller. It predicates 'fuckers'."

"Judy's really proud of you, you know."

"Thanks. How are things coming on the baby front?"

"We're catering two parties next week. It's a lot of stress."

"Mary's on my case."

"I know that."

"She's an impatient woman."

"I'm doing a Mardi Gras dance next Saturday."

"I'm not the one pressuring you."

"I know that, Sam."

"Do people actually eat at Mardi Gras? I thought they danced."

"They eat, too."

"What are you making?"

"Cayenne shrimp and jambalaya. Maybe a gumbo."

"You're going to stink up the house, aren't you?"

"Probably."

"That's what I thought."

# Chapter 75

The early reviews on the book aren't great. Mostly, I've been accused of covering old ground. One reviewer called it *Seusshackery*. Another referred to it as *cartoonfoolery*. Surprisingly, it hasn't affected the sales. Frank's thinking we'll probably go into a second run by the spring, hopefully fanning out to the international markets. He's interested in Japan. He says they're crazy about cartoon books, especially ones that help them learn English. Frank figures we're killing two birds with one stone. "I love this shit," he says.

Iris is trying to tone down his language, especially in emails. She tells him people could be hacking into their computer. A newscast the other night reported a surge in hacking from Russia and Uzbekistan. "What do those fuckers want with my emails?" he says.

Frank's even considering an international reading tour. I'm not crazy about the idea. Travelling doesn't interest me anymore. I've gotten used to hanging around the house, doing my own thing. Even dancing is fun now. Silvio still sees me as a klutz, but he does his best, calmly adjusting my stance so I won't send Mary flying. Two of the older intermediates were held back. Silvio makes them work on their steps in the corner. He tells them they lack *machismo*. It's probably arthritis. They dance next to us, and I catch the guy's eye. I recognize a kindred spirit, a fellow interloper. He's doing his best, but you can't fake natural rhythm. Either you've got it or you don't.

I see people dancing on these television shows. The men toss the women around like rag dolls. You'd think they'd all have dislocated discs and pinched nerves. I asked Krupsky about it last week when

I went in for my physical. "What have you got against dancers?" he says.

"Nothing."

He listens to my heart, my lungs, the groaning of my joints. Then he tells me I'm good to go. "You take up jogging or something, Sam?" he says.

"Tango."

"You tango? I didn't think you had it in you."

"I could tango you under the table."

"Is that so?"

"I saw you twist, Krupsky."

"You think I don't know how to tango?"

"Not if your twisting is any indication."

"Try me."

"Come to the studio tomorrow night," I say. "Seven o'clock. I'll tell Silvio you're checking the place out." I write down the address on his prescription pad. "What are you grinning at?"

"Nothing, Sam," he shrugs. "See you tomorrow night, *amigo*."

"Stop grinning, for chrissake."

"Why? I'm happy."

"You're too happy."

"Then go forth and multiply."

# Chapter 76

Krupsky and his wife are there in front of the dance studio when we arrive. They look like two little elves all dressed in their finest clothes. "Didn't think you'd have the guts to come, Krupsky," I say, and he smiles away, giving Mary a wink. "You've met Mary and Muller," I say. "This is my daughter, Judy."

"Very nice to meet you, Judy," Krupsky says, doing a slight bow. "My wife, Emma. Are you ready to be dazzled, Sam?"

"We'll see who dazzles."

"Lead the way." We get inside and I introduce them to Silvio and Carmen. "A pleasure," Krupsky says. "My wife and I spent many pleasant years in Buenos Aires. Sam says you're quite the dancers."

"He's very kind," Silvio says. "I hope we measure up to what you've seen in Buenos Aires. Come, we'll get started." Silvio assembles all the couples out on the floor. Krupsky leads Emma by the hand like she's royalty while Judy rubs Muller's back.

"Stop looking so smug," I say to Krupsky. The music starts and Krupsky goes into a stance, tilting Emma slightly. Their bodies lock, Krupsky brings her forward, elbows out, feet sliding into position. Then they're off, around the room, little legs practically flying. Everyone turns and watches. Even Silvio and Carmen are staring. Krupsky flows like a river, taking a spin around the eddy. He's a virtuoso and a bloody show-off. He glides close to Carmen, giving her a wink and she claps her hands. "Olé," she says.

"Sam, they're wonderful," Mary says.

"Bloody hell."

"I thought you'd be pleased."

"I was calling his bluff."

"Look—he's trading with Muller."

Krupsky has Judy in a promenade hold. He barely comes up to her shoulders, but they swirl and glide, dipping, touching toes. At the end of the song, Krupsky goes over and asks Carmen to dance. Silvio stands at the side, looking half amused and half amazed. Krupsky dances right by him, eyes half closed in bliss. On the next song, Silvio guides Krupsky's wife out on the floor. Krupsky and Carmen pass by, then Silvio and Emma. They step, turn, and bend, all in a fluid motion.

On the next number, they exchange partners again, Silvio and Carmen do a dance step that takes them right across the floor. Krupsky and Emma follow, their little legs going like crazy. We all clap at each pass, gasping when Krupsky dips Emma and brings her up again. Silvio takes out a handkerchief. It's perfectly folded and monogrammed. He dabs his forehead, puts it back in his pocket, and starts again. Krupsky directs Emma over towards Silvio. "Magnifico!" he calls out. When the music stops, both couples bow, holding up their hands. They come off the dance floor.

"You were wonderful," Mary says to the Krupsky and Emma.

"Thank your husband," Krupsky says.

"Stop looking so damn smug," I say.

"Smug?" Krupsky shrugs. "Who's smug?"

# Chapter 77

*G*rammarians are all up in arms over the stupid book. They're such tight-assed little twerps. One of them claims I mixed past and present tenses. Another takes issue with my comments about adjectives. "They are *not* something we can do without!" he writes. Still another contends that not all proper names are special. "Would you call the Klu Klux Klan special?" he says. "Or the Kuomintang?!!"

Frank hates academics. His own education ended in the eighth grade when he was caught pissing in the sacristy. He's never walked past a Catholic priest since without giving him the finger. "Don't worry about it, Sam," Frank says. "Let the fuckers bitch. They aren't our audience, anyway." Last week, Frank did a talk show, telling the interviewer our character is called Mr. Quiggles. A reviewer called it the stupidest name in children's literature. Frank told him to go fuck himself. "At least Frank O'Conner starts with an active verb," the reviewer said.

The house over on Cedar looks brand spanking new, smelling fresh from Max's room deodorizers and scented candles. The owners stand in amazement. Around back, Zack's taken over gardening duties since his seafood business was a flop. Now he mows the grass and trims the hedges, still wearing his security guard boots. We celebrate later with a new batch of brownies and milk. Muller sent them over with a note congratulating Ruby. Judy did up a little floral arrangement to go with it. Otis gets sentimental on the third brownie, telling Ruby she's his one and only. "Dry up," Margot says. "How about a toast to our author here." I get up and take a bow. Bisquick squawks out, "Tit action!" The bird's nothing but attitude these days. Margot has to get back on the air. "I've got some flagellating youngsters who need sorting out."

Otis and Max pass out on the rug. Zack's head hits the table. Ruby walks me to the door. "We're starting the house out on Madison tomorrow."

"Sounds good."

"You won't be tied up with Mr. Quiggles?"

"I'd rather not think about Mr. Quiggles." Mr. Quiggles can go schtup a T.

# Chapter 78

The occasional sombrero still slides off the cabana roof over at Riley's. A streamer flutters in the hedgerow. Other than that, we're pretty much back to normal. I get up, check the forecast, and put coffee in a thermos. The house on Madison is a big place, split-level. All of us are working over there. Zack's been trying to sell the last of his seafood off the back of Ruby's pickup. It's all packed on ice in a cooler, smelling like a ship's gunnel. "I was looking for some Gatorade and pulled out a lobster tail," Ruby said the other day. Zack tried putting a sandwich board next to the truck, but Ruby told him to knock it off. "Sell it on your own time," she said.

Otis is promoting his latest brainless idea called "Otis's Cry Off." He wants people sending in video clips of their best cries. The winner gets dinner at a local steak house. The owner's been advertising on Otis's site. "It's called cross promotion, Sam," he says. "We scratch each other's backs."

"I know what it is, Otis. I worked in advertising, remember?"

"Mr. Big Shot."

"You're a lame brain."

"I don't see you cross promoting anything."

"This says only the appetizers are free."

"So, sue me."

"You're telling people they're getting a free meal."

"I repeat, sue me."

Margot comes over and honks the cattle caller in his ear. His dentures fly across the room. "We don't need lawsuits," she says.

"Get your bird away from my teeth," Otis yells. "Christ, Margot, I can't hear anything now. Where in blazes did that bird go? Ruby? Is Bisquick up there with you?"

"I'm trying to fix the can opener, Otis," she calls down.

"Dammit," Otis says. "Folks, I need to get my teeth back. Here's Johnnie Taylor doing—appropriately—'You Can't Win.'" He runs upstairs and Bisquick flies down. "Where's my teeth, Ruby?"

"Probably behind the couch."

"Stupid bird."

"I bought you some denture adhesive."

"It tastes like mint crap."

"Well, buy your own denture adhesive from now on."

The song ends and Bisquick bobs at the computer monitor. Videos pour in like you wouldn't believe.

# Chapter 79

"Here's one from the great Eddie Floyd," Otis is saying. "A Stax original out of Montgomery, Alabama. Mr. 'Knock on Wood' himself. He wrote the song with Steve Cropper and it was intended for Otis Redding. Then Jerry Wexler heard Eddie's version and said, 'This boy's got a hit on his hands.' That being said, I thought I'd play another of Eddie's songs, a favorite of Ruby's called 'I Never Found a Girl (To Love Me Like You Do).' Here you go, Ruby, and remember, folks, I'll be judging the entries for *Otis's Cry Off* this Friday. Send in your video clips and maybe you'll win a steak dinner."

Ruby enters the frame and kisses Otis on the head. "Go brush your teeth," she says to him, and he disappears while Margot dances and folds sheets. I watch, drinking coffee in the kitchen.

Frank called earlier to say the books are selling well. In some ways, I consider our success a bit of a bunko. I'm no grammarian. Nobody gives a shit about adjectives, anyway. Descriptives are supposed to help us form mental pictures. Who forms mental pictures in this day and age? Pamela Anderson's boobs are right there on YouTube. The other morning, I found Mary and Judy watching a couple dance the tango down in Columbia. It was all in real time. The man talked between songs, describing each *corte* in broken English. "Look at them, Sam," Mary said, watching them float across the floor, sending out these big, toothy smiles. Because it's in real time, it's like you're there. People don't have to day dream anymore. They don't have to *imagine*. It's all there in front of you. You can skydive, walk around Machu Picchu, or have a dolphin to take you skimming across a lagoon in Key West.

There's even a program called "Second Life" where you exist in a parallel universe. Muller's a fireman. He has a mask strapped to his face, entering buildings, pulling out babies and small kittens. Judy is some sort of Rapunzel. She wanders around castle ramparts, waiting for her knight in shining armor. The whole thing gets pretty silly. Judy keeps calling to Muller, telling him to save her from some fire-breathing dragon. You half expect him to show up on her screen in his firefighter's uniform with a tabby under his arm.

I'm surprised Mary isn't doing something like that. Maybe the tango's enough for her. You never know with Mary, though. Sometimes she's perfectly content sitting in the sunroom. Other times, she wants to dance across the kitchen floor. She still corners me in the bedroom. "For crying out loud," I say, "it's two in the afternoon. Why can't you boff someone online like everybody else?"

"Who's boffing online?"

"The whole world."

"Are you boffing online, Sam? Tell me the truth."

"No, Mary."

"I'll find out."

"I'm not boffing anyone online, for chrissake."

"I'm watching you, Sam."

I'm not even sure I'd know how to boff online.

# Chapter 80

*I* take the bus to work. Muller and Judy are using Mary's car for a catering job. Theirs is still dribbling oil down the driveway. I lent mine to Mary so she can check out industrial kitchens. My hope is she'll find one with an apartment upstairs, but saying that really raises her hackles. "They're staying here," she says. "I've already told them we can turn the den into a nursery."

On the bus, I'm sitting next to a girl who texts with one hand and flicks through songs on her iPod with the other. Her fingers are perfectly coordinated. She texts, checks song lists, then texts some more. The music comes out sounding like an overcharged mosquito. Looking around the bus, I realize most of people have something in their ears. At my stop, I step out on the sidewalk and see Ruby and Max putting paint cans into the truck. I help with the ladders.

The owners on Madison are waiting out front when we arrive. They have these two enormous sheep dogs that gallop around like long-haired ponies. "I'm Ruby," Ruby says to the couple. "This is Max and Sam."

The couple can't do a thing with those dogs. They run around, bumping into everything. One of them sticks its nose in Ruby's crotch. "Gilbert!" the woman says. "Stop that."

We go around the house, Ruby taking notes. From what we can see, the upper floor needs a full paint job, foundation included. I help Max get our stuff out of the truck. The dogs follow me, knocking over one paint can. A few minutes later, they crash into a ladder. "Can you ask them to take the dogs inside, Ruby?" Max says.

"I can try." Ruby comes back five minutes later. "No dice. She says they'll settle down."

We can't leave anything on the ground. As soon as we do, they run off with a roller or knock over something else. It goes on all day. Max is getting more and more frustrated. "We're losing money every time they go by, Ruby," he says. We have to bring everything back with us that night. "I'm gonna figure something out," he says.

Next morning when we arrive, the dogs come running around the side of the house. Max is waiting with two brownies wrapped in tin foil. He takes one out, breaks it in two, tossing half to each dog. We sit in the truck, drinking coffee, while the dogs go off behind the garage. We find them later under a tree on their backs.

The woman comes out of the house. "What's wrong with Gilbert and Freddy?"

"They're just resting, ma'am."

"On their backs?" She starts rubbing their tummies, calling them her "little boys." The stupid things don't even recognize her. "I've never seen them like this before," she says.

"They look pretty happy," Max says.

"You don't think they ate paint, do you?"

"No, ma'am," Max says. "They'd be puking all over the place. We've seen it before, haven't we, Sam?"

The rest of the day is a breeze. Gilbert and Freddy barely move the whole afternoon. Towards four o'clock, Freddy makes a half-hearted attempt to stick his nose in Ruby's crotch. It's too much for him. He falls asleep with his ass in the koi pond.

Next morning, the dogs come galloping out of the house: tufts of grass fly, slobber is everywhere. Max doesn't even bother getting out of the truck. He tosses the brownie, lights a cigarette, and waits for them to fall over. Ruby isn't thrilled. Giving those dogs pot is cutting into our profits. Otis went nuts when he found out. "You're wasting good grass on a couple of mutts, Max?"

"They're purebreds, Otis."

At least we're back on track. We paint the rest of the day with Gilbert and Freddy sleeping away. The woman comes out occasionally, rubs their tummies, then goes back inside. Ruby takes Gilbert and Freddy a bowl of water. They slurp half-heartedly. "You've turned them into idiots, Max."

"They'll be okay in a few hours."

"You sure about that?"

"Pretty sure."

"You said the same thing about Otis."

"That's true."

# Chapter 81

Frank is throwing a swank party at his cottage. He's invited the current investors and a bunch of corporate friends. We need capital for the next book. Frank figures he'll get it with a bunch of champagne and a shrimp waterfall. "It's your chance to shine, Sam," he says. Muller's been asked to cater. The menu's being left up to him. Frank wants floral arrangements, too; a "dash of Irish", as he puts it. He sent me an email from the airport on his way to Tokyo.

> *Sam,*
> *This is an important meet and greet with the investors. They want to see the man behind Mr. Quiggles. I've got business in Tokyo until the fifteenth—should be back in time for the party. Any questions, talk to Iris. We still haven't had our drink and steak dinner, have we? It's coming. Let's get through this first. See you when I get back into town. Give my best to Mary, et al.*
>
> *Frank*

I'm terrible at schmoozing. I don't have Frank's gift for the gab. Half the time, I just stand there staring at my shoes, then say something stupid like, "Let's hope this does the trick." It used to drive clients up the wall. I'd hear them talking to Frank after a meeting, saying, "What's the deal with that writer of yours?" Frank would tell them I was a genius. "You can't talk to geniuses; you know that, Sherman." he'd say. Fortunately, according to Frank, the numbers will do the talking. He hired one of the top research firms in Chicago. To quote them, "The Mr. Quiggles franchise should see solid growth over the next year. These books are enjoyed by all ages and cultures, clearly the result of their simplicity and accessibility."

I've been reading the full report, hoping it'll give me something intelligent to say. There's a lot of money involved, most of which Frank's already committed to advertising and public relations.

Meanwhile, Muller goes over the menu in the kitchen. Cookbooks are spread out on the table, pans inspected. Iris sent over their chef, a Somali named Mustafa. The guy's close to three hundred pounds with big white teeth and a hairline moustache. He and Muller try different recipes, throwing stuff away, starting again. Mustafa stays over one night and sleeps in the basement.

Muller's going with a roasted chicken covered in honey, apricot and tarragon sauce. The side salad is blue cabbage with cashel blue cheese. For dessert, he's making chocolate cake laced with cinnamon and chilies and topped with compote of maraschino cherries. The dishes themselves will be cooked up north in Iris's big ovens. Muller and Mustafa are going up in one car, Judy and Mary in the other. Max loaned me his to take up the warming trays. It looks like a small cavalcade, complete with a grinning Mustafa, and Judy's floral arrangements almost sticking out the side windows.

Frank's cottage is on Lake Geneva. You go past these big homes with iron gates out front. Frank's place isn't hard to find. The house itself goes to a peak, then flairs out at the sides. There are levels everywhere supporting huge windows. Iris meets me at the door. She looks good with her red hair pulled up in a bun. "The troops have arrived," she says.

There's a fieldstone fireplace, big sofas. I follow Iris around to the living room. Through the picture windows, I can see three levels of deck and a flight of stairs zigzagging down to the water.

Judy starts hanging garlands of wisteria and local ivy everywhere. Seating for the guests has been arranged on the main deck, tablecloths luffing in the breeze. People arrive and Iris guides them through the house. Expensive cars and limousines fill the driveway. While Iris is giving them the tour, Frank calls, saying his plane's just landed. "Frankie's on his way," she says.

I go check on Muller. The kitchen is a sunken room holding two ovens, gas stoves and microwaves. While Muller works away under a slick layer of sweat, Mustafa smiles like a fucking junkie.

More guests arrive, more cocktails, the balconies are full of dangling jewelry. A guy wearing an ascot grabs my hand. "You must be Sam," he says. "You look like a writer. Well, Sam, how does it feel to be Mr. Quiggles?" I tell him it's a pisser. His colleagues gather around. "Frank's told us about the next project," the guy says, "Nobody's in the dark here. So give us some details. Who's this woman Frank says is taking the world by storm? She used to be his accountant?"

"Margot?" I say.

"That's her," the guy with the ascot says. "Got a show on the Internet or something. Quite a hit, I hear. Are you taking existing quotes from her show? Or is everything new in the book?"

"I'm not sure I follow."

"Her advice book," another says. "Frank says Margot really lets people have it. Give us the poop on this gal. What're you planning?"

"Well, I guess we'll be using her quotes."

"Is it going to *sell*, Sam?"

"Let's hope it does the trick." I excuse myself and find Iris on the phone with Frank. The airport's mobbed. All the highways are packed. Frank can't even charter a plane. He's finally found a cab driver willing to make the trip. He hangs up before I can talk to him.

Iris tells the maids to start putting the appetizers outside. Muller's made prosciutto wrapped around figs and a smokey gruyere. Bottles of champagne are brought out in frosted ice buckets. I help Muller with some of the pots while Mustafa whistles through his big teeth and Iris stands in the living room with a drink in her hand.

Frank calls twenty minutes later to say the cab's broken down. A tow trucks on its way. Iris puts me on the phone. "Frankie's screaming like a banshee," she says. "Try to calm him down."

Frank says he's in a ditch, kicking tiger lilies or something. "Take it easy, Frank. Everything's going fine."

"What are the investor's doing?"

"Talking about our next book."

"Which one?"

"The one I'm supposed to be writing with Margot. When did this happen? Have you even talked to Margot?"

"Christ, no. I was blowing smoke. I had to tell the investors something. And don't go blabbing to Margot—fuck, I just kicked my shoe into a field. Who do you know with a car?"

"I don't know anyone, Frank."

"I'm standing in a fucking ditch here. Find me a friggin' car. I'll pay whatever it takes. I'm on highway twelve, just north of ninety—" He's swearing away. "What the fuck did I just step on? Call someone, Sam!"

I hang up and get on the phone to Max. "You feel like being a chauffeur?"

"For who?"

"Frank O'Conner. His cab broke down."

"Where is he?"

"Highway twelve, just north of ninety."

"What's he paying?"

"Let's just say you could start a college fund."

"I'm not at home, Sam. Zack and I stole the wiener van again."

"What the hell for?"

"To pick up shrubs. Ruby's out in the pickup."

"Where are you now?"

"In the west end. I can cut up to ninety, no problem."

"Well, dump Zack, for chrissake."

"I'm on it, Sam."

I hang up and dial Frank's cell. "Max is on his way."

"Who the hell's Max?"

"Your old security guard."

"Did I fire him?"

"No, he took off."

"That little fucker? Tell him hurry up. I'm standing in a bog."

I hang up and return to the party. The guests are sitting down to dinner. Chicken bubbles in the warming trays. Dishes clatter. "How's Frankie?" Iris asks.

"He says he's standing in a bog."

Twenty minutes later, Frank rings again, screaming his head off. "Where's that little wanker?" he yells.

"Should be there any minute."

"Jesus wept! What's everybody doing?"

"Drinking."

"Watch them, Sam. Half those bastards have screwed each other's wives. I wouldn't put anything past them right now."

"Calm down, Frank."

"*You* calm down. I'm ready to kick the shit out of this cab driver. He's out in the field eating carrots. Watch that fucker, Harry, in particular."

"Which one's he?"

"Our main investor—fuck, Sam, are you talking to those guys? I told you to keep them sweet. Lay some crap on them. Tell'm Margot's the next coming of Christ. I'm counting on—what the fuck is that?"

"What?"

"Jesus wept—is that my fucking wiener van?"

We get disconnected. I find Iris in the living room. "Max is bringing Frank up now," I say to her.

"Oh, that's wonderful," she says with a hazy smile. "Frankie's on his way. Have you eaten yet, Sam?"

"I'll get something in the kitchen."

"Tell Muller everyone loves his food."

People are all over the balcony, food is consumed, and champagne glasses tilt. I go down in the kitchen and eat something off one of the serving plates. Muller and Mustafa keep bumping into each other.

"Iris says everyone loves your food," I say. "Anything you need me to do?"

"We're okay, Sam."

I got back upstairs. Iris is swaying to the music. "You seem to be enjoying yourself," I say to her.

"I am," she says. "This is the best I've felt in years. Your Mary's one in a million, Sammy boy. A Christian goddess."

"I wouldn't go that far. She's not Christian, for one thing."

"You be good to her, Sammy. I mean it. I was depressed as hell. Then, puff!"—snapping her fingers—"Mary lifted me up."

"Are you sure it was Mary?"

"None of your smart-alecky stuff. Mary's an angel. And stop looking so serious. Here," she says, bringing a plate out from behind her back. "I had Muller bake these. Don't tell Frankie."

"Christ, Iris."

"Relax," she says. "Go take a dip. The food will be eaten, drinks will flow and the cow will jump over the moon."

I bump into Mustafa bringing out trays of brownies. The fucker's grinning like an old derelict. Muller's drizzling some sauce over strawberries. "You didn't tell me you were making brownies," I say.

"Iris asked."

"Frank's got all the investors out there."

"I think Iris knows that, Sam."

"They've all shagged each other's wives, for chrissake. Where's Mary and Judy?"

"I don't know."

Iris is still swaying to the music. Mustafa's fat head moves through the crowd on the deck. "There you are again," Iris says to me. "Did you have your dip?"

"Is everybody eating brownies?"

"Like Dog Chow."

I look outside. A woman's pole dancing a light standard. "Where's Mary?"

"Down at the dock. Relax, Sammy. Have some fun."

It's an ugly scene on the dock: tuxedos on the railings, ties in bushes. Someone's naked in a canoe. Others joust with paddles. Mary's over on some rocks with Judy. "What's wrong, Sam?" Mary says.

"Frank says this crowd could turn ugly."

"They're having fun, Daddy."

"You don't know their idea of fun, sweetie."

People disappear into the shallows. Bottles teeter on the dock. One of the guests starts swimming across the inlet. A woman in the water squeals, a man cannonballs to her rescue. The investor I met earlier is singing show tunes to a gold lamé gown floating by.

Up above, a long strand of icicle lights dangles from one of the trees. The other end is wrapped around a woman's leg. She falls into a juniper bush. Something crashes on the upper deck. Probably one of the warming trays. A passing paddleboat is upended, the owner pulled to shore. He's given mouth-to-mouth despite his protests. Mary and Judy giggle as a naked woman swims past. I keep checking my watch. "What's wrong?" Mary says.

"I should try calling Frank."

"Forget Frank," Mary says. "Let's go in the water."

"Are you two getting naked again?" Judy asks.

"What do you mean 'again'?" I say.

"You were naked at Riley's party."

"No we weren't."

"Just go in, Daddy."

Mary pushes me in the water. My head goes under and I imagine Muller down there, hair going up and down, cheeks inflated. I come up sputtering. Judy does a cannonball, her white knees up to her chest. She surfaces and says, "Come on Daddy." Then she and Mary swim towards the neighbor's dock. I follow and we hang from the ladder, wiggling our toes. A diving contest of sorts is taking place. Just a bunch of granny dives. We watch for a while, then I hear a backfire around the other side of the inlet. Naked bodies go up trees. Mustafa slides down the hill on his ass. "What's that, Daddy?" Judy says.

I dress and run up the stairs. A crowd is gathering out front. Chugging up the driveway, I see the wiener van with the passenger door open. "You stupid, git," Frank yells, jumping out. "Fucking arse almost took out my front gate!" He grabs my arm. "How's it looking, Sam? Never mind, I'll see for myself. Tell your little fucker friend to get that piece of crap out of my driveway. Park it in the neighbor's yard or something." He stomps off into the house. Max gets out.

"How's the party?" he says.

"Iris got Muller to make grass brownies. Everyone's stoned out of their gourds."

"Any left?"

"Check with Muller."

Frank is being led down to the water by two naked women. Iris is laughing. Frank's uttering oaths, telling everyone they're destroying his property value. Then there's a loud splash and Frank's in the water going after Mustafa with a paddle. Mustafa makes for open water.

# Chapter 82

*M*orning comes, streamers dangle outside my window. Confetti blows in the breeze next to the wiener van. Someone downstairs says a Supreme Court judge is still lost in the woods. I go to the back balcony and see a naked figure across the inlet. Frank stands on the dock, yelling, "You wanker!" Muller's on the second level deck, pulling warming trays out of the hydrangea bushes. A police launch returns Mustafa. Frank helps him up on the dock and kicks his ass.

I go downstairs in Frank's dressing gown. Iris is tending to minor scrapes and poison ivy while Mary and Judy bring in the broken crystal. A steady stream of people emerges from different nooks and crannies, stumbling outside to their cars, driving off past a man fast asleep in the junipers. Frank comes inside, pours a brandy, then Max appears with a mouse under one eye. I guess he slept in the wiener van. "What happened to you?" I say.

"Somebody hit me."

Iris puts a cube steak on his eye while Muller brings in the last of the warming trays. He takes them to the galley and starts making scrambled eggs with artichokes. "What's Muller charging me, anyway?" Frank says.

"Talk to Mary," I say.

Mary's shaking the tablecloths on the deck. Frank goes out, they talk, he pulls his hair, then comes back inside. "The woman's a monster, Sam," he says, holding Mary's written estimate. "This is flat out robbery."

"Don't you go shortchanging them, Frankie," Iris says. "They worked very hard. You should be grateful."

"I know that, Iris—"

"Pay it."

"There's nine hundred dollars in desserts alone."

"Worth every penny."

"I never even got any dessert. What did we have?"

"Chocolate cake."

"Nine hundred bucks for chocolate cake?" he yells, then spots Max on the couch. "And what do I have to pay you, you little bastard?"

"Sam says you're sending me to college," Max says.

"I'm what?"

"You're sending me to college."

"In a pig's ear."

"You're lucky he got you up here at all," Iris says.

"I know that Iris, but—"

"What would a chartered plane have cost you?"

"Iris—"

"Four grand?"

"Don't go giving that little snipe any ideas."

"Two grand's fine," Max says.

"Over my dead father's arse."

"You dragged him out on a weekend, Frankie."

"Bloody hell, Iris . . ."

"He got you up here, didn't he?"

"He almost killed us doing it."

"You wanted me to pull out all the stops," Max says.

"*Pull* them out, not hit them."

"Watch your blood pressure, Frankie."

"Christ, I've still got a judge wandering around out there—"

"He'll be fine. Have some breakfast. Then you can write everyone a nice big check."

Muller brings out the eggs, roasted potatoes, prosciutto and garden salad. People gather around the table. Coffee is served with cinnamon toast on the side. The investors emerge from their rooms just as Mustafa brings in a bowl of fruit, grinning away. "What are you smiling about, you fat bastard?" Frank says. "Tried to drown me last night, didn't ya?"

The investors gorge. Someone comes out of the garden shed. He looks around, then walks inside. His right eye is swollen. "What happened to you?" Frank says.

"I wanted a hot dog. That guy hit me."

"You hit me first," Max says.

"You struck my lawyer, you little fucker?" Frank says.

"I told him I didn't have any hot dogs."

"It's a hot dog van, isn't it?" the lawyer says.

"I have to get going," Max says. "Ruby wants me back for dinner. Are you paying me or what?"

"I'll get his check book," Iris says. She goes to the den and comes back laughing.

"What's so funny?" Frank says.

"There's a love connection going on in there."

"On my couch? Tell them to get the fuck out of there!"

"*You* tell them, Frank. They're your friends."

"Bloody hell! What do I owe you again, you little bastard?"

"Two thousand."

"I'll give you five hundred."

"One thousand."

"Eight, and not a penny more."

"Sold."

"Fucking weasel."

"Frank," Iris says.

"Don't Frank me. The little bastard's killing me."

"What do you want done with the wiener van?" Max asks.

"I don't care. Burn it. Fuck it up the tailpipe."

"Language, Frankie," Iris says.

"I'll figure something out," Max says.

"Take your money and go, you bloodthirsty little prick."

"You forgot to sign it."

"Give it here. Eight hundred dollars for a ride in my own vehicle. Remind me never to hire outside help again, Iris."

"Be thankful you got any help at all."

"You're enjoying this, aren't you?"

"Write Mary a check, too."

"We could have gone to Spain on this."

"Write it and stop bitching."

Frank writes Mary a check. "Anybody else?" Frank says.

"You covering dry cleaning?" his lawyer says.

"Go fuck yourself, Desmond."

Max puts some scrambled eggs between two pieces of cinnamon toast. "I'll see you tomorrow, Sam."

"Okay, Max."

"We should get moving, too," Mary says.

"Let me get dressed."

The wiener van backfires while I'm putting on my clothes. A woman screams and something goes thump in the den. When I come downstairs, two people emerge, moving along the wall to the door. "We're not bad people," the woman says. They go outside and disappear down the driveway. We load everything in the cars and head out. Down by the gate, we see limos parked at odd angles.

When we get home, Margot's on the air, giving somebody shit about their student debt. "You bought a car, for God's sake? No, it's not okay. No, student loans aren't forgivable. Who told you that?"

In a few months, she'll be a reviewer's dream. Frank's going to promote the hell out of her book. "Just write down what she says," he told me, which is a problem in itself. Margot works off the cuff. I'll probably have to sit with Margot, recording everything. The language might have to be toned down. Margot gets pretty ripe when she's on a roll. On the other hand, Frank likes ripe.

There's no point worrying about it at this point. Margot hasn't even agreed, and you never know with her. She may tell Frank to go shove it. Then again, she might think it's a hoot. Margot gets a kick out of Frank sometimes. She used to laugh like crazy when he'd come into the office with a new idea. You'd hear her cackle, and Frank would bang on the wall saying, "Shut up, Margot, it's a good idea."

Anyway, I'm just the writer here. My job is to get Margot's words down on paper, put them in logical order, then let Frank take over. And wait for the feminists and lawsuits.

# Chapter 83

*M*oney keeps rolling in from the grammar books. Frank's no fool when it comes to percentages. Even after distribution and taxes, he's about to make a good profit. It's got all the trades and tabloids talking. They say Frank's on a new kick, lambasting kids over their texts and blogging. One reporter wrote: "It's about time someone nipped this texting thing in the bud."

Frank's still wants to take the books on the road. God help us if anybody asks Frank a grammar question. The man couldn't tell a split infinitive from a split pea. They're already asking about his next project, which he says is a book about social conduct, served up by a woman who doesn't stand on ceremony. "She has her own online show," he says. "Her name's Margot Simmons and she doesn't take guff from anybody. You got a problem with your kid, talk to Margot. She'll straighten the little bugger out. I have her on exclusive contract."

Margot hasn't signed the contract yet. Knowing Margot, she plans to fleece Frank but good. "The woman's a fucking menace," Frank said after their last meeting. "She's taking me to the cleaners." Margot thinks it's funny as hell. She doesn't need his money. She's got a new account called Bendex condoms. They're multicolored and look like old barbershop signs. Affiliated marketing is definitely working for her. She gets five cents for every hit. The money's rolling in and, with her new publishing contract, she could rake in plenty.

Otis has something going, too. A pharmaceutical company figured *Otis Cries for You* must attract a lot of depressed people. They want him to help advertise a new happy pill. Knowing Otis, he'll probably take more than he sells.

Muller and Judy have catering parties booked right through the winter. They sold their house in Seattle put the money towards an industrial kitchen and they should be up and running soon. As far as living arrangements go, they're happy staying here. Judy found out she's pregnant. She's expecting next June. Mary's turning the den into a nursery.

Max enrolled in night school last month. He's taking a marketing course for young entrepreneurs. Now he plans to expand, putting Zack in charge of the gardening. He calls it the *Total House Manicure* and plugs it on both Otis's and Margot's shows. Margot's handling the business side. She's incorporated everybody under the same umbrella, calling it Margomax. We're all listed as officers—even Otis, who got his nuts in the wringer for not paying royalties on his songs. Margot's taken care of that, everyone's paid off, or they think they are, anyway. Margot's as sneaky as Frank, which is pretty sneaky.

Ruby and I are finishing the house with those crazy dogs. The outside is done, just a door or two left to paint. The dogs wait for us to arrive, looking like junkies. Max is cutting back on the brownies, but those dogs are demanding brutes. Around three o'clock, they snap their heads up, get the munchies, and then it's bedlam. "They never used to be like this," the woman keeps saying. She sits on the grass, patting their tummies with Gilbert getting an erection the size of a paint roller. "Give mommy a big kiss," she says.

You'll get more than that in a second.

# Chapter 84

---

*M*argot's decided to lease vans for everybody: names will be painted on the sides, logos designed, and the Margomax insignia on the back doors. Something tells me Frank has his finger in this. They have secret meetings in her bedroom and Frank emerges, screaming away, saying she's fleecing him. Sometimes this plays out while Otis is on the air. Frank appears behind Otis, retreating upstairs. Margot comes out snickering away. "Everything okay, Margot?" Otis says.

"Right as rain," Margot says.

Frank's on the phone to me later. He wants Margot's quotes by late November. If everything goes according to plan, her book should make the bookshelves by Christmas. I wait until Margot's show ends and we sit at the kitchen table. I'm recording everything on a little tape recorder. "What do you think of child psychiatrists?" I ask.

"Assholes."

"Why's that?"

"They're in la-la land, Sam. They still think babies come from storks. Nothing but meatheads, the lot of them."

"Care to expand on that, Margot?"

"You know what ADD stands for, Sam?"

"Attention Deficit Disorder."

"No, it means A Dickhead Delinquent. These kids don't need pills. They need a swift kick in the pants. Everything's got some underlying cause with these child psychiatrists. Kids need discipline."

"What if the kid really has ADD?"

"They all do, for God's sake. Who doesn't at that age?"

Bisquick swoops in on Otis for a nipple grab. "Frickin' bird."

"Give him a grape," Margot says.

"I tried giving him a grape. He doesn't give a shit about grapes anymore. Get him away from me."

Margot picks up the foam finger and Bisquick goes for it. "There, you big sissy," she says to Otis.

"He's not grabbing *your* nipple. Why can't we tape his beak?"

"For the same reason we don't tape yours."

Otis goes to the fridge. "What's the story on the brownies, Sam?"

"Muller's too busy, Otis. Riley's pot is all used up, anyway. Max's looking around for another source."

"Where's Max now?"

"Your guess is as good as ours."

"We're trying to work here, Otis," Margot says. "Go fix the tap in the laundry room. I can't sleep with that thing dripping away. It gives my bladder ideas. Where were we, Sam?"

"Something about dickhead delinquents."

# Chapter 85

―――――――――――――

$\mathcal{T}$welve hours of tape, eighty quotes of mixed quality. Within five weeks, we'll be looking at a book ready to ship. Margot holds the manuscript like it's a used diaper. "If this sells, I'm a bigger dope than they are," she says. Frank keeps calling her a "bloodsucker" and she calls him a "bog trotter." It plays out in the basement with Ruby doing the laundry. Margot had a heavy duty washing machine and dryer put in last week. She's writing it off as a laundry mat.

Meanwhile, I'm getting our driveway resurfaced and buying paint for the nursery. The bill to resurface is over a grand. Margot says she'll bill it under sundry items. Everything we spend seems to be written off, even Muller's catering expenses. Mary works on his schedules using a new program. The jobs have timers scheduled to go off a day before the event. She turns everything into a pie chart at the end of the month.

We've made a good start on the nursery today. I'm getting to the point where I don't use tape anymore. Mary's impressed with my steady hand. "You're quite the pro," she says, following me around the room with a roller. We get the first coat on the walls before we have to get ready for our dance lessons tonight.

Krupsky and Emma are at the dance studio when we arrive. He's dressed in a suit with a pink carnation, kissing every woman's hand. Mary thinks it's charming as hell. "How are you, Sam," Krupsky says when we go over. "I thought I told you to wear a hat? Your skin looks like a breeding ground for carcinoma."

"I wear a hat, Krupsky."

"Get something bigger. Maybe a sombrero."

"I saw you twisting."

"Where?"

"In your office."

"No law against it, is there?"

Silvio claps his hands. All the dancers take their positions. "Today we'll concentrate on our *ochos*," he says. "Begin with your promenade holds. A little higher, Sam."

The music starts and we move about the floor. Krupsky and Emma dance closest to Silvio. Muller and Judy are on the other side. I nip the corner of Mary's toe and get a snarl. After three songs, the floor is open. Some couples stay together, others exchange partners. Krupsky asks Mary to dance. Emma stands with me. We've danced before. She's excellent, but you can tell she wants to watch her husband guide Mary around the room. They go floating by, doing a *caminando*, before he starts showing off his *cazas* and *baldosas*, a foot going in and out between Mary's legs, tapping her ankles. I wish Silvio would put him in the senior's class or ban him altogether. Everyone loves the little prick, especially Carmen. When the music stops, Krupsky leads Mary over to our corner by the hand. "She's as graceful as she is beautiful," he says to me. "You're a lucky man, Sam. All the more reason to wear a hat before you lose your nose."

"I got plenty of hats," I say, which is true since Riley's been tossing sombreros over the hedge. He's heating the pool for New Year's. At the stroke of midnight, we're all invited over. Judy and Mary aren't keen on the cold, but Muller's game. I have to admit, he's been acting a lot more serious lately. It's a bit of a relief and slightly unnerving at the same time.

Silvio and Carmen have the studio decorated for New Year's Eve. Streamers cross the ceiling, the punchbowl is full. Silvio stands in the middle of the floor. "As this year ends," he says, "we should reflect on what we have in our lives"—he takes Carmen's hand—"including our loved ones, food to eat, and, most of all, our health. That gives us the greatest gift of all. Please, everybody, join my wife and I and let's dance. Let's celebrate this time together."

Krupsky blows his nose and wipes his eyes. Emma puts her hand on his shoulder. I don't know what's wrong with the guy. He starts blubbering away. "The poor man," Mary says to me. "Say something, Sam."

"What do you want me to say?" She gives me a shove and I go over. "You okay, Krupsky?"

"Emma and I," he says, blowing his nose again, "we arrived in Buenos Aires this day fifty years ago. They kept us in Israel for two years waiting for visas."

"Sorry to hear that, Krupsky."

"Practically children, Sam. That's all we were. Without any family left. We had each other. Otherwise, bupkis."

"Can I get you some punch?"

"I think we'll dance now, Sam. Thanks for the offer."

He takes Emma out on the floor and they dance. They hold each other close, foreheads touching. "Invite them over after this," Mary says to me. "Go over and ask. Don't give me that long face, either."

"Fine, I'll go over and ask."

"And smile."

"He's not smiling."

"That's why I want you to smile."

"If I keep doing that, I won't be Cranky Face anymore."

"Just go over there."

# Chapter 86

We all sit together in the sunroom, Krupsky rubbing Judy's stomach, a smile on his face as big as the moon outside. It'll soon be New Years. Looking at my daughter now, I think back to the day she was born. The agency was pitching a new account and Frank kept coming down the hall, yelling, "What's taking you bastards so long?" I was in the art director's office, getting the last of the layouts together, when our receptionist came over the intercom: "Sam, Mary's in labor." I dropped everything, grabbed my coat, and headed out the door. "Where are you going?" Frank said, and I told him Mary was about to give birth. "Go on then," he said. "You probably want to take a few pictures. Go on then, you git. Hand out your cigars."

That afternoon, Judy came into the world, seven pounds, six ounces. The rest happened in a blink of an eye: nappies turning into underwear, t-shirts turning into bras, a graduation and then she was gone, off to Seattle to meet the man of her dreams. She looks up at me now and smiles, the dimples growing. Krupsky pats her hand and stands up. "You should be very happy, Sam," he says.

"I am, Krupsky. I'm tickled." The lights are on around the pool. Steam floats through the trees, disappearing into the blue-black sky.

"Imagine that," Krupsky says. "Swimming on New Year's Eve."

We go outside for a cigar. "Any plans for the New Year?" I ask. "Resolutions?"

"At my age, Sam? What do I have to resolve?

"Probably right."

"What about you?"

"I still get dizzy spells."

"So, sit down when it happens."

"Mary thinks I need medication."

"Do you think you need medication?"

"I don't know what I need."

"Look out there, Sam," he says, pointing up with his cigar. "Lots of stars. Thousands—millions. We've seen a few galaxies beyond Pluto. After that, bupkis, Sam, bupkis."

"What are you saying, Krupsky?"

"We're specks in the universe, Sam. Most of our decisions are made for us. It's called the earth's rotation. The world spins around, we spin around with it."

"Not very encouraging."

"So it's not very encouraging," he shrugs. "You know what I'd like to do, Sam?" More than anything else? I'd like to swim."

"If that's what you want. I'll find you some trunks."

"I thought this was a naked deal?"

"So now you're a hedonist?"

"What have you got against nudity?"

"Depends who's naked."

"Again, sue me."

Five minutes later, wrapped in bathrobes and snow boots, Krupsky, Muller and I cross the lawn. People are running out of Riley's house, dropping towels, jumping in the deep end. Riley and Pam are naked. "Eighty-six degrees, Sam," Riley says.

Krupsky laughs and drops his robe. He jumps in the pool with his cigar. Muller and I jump in after him. Krupsky moves to the shallow end. "Pam, this is my doctor," I say. "Krupsky, this is Pam."

"Glad to meet you, Pam."

"When did you start hanging out with your doctor?" Riley asks.

"We've been dancing together," I say.

"Not with each other, of course," Krupsky puffs away.

"Riley, Krupsky," I say. "Krupsky, Riley." They shake hands. Muller swims over to the diving board. He gets out and does a belly flop. Krupsky laughs himself silly.

More people emerge from the house, shaking their thighs, jumping in the water. They're counting down in the house. Then someone yells out, "Happy New Year!"

Krupsky's eyes shine. "Happy New Year, Sam," he says.

"Happy New Year, Krupsky." Now he's blubbering again and Pam's giving him a hug. Lucky prick.

# Chapter 87

Ruby calls the day after New Year's. "We've got a bit of a panic, Sam. You up for painting a store? A crew's coming in with the fixtures and counters on Tuesday. The owner wants two coats on the walls tomorrow. Max is already over there doing some prepping. You in?"

"Sure," I say. "Pick me up around seven." I get off the phone, joining Mary in the sunroom. Muller and Judy are watching Margot talk about New Year's resolutions. Behind her, Otis dances with his arms going like windmills. Ruby bought him an iPod for Christmas. Now his New Year's resolution is to have fun. "Knock it off, Otis," Margot yells. She throws a pen and it bounces off his forehead.

"I'm doing my thing, Margot," Otis says.

"I didn't do my thing when you were on."

"I didn't know you had a thing."

"Here's my thing"—stomping on Otis's toe—"how's that?" Otis goes hopping around the room. "Now," Margot says. "What are your New Year's resolutions, folks? Any new projects? Anyone joining a health club?" The pings go off like mad. Margot reads away, her bifocals slightly askew. "Half of these aren't worth going into detail," she says. "The others I can sum up with three words. Get a life."

More pings. "Look, knock off the stupid stuff. Is anyone doing anything constructive?" Ping, ping, ping, ping. "Here's one from Lola. She's expanding her business. Nothing wrong with diversifying. What sort of business, Lola?"

Ping.

"Oh, you're *that* Lola. How exactly are you expanding?"

Ping.

"Bigger tits isn't diversifying, Lola. Otis, get your keister over here. I don't know what's wrong with everybody . . ."

Ping.

"Well, thank you for the compliment, Mitch. I do sit ups and push-ups according to the U.S. Military Training Guide. My birthday's in June. Which, by the way, is when my friend, Sam's daughter, Judy is having her baby. Great news, Judy."

Ping.

"Of course she knows who the father is—"

Ping, ping, ping, ping.

"Bunch of dingdongs. Get over here, Otis."

Otis limps over to the computer. "This goes back to 1966, folks. James Carr doing 'You've Got My Mind Messed Up', one of his best. Enjoy, folks. Be right back." He leaves Bisquick watching the record go around and around.

Mary turns off the computer. "That was very sweet of Margot," Mary says.

"Maybe I should do butt squeezes," Judy says.

"Just do them in private, sweetheart," I say.

Muller stretches and yawns. "What did Ruby want, Sam?" he says.

"Another painting job starting tomorrow."

Judy starts doing butt squeezes. Muller drifts off to sleep. Meek and Beek sit there like a couple of stuffed birds.

# Chapter 88

The doorbell rings at seven o'clock the next morning. I'm just finishing my toast and coffee. Muller goes to the door. "Morning, folks," Ruby says, tossing me a pair of clean painter's pants. "Let's boogie, Sam. Max's already over there. He was priming until two in the morning. How about you, big fella? Need some extra cash for that baby of yours?"

"Can I go with them," Muller asks Judy.

"Sure, Muller," she says. "I've got baby booties to knit."

Muller grabs his coat and follows us outside. We crowd into the pickup, Muller in the middle, me pressed up against the door. Ruby hasn't started driving the new van yet. She says she can't see out the back windows. She'll keep using the pickup until she gets more practice. Muller's legs are practically up on the dashboard. "You and those big drumsticks of yours," she says. "We're not going anywhere if I don't get this thing out of reverse."

"Sorry, Ruby."

"I'm not mad, you big lug. I missed you."

"I missed you, too, Ruby."

"I gave up smoking, Sam."

"Good for you, Ruby. I'm next."

"Was that your New Year's resolution?"

"I'm not big on New Year's Resolutions."

"Excited about the baby, Muller?" Ruby asks. "What pediatrician are you using?"

"I asked Krupsky if he'd deliver the baby."

"You what?" I say. "When?"

"In the pool the other night. He said he has to brush up. He hasn't delivered a baby since the sixties."

"Since . . . since the sixties?"

"Easy, Sam,"

"The sixties? Jesus Christ, Muller. You're telling me Krupsky's *brushing up*? Why, for chrissake? Why Krupsky?"

"I like the way he touches Judy's stomach."

"Does Mary know about this?"

"Judy told her this morning. Did you know he delivered three babies on the boat going to Buenos Aires?"

"That was fifty fucking years ago."

"We're also thinking of having a home delivery."

"Pardon?"

"Home delivery. Maybe a water birth—"

"A what?"

"In the bathtub, Sam. Krupsky says he's fine either way."

"Fucking hell, Muller—stop the truck, for chrissake. I can't breathe. Stop the truck." Ruby pulls over to the side of the road. I get out and fall on the ground. Muller's got his paper bag out. He puts it over my face. "Breathe, Sam. Take deep breaths."

"Is he going to be okay?" Ruby asks.

"He's having a panic attack."

"I didn't know he had panic attacks."

"Nice and slow," Muller says. "You have to calm down."

"I'm . . . trying to calm down. You keep . . . you keep . . . pushing my God damn buttons . . ."

"Do you want to go home, Sam?" Ruby says.

"I'll . . . be . . . fine in a minute."

"Maybe we should take him over to Dr. Krupsky?" Ruby says.

"Christ no, Get that bag off my face, Muller. I'm fine . . . Let's just get back in the truck, okay?"

"You sure?"

"Just get in the truck."

The painting gets done faster than we expected. Max stays behind to do the trim while Ruby drops Muller and I back at the house. Judy and Mary are busy in the nursery putting up curtains. In the kitchen, I splash cold water on my face and sit in the sunroom. Margot's talking to some blogger who thinks she's addicted to herbal enemas. A song is going through my head, a tune sung by Tony Bennett. I watched him on a special the other night. It was old footage, shot around the time he joined Martin Luther King Jr. during his March on Washington.

The song keeps going around in my head, something about every head being held up high and sunshine in their skies. Lyrics always give me trouble, mostly because I mix verses up. Mary remembers the first line of a song, then goes, *dum diddly dum*, or *la, la, la*, until I'm about ready to scream. She's probably doing that now although, knowing her, she's thrown in a couple *ba booms* just to scuttle any suspicions I might have that she's a one-trick hummer.

I pour myself a drink and look out the window. Steam rises from Riley's pool. It must be costing him a fortune. I sit down and pretty soon I'm drifting off with Tony singing in my head.

"Sam?"

I open my eyes. Krupsky's standing there with a pill bottle in each hand. Mary and Judy are standing next to him. "Heard you had an episode today. What gives?"

"I'm okay."

"Muller says you gave him goose bumps."

"He told me you're delivering the baby in the tub, for chrissake."

"That's what this is about?"

"It's just an idea, Sam," Mary says. "You didn't have to go loopy."

"I didn't go loopy."

"What's wrong with home delivery, Daddy?"

"I didn't say there was anything wrong with it."

"Water birth's no biggy," Krupsky says. "Have a pill."

"I don't need pills."

"Glad to hear it, Sam. Anyway, get some sleep. I'll pop around again tomorrow. Bye, Mary. And you, my girl,"—he puts his hand on Judy's stomach—"let's keep up the good work, huh?" He goes out humming some song that sounds suspiciously Latin.

"I like Krupsky now," Mary says.

"What changed your mind?"

"He's a kind and giving soul."

"He still irritates the fuck out of me."

"So, what else is new? You'll never change, Sam."

"Why do I need to change?"

"You're a downer."

"Am not."

"You can be, Daddy," Judy says. She's going through cookbooks, helping Muller sort out his menus. To see them in the kitchen, you'd think everything was rainbows and sunshine, nothing but love, love, love. I'll tell you, Judy, you need a downer now and then, someone to drag your husband out of the lake. As for you, Mary, I've been up more than down, lately, if you know what I mean. At least I haven't wilted.

# Chapter 89

*W*e're all going to this Mardi Gras party Muller's catering. It's open to the public and promises to be quite the affair. Krupsky and Emma are coming, too. He figures it's a good chance to practice our rumbas. Once word got over to Otis's place, the whole gang decided it would be a blast. Ruby's even taking a few days off to make outfits. When I dropped over there earlier, everyone was in the rec room getting fitted. Material covered the floor. Ruby was hemming sleeves and collars while Otis blubbered away on air. "Get over here so I can fit you, Otis," she said. "You've cried enough for one day."

Margot and Ruby are wearing these crazy gowns, Otis looks like a gay pirate, Max and Zack resemble stable boys on crack. Mary and Emma are sewing away here at home, trying to get enough material to go around Muller's waist. Krupsky and I are going as gauchos. Mary hopes we'll get a chance to do the tango.

The palladium is up near Berger Park, a long building by the water with marquis flashing, spotlights beaming across the sky. Inside, it's all beads, headdresses and masks. Max and Zack head for the bar, Ruby drags Otis out on the dance floor. We see Muller at one of the serving tables with feathers in his hair. Music plays, people dance, drinks are poured. A rumba chain forms and we all join in. Bums go up and down, glitter drops on the floor. Outside, big heaters glow red on the patio.

I go out for a cigar and Krupsky follows. We stand against the railing and look at the water. "You know, Sam," he says. "I must thank you."

"For what?"

"This," he says. "All this,"—pointing his cigar— "the whole works. You got me tangoing again. I'm indebted, I really am." He looks at the sky. "The moon is up. All is well."

"I think you're drunk, Krupsky."

"Have it your way, Sam. I know what I am. How about you? Have you figured out what you are yet?"

"I've got the same last name as Tony Bennett."

"Does it help knowing that?"

"Not particularly."

"Sam"—putting his hand on my shoulder—"what would make you happy?"

"Seriously?"

"Shoot."

"I'd like, just once, for you to fall on your ass."

"That's it?"

"That'd do it."

Ruby drags Otis out on the deck and pins him to the wall. Otis squeals like a pig. Krupsky tosses his cigar over the railing and goes inside. I look across the parking lot. Just beyond the point is the place where Muller tried to drown himself last summer. I can't imagine him doing anything like that now. Krupsky says it's a big universe. That's all we know. I guess he's right. Just eat what's solid, and spit out air. I go inside and find Mary. Krupsky's dancing with Margot. "Come on," Mary says, pushing through a group of people throwing balloons in the air. "Watch my feet this time."

Margot's not much of a dancer outside of the crazy shake-a-leg stuff she does in Otis's basement. It's still amazing how Krupsky leads her through cazas and baldosas. The other dancers are giving them room, clapping and banging on tambourines. Krupsky caminandos Margot between different couples. Voices yell *Como vai* and Krupsky moves faster, spinning Margot, going off in one direction, then another. We lose sight of them as they move between feathered heads. Then there's a crash. A table topples over, glasses smash. We push through the crowd. Margot and Krupsky are on the floor. "Are you two okay?" I say.

Margot tries to stand up. Her dress is caught under Krupsky. "We were chugging along just fine," Margot says. "Then we dropped like a bomb."

"Are you okay, Krupsky?"

"Just fine, Sam." Krupsky sits up and wipes his jacket. He smiles at me. Then the crazy bastard winks.

# Chapter 90

*I*'m in my living room, covered in feathers. I fell asleep on the couch earlier while Krupsky and Margot tangoed through the kitchen. The rest of the crew, beads around their necks, danced in a rumba chain with Muller leading. Now I'm looking at crushed beads all over the floor. Mary, Judy, and Muller are asleep. Through the window, I see the moon above Riley's cabana. It's staring down at me, like the man in the moon, as the song goes, when the moon beams.

I take the dustpan from the cupboard and start sweeping up the beads. Krupsky's gaucho hat hangs on a lamp. Mine is crushed on the floor. At some point last night, Krupsky said to me, "Good people are around you, Sam," he said. "You should be thankful. A man with friends is rich. Have you ever counted them?" Muller was leading a rumba chain through the sunroom. "I'll leave you to ponder that," Krupsky said and joined the end. As I was drifting off, I remember Emma standing the kitchen, her hands in a dishcloth.

I mix a drink and sit at the kitchen counter. Muller must have left the computer on. A shape move across the computer screen. It's Otis sitting down in his bathrobe. Confetti twinkles in his hair. He stares at the screen, clearing his throat. "I know I'm talking to a limited number of you out there," he says. "Maybe this is a good time to get something off my chest. I've done some bad things. I slept with Max's girlfriend. We slow danced to James Carr. Just want to send an apology . . . sorry, honey . . . I was bad. Here's *Dark End of the Street* . . .

Bisquick appears beside the turntable. He jumps on the record as it starts going around and around. "Bugger off, bird," Otis says. The bedroom door opens in the background. "You got Bisquick with you?" Margot calls out.

"Stupid thing's on my turntable—" Bisquick flaps about as Otis swats at him. "Get off there—" He makes a grab for Bisquick and falls out of his chair.

Margot comes out in a negligee. "Are you on air?"

"What the hell did you think I was doing?"

"I'm standing here in my bare minimum."

"Well, cover up."

"Come on, Bisquick," she says. "Leave Otis to his birdbrains."

"Dammit, Margot, they can hear you." Bisquick flaps over to her arm and Otis gets up. He puts the stylus on the record and it pops. "Here it is, honey. Once again, I did you wrong. That's a fact."

"Who the hell are you talking to, Otis?" Margot says.

"None of your dang business. Go to bed." The bedroom door slams. Otis takes out a handkerchief and blows his nose. Confetti falls like dandruff.

# Chapter 91

"I thought we were starting early today?" I say when I come through Otis's back door. Max is the only one up. He yawns and scratches his chest. Then Ruby appears in her dressing gown. "What time is it?" she says.

"Eight o'clock," Max says. "We told Sam we were starting early."

"Let me get ready," she says. She goes off while Max sits and drinks his coffee.

Margot comes upstairs with Bisquick on her shoulder. "Morning, Sam," she says. "God, my head hurts. Krupsky came back with us and made hot toddies. The man's a machine." She puts bread in the toaster. Bisquick tries to pull it out. "Buzz off, Bisquick. Go on, get down."

Otis stumbles through to the washroom. "Otis, I'm doing something here," Ruby yells, and he bounces off walls coming to the kitchen.

"Keep that bird away from me this morning, Margot," he says.

"Keep him away yourself. I'm not your bodyguard."

The toilet flushes and Ruby comes out in jeans and a flannel shirt. Her hair is up under a bandana. "Let's go if we're going," she says.

In the truck, I roll down the window and light a cigarette. "Damn, that smells good," Ruby says. "Give us a puff."

"I thought you weren't smoking anymore?" Max says.

"I just want one puff."

I feel the sun warming my face, the light against my eyelids. I picture the rooms we're painting now, each one needing a little sanding, a little priming. I can feel the brush in my hand. "Where are we going, Ruby?" I say.

"A new job, Sam. I thought I'd keep it a surprise."

"Why?"

"Because it's someone you know."

"She's talking about Iris, Sam," Max says.

"Iris O'Conner? When did she call you?"

"Just before New Year's. She wants some painting done."

We're driving up past Lincoln Park. Frank's place is a big old Georgian with white columns. Over the years, Iris has fixed it up, extending the gardens and putting an atrium off the back. It wasn't that big when they bought it, but there have been additions. Frank would always come in the office saying, "Iris is up to her old tricks again. Look at these bills, for crying out loud." As much as he complained, he had pictures of the house framed on his wall. The shingles on the roof were replaced with tile, the front door painted an ivy green. I've only been over there a few times. We pass big houses, each with low flagstone walls. Frank and Iris live down near the end. Max starts unloading things from the truck while Ruby and I go up to the front door and ring the bell. Frank opens the door in a purple cardigan, looking like he hasn't slept. Loose skin surrounds his jaw, the shine replaced with stubble. "Sam," he says. "What are you doing here?"

"Iris wants some painting done," Ruby says.

"Painting?" he says. "She never told me."

"Who's that?" Iris says from another room.

"What are we painting?" he says. Iris appears in silk pajamas and a yellow dressing gown. Her hair is pulled back, face drawn, no makeup. "Don't leave them standing out there," she says. "Come in, Sam. You must be Ruby. Mary's told me all about you. Just push Frankie out of the way. He's always getting under my feet. Come in the atrium, we're having tea."

"Max is getting things out of the truck," Ruby says.

"That little bastard?" Frank says. "Christ, why didn't you tell me you were painting, Iris? Now I've got to deal with that little fucker."

"Come through to the atrium, Ruby," Iris says. "We'll talk in there. Do you want tea, Sam?"

"Sure."

"Don't just stand there, Frankie. Have Max bring everything to the servant's door. We'll start the tea."

"What did he do with the wiener van, Sam?" Frank asks.

"Took it to the wreckers finally."

"Good riddance." Iris and Ruby go to the atrium. "Sam," Frank says. "A word." He pulls me over next to his den. "Look," he says and pauses, "Iris isn't doing so well. She's going in for more treatments. We thought we had it nipped in the bud."

"She looked great up north."

"I thought so, too. Why's she getting stuff painted, anyway? The place looks fine."

"I don't know. I just found out about it."

"She can't have paint fumes, Sam. Or the noise." Max bumps against something out front. "Jesus wept," Frank says. "Now I've got him around." He opens the front door. There's Max with a ladder. Frank's cell phone rings. "I have to take this, Sam," he says. "Probably New York." He goes down the hall.

"Where do I put this stuff, Sam?" Max says.

"Take it around the back. I'll find out where Iris wants us to start." Max backs down the steps with the ladder. I go out to the atrium. Ruby's taking notes. "Have some tea. Sam," Iris says. "Where's Frankie?"

"He's taking a call."

"All upset, is he?"

"He's worried about the fumes and the noise."

"We'll be at the other end of the house, Sam," Ruby says.

"What did Frankie think I was doing?" Iris says. Her face is so drawn.

"Anything else?" Ruby says to Iris.

"Frank's den could use some freshening."

"My den needs what?" Frank appears.

"It needs painting, Frankie."

"Like hell it does. I don't want that little bastard in there." Max passes by the atrium windows, stumbling over his bootlaces.

"They're here now, Frankie. We might as well get it done."

"Iris, you're in no condition—"

"No condition for what?"

"Just—" he says, rubbing his chin and sitting down. "Never mind. You know what I was about to say."

"Frankie thinks I'm going to drop dead."

"That's not what I meant at all."

Ruby looks at me. "I've got lymphoma, Ruby," Iris says, pouring more tea. "I need treatments. That's what the specialists say, anyway."

"Crackpots," Frank says.

"You poor thing," Ruby says. "I was diagnosed with lupus three years ago. Turned out to be nothing. Didn't let me know for two weeks. Otis cried every day."

"Otis is Ruby's husband," I say.

"*Otis Cries for You*?" Iris says. "He's funny as hell."

"That's my Otis," Ruby says.

Iris coughs. "We spend all this money on specialists," Frank says, "and they can't tell us anything, for chrissake." He takes Iris's hand.

"Why don't you see Dr. Krupsky?" Ruby says. "He's wonderful. He told me I'm the brightest star in the galaxy."

"Krupsky's my GP," I say.

"He any good?" Frank says.

"He's not a specialist, Frank."

"I don't care what he is. I asked if he's any good. I want answers, not somebody picking their arse for a thousand an hour. What's that little bastard doing out there?" Max is trying to get all the drop cloths untied.

"I'd better go out and help," Ruby says.

"Sam," Frank says. "See me in my den before you get started. I have to make one call. Finish your tea."

Iris sits with her hands between her knees. "Frankie doesn't handle these things very well," she says.

"He's scared."

"You know what they say in Belfast? Anything can be solved by raising your voice."

"When will you start treatments again?"

"Soon. I swore I'd never own a wig," she laughs. "I'd rather wear a big fur hat."

"Frank will buy you a whole mink farm."

"No doubt he would."

"Listen, Iris. What Ruby said about Krupsky. He's a nice guy and everything. I don't know what he can tell you. He's not an oncologist. He probably knows more about tango."

"He tangos?"

"Like a born Argentine."

"He sounds like quite the person."

"I'd better go talk to Frank and then get to work."

"Thanks, Sam." She stares out at Max cutting cords with a penknife.

Frank is sitting in the den with his arms behind his head. "What's up?" I say.

"New York," he says. "Everything's gone through. I'm fucking rich. Even Margot's book is doing great. Yours? Not so much. The Japanese market isn't doing as well as I expected. Now, Sam, this doctor Ruby was talking about?"

"Krupsky," I say. "I just talked to Iris. He's not an oncologist, Frank. I don't know what he can do for her."

"He's got to do something, Sam," Frank says.

"Like what?"

"Something, for God's sake. I'll get fucking voodoo doctors if that's what it takes. You got Krupsky's number?"

"I'll call him."

"Do it now."

"He's probably with a patient."

"Leave a message. Get him to call back."

I phone and Krupsky answers. "Hello, Sam," he says. "Saw your name on the call display. My secretary's off today. You need medication?"

"I'm calling about someone else. A friend of mine. She's got lymphoma."

"Nasty stuff. What do you want me to do?"

"I don't know. Her husband doesn't think he's getting enough answers from the specialists. We're here painting now. Could you possibly come over after work?"

"I was going to drop in on Judy anyway."

"Maybe before that?"

"I'll come by around four o'clock. What's the address?" I give it to him while Frank eyes a cigar. I hang up. "He'll be here around four," I say to Frank.

"Thanks, Sam," he says.

"Listen, Frank, this probably isn't the time. I made a decision the other night."

"About what?"

"No more grammar books. I'm done."

"Not surprised. It's all a load of rubbish, anyway. Not you, just the business itself. I did you a favor selling out, you know. Gave you your fucking life back. I didn't think you'd pick up a paintbrush, but to each his own. Go on, you wanker. Go paint."

Ruby takes us to the old servant's entrance. It leads up to a large open studio above the garage. We bump up the stairs with the ladders, drop cloths and paint cans. The room has a cathedral ceiling and four dormers. Ruby mixes paint while Max and I lay down the drop cloths. "Start around the windows, Sam," Ruby says. "Max and I will do the ceiling. I have to go get another paint color Iris wants. Maybe I'll do that now. You guys get hustling. I'll be right back."

We paint through the morning. Ruby returns around noon. "They didn't have this color anywhere," she said. "I had to get it made up in the end." It's a shade of violet I've never seen before. "Nice," Max says. Iris's housekeeper comes upstairs with sandwiches. They're all cut like the ones served at cocktail parties.

Just after four o'clock, Krupsky shows up. I find him sitting with Iris in the atrium. He's holding her hand. "I'll see what I can do," Krupsky's saying. "I have a friend at the General. One of the best. He'll look at your charts." Krupsky sees me standing there. "Hello, Sam," he says. "How's your painting going?"

"We've made a good start," I say. "How's everything here?"

"Absolutely marvelous," he says. "Iris and I are having a nice chat. She's a tango dancer. Imagine that. We're going to dance once she gets through her therapy. Are you off now?"

"Just cleaning up. You coming back to see Judy?"

"I'll be along in a bit."

Frank comes in the atrium. "Everything sorted?" he says.

"We're fine, Frankie," Iris says. "Go do your work."

On the way home, I light a cigarette. "Give me a puff, Sam," she says. "Ruby," Max scolds.

"This is it," I say. "I'm stopping." We pass the cigarette back and forth. Max opens his window. He says the smoke puts him the mood for something charbroiled.

# Chapter 92

*K*rupsky is here at Frank and Iris's every day. He's cutting down on patients. He says he'd rather spend time with friends.

The room over the garage is finished. Once Iris feels better, Krupsky wants her to start tangoing with him. They're turning the room into a tango studio. Krupsky's already brought over his tango records, and he and Iris sit in the atrium listening to the music. Frank's on his cell phone as usual, talking away. We're working on Frank's den now. He hates having us around, especially Max. Knowing Frank, he thinks Max is after his cigars and liquor. "I don't want your cigars, old man," Max says to him.

"Who are you calling old, you little bastard?" Frank says.

He got up on a ladder yesterday, showing Max he could paint a straight line. "What do you think about that?" he said. "I painted for a living back in Belfast. Did plaster, too. Try that, you little prick."

"You missed a spot," Max said.

"I did not."

"Over there. You need glasses."

"I'll punch your lights out in a minute." Frank stepped off the ladder and took a header into the wall. Ruby laughed her head off. Paint dripped down Frank's cardigan. "My auntie knitted this, for chrissake," he screamed.

"Give it here," Ruby said. "I'll get it out."

Frank took the sweater off, then tried to kick Max in the ass for calling him an old man. "Little snipe," he said. He went off in a huff.

"How are you going to get the paint out, Ruby?"

"I don't know yet, Max."

"Want some turpentine?"

"That'll fade the color."

"How about urine?"

"That gets out paint?"

"No, I just wanted to piss on Frank's cardigan." Ruby laughed herself silly. I laughed, too. Why not? Frank's pissed on enough things in his day.

# Chapter 93

Krupsky and Iris are starting to tango. Late last week, Emma came over and was introduced to Frank. They actually get along. Emma speaks six languages. She's teaching him Russian and Polish, just in case he wants to tour with Margot's book. They're out in the atrium every day.

We've been going over there some evenings ourselves. The studio has a decent sized tango floor. Krupsky's set up lanes with chalk, showing us how to move up and down the room. Frank sticks his head in every now and then. Emma even got him out tangoing a few times. "Look Iris," he said, "it's a piece of cake," and promptly fell on his ass. Sometimes, when we finish up, Frank takes Krupsky outside for a cigar. I've given up smoking altogether. "I'm glad you've stopped," Mary says on the way home.

Muller and Judy still play Scrabble, but they don't argue anymore. Muller can use all the proper names he wants. Judy's face is this bright pink, the color of motherhood. As soon as the baby comes, they want to start tangoing again. "Muller's going to get fat otherwise," Judy says. He's already fat, but he's her Big Bear. The rest of the crowd misses him, or his brownies. On our way to a house on Evergreen Avenue, Ruby said, "He grows on you, doesn't he, Sam? Just like Otis." Krupsky put Otis's arm in a sling the other night. Otis pulled something doing that stupid windmill dance.

We've got a long day ahead of us. It's outdoor work, but now it's getting warmer. I can't wait to get on the ladder. I like being up there with the bees. I've also bought an iPod and downloaded some songs. I sing along, making Max look at me funny. I'm probably off key, but I move with my brush, hitting high notes with an upward stroke. "You missed a spot," Max says.

"Where?"

"Over by the corner."

"I'll get it on the next coat."

"You're pretty tone deaf, you know."

"I'm holding a loaded brush, Max."

"Who're you listening to?"

"Tony Bennett."

"Isn't he dead?"

"He's doing fine, Max."

"What is he?" Max says, "A hundred or something?"

"He's not a hundred."

"How old is he then?"

"I don't know, Max. We don't celebrate each other's birthdays."

# Chapter 94

The winter and spring practically flew by with work, putting the final touches on the nursery, and Muller catering. Mary rented an industrial unit, hiring people to help Muller out. It's all covered under Margomax. We jokingly refer to each invoice as "Frank's concern." He and Iris have started travelling, but Frank's a Skype addict now. Margot likes to put him on mute while she watches his lips move.

She's bilking the hell out of him. As she says, the man's been bilking people for years. "I outta know," she says, and does up another invoice on the new Margomax letterhead. Frank added an ivy green banner at the top. That's just in case Margot forgets it's his money she's throwing around. She gave us bonuses last week. Frank just about had a fit. He called Margot an "old bat" before she put him on mute and mouthed the words, "Suck on it, Frank."

We gather over at Frank's on Friday nights, at least when Frank and Iris are in town. We're getting pretty good at tangoing. Frank and Margot go out on the floor occasionally. It looks more like jitterbugging than a tango. Krupsky tries introducing some form, holding up Frank's arm, turning his chin. Frank looks like he's waiting for a snapshot.

It's nice with the windows open, a breeze coming in off the lake. Iris still can't overdo it. She likes to sit with Judy while Muller dances with Emma. Judy calls her Auntie Emma and Margot Auntie Margot and now Ruby's Auntie Ruby. You'd think she'd have enough aunts, but now she's calling Emma, Gramma Emma. It doesn't seem to bother Emma one bit.

Max finished his business course and now has three people working for him, including Zack. We suspect Zack's selling seafood out the back of the van again. It smells like a tuna boat.

Another bit of news: Max's expanding into interior decorating with a woman he met on Otis's show. He was filling in for Otis one night and she called in to say she liked Max's choice of song, The Tempree's "Dedicated to the One I Love". It's still early days in the romance department, but he brought her over once to Frank's, and Krupsky got them doing a basic samba. Frank still calls Max a scheming little git, blaming him for his purple sweater smelling like a marsh. "I didn't do anything to your stupid sweater," Max says.

He doesn't push it, though. Frank is paying for the *House Manicure* advertising, although he doesn't know it. Margot slips everything through under general expenditures, something Frank suspects, but he's too busy taking care of Iris.

Last month, we received three gold stars in one of the trade publications for "Best House Painters in North Chicago." That brought in a lot of calls. We'll be painting solidly right through the summer, then Iris wants us staining their decks up at Lake Geneva. Otis isn't crazy about the idea, telling Ruby her absence will leave him "sorely in need of human interaction." Margot says that's a hoot. "You can't even spell interaction," she says.

Frank thinks he's getting a deal on the staining, but Margot's charging him through the nose. They argue over pricing while they dance. Sometimes Frank tries to strangle her. They end up smoking cigars on the patio.

The grass brownies are a thing of the past. Everyone's been weaned off except Otis who's been trying to bake them himself. They look like flattened turds. Bisquick won't even touch them. "Ain't we hoity toity," Otis says. Bisquick doesn't think much of Otis's nipples now, either.

# Epilogue

*U*pon this writing, we are a family of five, a new arrival coming this evening. It happened at exactly seven thirty-five. Krupsky delivered a nine pound, four ounce baby with lungs the size of pontoons. Muller fainted and landed on Krupsky's foot. As soon as she could, Emma moved in with blankets, wrapping the baby in one and throwing the other over Muller. A round of applause came from the living room. The lovebirds sang and Otis sounded like he was choking on a peanut. Then Krupsky came out with Emma holding our new bundle of joy. "Congratulations, Sam," Krupsky said. "You must be very proud. Gather round, folks. He's a healthy little bubala."

Margot, Ruby, Otis, and Max crowded around. Frank was sitting on the couch with Iris. He made a nice toast to little Anthony (after Tony Bennett) and Iris put her arms around his neck. "Nice, Frankie," she said. She looks better now, wearing a silk turban instead of a wig. When Otis almost fell on her, she let out a loud Belfast laugh. Then Krupsky came over and sat next to her. He patted her knee. They've become best friends.

Muller appeared, grinning like a chimp. He sat in a chair and Emma put the baby in his arms. He can't hold Anthony worth a shit, head rolling like a pom-pom, but I'm proud of him for being more than a cumquat using an oxygen tank for a security blanket.

Riley and Pam popped over with the kids. When Emma took little Anthony back to Judy, Krupsky raised his glass, saying this was how life should be. "To your family, Sam," he said. His eyes glistened. Everyone raised their glasses, too. Even Bisquick seemed to understand what was happening. He stopped hurling invectives at Meek and Beek and sat on Margot's shoulder.

Krupsky is standing in the middle of the rug now, an unlit cigar in his mouth. "You know, Sam," he says. "I saw something years ago in Peru. Small village near the Yavari River. A baby was born and the villagers took it down to the river. Wasn't sure whether they were going to baptize it or drown it. Anyway, they put the baby in this reed basket. Then everyone got in the water, passing the basket from one to the other until they'd all touched it."

"Why did they do that?" Riley asks.

"Everyone shares responsibility for each child."

"How wonderful," Iris says. "Isn't it, Frankie?"

"We can do the same thing next door," Riley says. "The pool's ninety degrees. What do you think, Sam?"

"It's my first grandchild, Riley," I said. "Wait til the next one."

"I think it's a wonderful idea, Sam," Muller says.

"So do I, Daddy," Judy calls from the bedroom.

Next thing I know, we're heading over to Riley's with my grandchild all swaddled up. The cabana lights go on, sombreros come out, and the girls start cutting holes in the Mexican towels for ponchos. Krupsky goes into the water, wearing a headdress left over from the Mardi Gras party. He stands there solemnly as Mary brings Anthony down to the shallow end. Frank and Iris are by the diving board, taking pictures. Then Muller comes through the gate with Judy. She's dressed in a white night gown, looking weak but beautiful. Muller's wrapped in two yellow beach towels like a toga. They step into the water next to Krupsky. Everyone else is around the sides, ponchos floating, cigars going. Otis slips and goes under. I guess he thinks his cigar is a breathing tube. He keeps blowing out smoke. Max fishes him out and holds his arm. Riley's daughters light votive candles and line them around the pool. Steam rises, mixing with puffs of cigar smoke.

"Hand me the baby," Krupsky says. Mary brings over Anthony, silent as a muffin. "This is going to look more like a baptism by a Jew," he says, "but here goes." Little Anthony is lowered into the water, letting out the first true scream of astonishment. Then towels are handed across and he's swaddled in those. "We don't exactly have a reed basket, so give me that air mattress there," Krupsky says. "Now Muller, you push the mattress towards Margot. Then each person passes it to the next."

We get in two rows. Muller pushes the air mattress towards us. I'm down by the diving board. Little Anthony barely moves the whole time. When the mattress comes to me, I take the end and hold onto the diving board with my other hand. "Now what, Krupsky?" I say.

"What do you want? We're done."

I lift Anthony up to Frank who stands with tears in his eyes. Otis lets out a whoop, tossing his sombrero in the air, then goes under again. Sombreros fill the air. Emma and the girls give towels to everybody and we head back to the house. Soon, we're all dressed and dry. Krupsky sits next to Iris, Emma brings around coffee and Mary sets out cups and saucers. I get brandies for everybody. Margot follows me out to the kitchen with Bisquick in hot pursuit. She links her arm in mine and lets out a sigh. "So how does it feel?" she says.

"How does what feel?"

"Being a grandfather, knucklehead."

"It feels pretty good."

"Look at them, Sam. Everyone's over the friggin' moon out there. I think Bisquick wants to make a move on Meek. That's the female, right?"

"Doesn't act like it."

"Iris looks good."

"She's not out of the woods yet."

Margot pours herself a brandy. "Krups thinks she's going to make it."

"It's Krups now, is it?"

"He's bringing me to the dance studio next week. Emma wants to babysit Anthony. Loves the little tyke already. Look at her."

"I thought Iris was his dance partner?"

"Frank doesn't want her overdoing it. He tell you about my book?"

"It's selling better than mine."

"What's he got you doing next?"

"Nothing. I told him no more grammar books."

"How'd he take that?"

"Glad, actually. Said he did me a favor closing up shop. Forced me to think for myself."

"How's that working for you?"

"I've decided I like painting."

"I could have told you that."

"How about you?"

"What about me?"

"Are you going to keep living with Otis and Ruby?"

"Suits me fine."

"And the show?"

"I got sponsors up the ying yang."

"Just stay away from those feminist rallies."

"Dually noted," she says. "You've got a wonderful family, Sam. You should be thrilled. Are you coming?"

I follow her to the living room and sit on the rug. Everyone's smiling. Judy has Anthony in her arms, dimples showing. In time, when the nappies start piling up, and the baby monitor blinks in the dark, I hope I'll make a good grandfather. As Krupsky says, "Life's a crapshoot, Sam, but at least you filled the cheap seats." I look at Judy and Mary, sitting there, pleased as punch, and I hope, when I'm passing along a few words of wisdom to my grandson, I'll believe, like the song says, that each day can be like the first day of spring. I'm not sure that's a direct lift or not. Let's just call it a tribute to the great Tony Bennett, my grandson's namesake.

Did I mention the song's called *If I Ruled the World?*
Have a listen. It's quite good.

Sam Bennett
Grandfather

# Acknowledgments

*I*'d like to extend my thanks and appreciation to Kathryne Hebb, Peter Riva, Nuala Byles, Myna Wallin, and Analisa Denny for all their hard work and unfailing belief that I would stop rewriting eventually.